COWBOY CREED
(Book 1, Cooper's Hawke Landing)

By

RHONDA LEE CARVER

www.rhondaleecarver.com

This book is a work of fiction. Names, characters, places, incidents and dialogue in this work are from the author's imagination and creation. Any resemblance to actual events, locales or persons, living or dead, is completely coincidental.

This book contains material that isn't suitable for anyone under the age of 17.

For more titles by Rhonda Lee Carver, please visit www.rhondaleecarver.com or see her complete list of novels at the end of this book.

Connect with Rhonda Lee Carver

Facebook: www.facebook.com/rhondaleecarver.author/

Twitter: www.twitter.com/RLCarver

Instagram: www.instagram.com/rhondaleecarver/

Pinterest: www.pinterest.com/rhondaleecarverauthor/

Amazon: www.amazon.com/Rhonda-Lee-Carver/e/B00CQLXKTO

BookBub: www.bookbub.com/profile/rhonda-lee-carver

Street Team: www.facebook.com/groups/471259293018665/

Newsletter: Subscribe here

BLURB:

Seconds chances come in their own time. For Mindy and
Creed the flame remains.

Newly divorced and empty nester, Mindy Sage, decided that her
hometown might be the perfect place to reinvent herself, or at least
find the wild and carefree girl she used to be before she moved away.

She's craving small town comfort, but the problem is, in Cooper's
Hawk, everyone knows everyone. Secrets can feel as tall and wide
as the Montana mountains that backdrop the friendly, picturesque
town where she'd left her heart in the hands of a handsome cowboy
nineteen years ago.

Search and Rescue team member, Creed Hawke, understood more
than anyone what saving a life meant, but who would save him from
the one woman he'd never gotten over? He'd moved on—or at least
he thought he had until those old emotions come tumbling back with
the vengeance of a forest fire. He's reminded of how much he'd loved
Mindy, wanted her, swore to marry her. Why couldn't he forget her?
Resist her? Deny her his heart?

Because he'd fallen for her at ten and never came back up for air.

How can he forgive her for stealing his daughter from him? Is love
stronger than the mistakes they've made? Or are they doomed
before they find forever?

Cover Design:
Rhonda Lee Carver

Stock Photo:
Period Images

Chapter 1

"RUN, MINDY. RUN! It's coming." The roaring of the twister as it barreled its way through the field engulfed ten-year-old Creed Hawke's words.

Mindy wouldn't have heard him anyway because she had all her concentration on the old beat up truck being sucked up by the massive swirling cloud from the field across the gravel road. She stood paralyzed with dirty, untied sneakers planted in the mud. She'd never seen something so scary and amazing all at the same time.

"What are you doing? Playing chicken with a tornado? Come on, dummy!"

A tug on her wrist made her turn around to blast her best friend a warning eye. "Who are you calling dummy, stupid?"

"You! Stop starin' and start movin'," he demanded.

Hearing a loud crashing of metal against dirt, she looked back to find the truck upended over on Hawke Farm where they'd been looking for a lost frog that morning. "Holy hot dog!" she muttered.

"We have to run!" Creed jerked her arm, almost making her fall.

He slipped his hand into hers and together they ran as the loud, freight-train rumbling ripped through Cooper's Hawk. Mindy's hair whipped around her face, stinging her cheeks. Dust particles blurred her vision and she squinted against the discomfort, but Creed kept pulling her along.

By the time they reached the rickety old barn her lungs ached and her legs were like limp noodles.

"In here. We'll be safe inside." Creed pushed her into the semi-dark space of the old barn. Her nostrils were assaulted by the strong odor of hay and decaying carcass.

"It stinks in here."

"Would you rather die out there?" He led the way across the worn floor, kicking up a couple of beer cans with the toe of his shoe. "Let's hide here."

They hunkered down behind the tire of a rusted tractor. Their ragged breaths mingled together and they still clutched hands. Mindy wanted to be brave like Creed, but she couldn't hold back the tears that came. They streamed down her cheeks as she hiccupped.

"What are you cryin' 'bout?" His pale blue eyes nailed her in accusation.

"I'm scared and it's loud."

He swung his arm around her shoulders. "It'll be okay. We'll be okay here. This place has lasted through a bunch of storms."

"This ain't no storm though. Mama said tornadoes are dangerous and if I ever saw one, I should run into the cellar." She pulled her legs up to her chest and laid her forehead against her knees.

"Don't be scared. Heck, this ain't nothin'. I'll never let anything happen to you. I promise." He patted her head.

The roof of the barn shook and the cracked windows rattled. A gust of wind blew the wooden door open, slamming it hard against the wall. She screamed and tucked her wet face against Creed's baseball shirt. "We're going to die! We're going to get blown away and I'll never see my mama or daddy again!"

"Just hang on. Here. Hang onto the tractor. It weighs a ton."

Without any argument, she did as he told her, wrapping her arms around the clunky tire. He stayed beside her, his hand on her back.

"I don't want to die, Creed. I ain't even been married yet. I want to get married first."

"Marriage is stupid," he sniffed loudly.

"To you it might be but not to me." Mindy had never heard anything louder than the tornado. It sounded like a train rolling right above their heads. Fear formed inside her and she could barely breathe. "It's here."

"You want to get married, Mindy? Fine. Hold on." He dropped his arm from her shoulders.

"Where are you going? You can't go!" she whimpered.

"I'm coming back. I'm lookin' for something." He picked an item up off the floor then came back with a thin metal circle that looked like something her daddy used to fix mowers. "This'll do. I'll

marry you, Mindy. Then you won't be so scared. Promise you won't be scared."

Her eyes must have grown two sizes bigger. "I can't marry you," she said wistfully.

"Why not?"

"Cause you haven't even asked. A girl can't marry a boy if he doesn't ask."

"Stop being so bull-headed. Do you want to get married or not?" The wind whistled through the cracks in the wood and windows.

"Fine, Creed Hawke. I'll marry you."

"Here's your ring. Don't complain because it ain't a diamond." He slipped the circle on her middle finger of her left hand and she stared down at it lovingly.

"You're s'pposed to say something."

"Like what?" His nose wrinkled.

"Like how much you love me. I saw it on a movie."

"Dang, I don't know what to say 'cept that you are my best friend. You make me laugh and you can throw a ball better than the boys, but don't tell them I told you so," he professed.

"I'll always be your wife, Creed. Even when we're big and grown up. But then I want a ring. A real ring. Like the one we saw in your mama's bedroom. The one with all those pretty diamonds that belonged to your grandma."

"What's wrong with that?" He tapped the oversized metal ring.

"It's way too big, Creedy."

"Don't worry, Minnow. One day I'm going to give you that ring you love. You watch and see."

A loud crunching sound brought their chins up. The metal shook wildly. Parts of the roof flew away, leaving a large, gaping hole. The rest of the metal shuddered and screeched against the force of the wind.

"It's going to carry us away," she whined.

"Heck, I ain't afraid of no tornado. Go away and leave us alone!" Creed yelled.

Her sobs returned. "I'm still scared."

"I'll hold onto you and never let go. We're married now. Husbands protect their wives." He held her tighter and, in that moment, Mindy believed that he'd never let anything happen to her.

"Mom? You okay?"

Mindy dragged herself from the memory and smiled at her daughter, Jane. "Yes. I'm fine. Just in deep thought."

"Have you been able to reach Pop Pop yet?"

"No, I haven't." The worry returned. Although she and her father didn't talk on the phone every day it wasn't like him to ignore her calls. "I left him several messages and he hasn't returned any of them."

"When are you leaving?" Jane tucked her legs up under her on the chaise lounge. Her long, dark, curly hair was pulled up into a topknot. Her beautiful eyes caught the sun's rays.

"In two days. After you leave for Columbia U." Feeling an emotional stab in her chest, Mindy wanted to hide the moisture in her eyes and looked out over the calm, blue water as a boat sailed by. Growing up in Montana, Mindy had always been more of a mountains type-of-girl, but after living on the beautiful shoreline of Lake Canyon for ten years she'd grown to love the peaceful area, although the too-big custom two-story house had been her husband's—or rather ex-husband's—dream and not hers.

She missed Cooper's Hawk. Missed the people, the small friendly town, and the mountains backdropped by wide open Montana skies. She especially missed Sage Ranch where her days as a child were spent barefoot and dirty, riding horses and raising goats. After chores, she spent a lot of time on the ice gearing up for figure skating competitions. That had been the carefree life she'd wanted for Jane, and she'd believed that was what Branch had wanted too. He'd promised Mindy they would buy a home in Cooper's Hawk, but a year turned into three, then five, and then more had passed at the blink of an eye.

The day he came home and excitedly told her he found a home on the lake that he "just had to have" her hope of going back "home" had vanished. Whenever she voiced her concern about a simpler life, he'd reminded her that he was the bread winner and her hollow work as a figure skating coach was more of a hobby than a contribution.

Sadness rolled through her at the loss of many years spent unhappy.

She often wondered if they'd had another child would things have been different between them. Would they have connected at a deeper level? He'd never wanted a child though. He always said his work kept him too busy, and she guessed there were other things that kept his attention outside of clients.

On days when memories flooded her, she wondered what ever happened to Creed Hawke. Pressing her palm against the necklace she had made from the metal "pretend" ring he'd given her during the tornado, she never took it off. Although their "marriage" at ten had been nothing more than play, in her heart she'd never been able to forget him and what he'd meant to her. He'd been her best friend. Her first love. Her first lover.

The last she'd heard he'd been on the rodeo circuit doing well for himself. She'd made it a habit not to ask her daddy too many questions.

"Does this have anything to do with a man?" Jane lifted a teasing brow.

My goodness, she looks just like him…

"Huh? What are you talking about?" Had Mindy shown some subtle sign that her mind had wandered to Creed?

"I've always had a feeling you've never gotten over someone. Is it my father?"

Mindy cleared her throat. "Jane—"

"Mom, it's okay. I'm joking. I know we've had this talk. You both were young, he wasn't interested in being a daddy, and he's riding bulls for a living."

Taking her daughter's hand, a heaviness crawled into Mindy's throat. "We've always been open about your father, but if you ever wanted to meet him…"

"No. Branch is my father, at least the only one I've ever known." She pulled her hand away then slipped on her mirrored shades that hid her telling eyes from view.

Seventeen years ago, Mindy and Branch had agreed to raise Jane as his daughter, but Mindy had carried the weight of guilt on her shoulders all those years. Her intention hadn't been to deceive Creed or keep his daughter from him. The night they'd shared in the back of his beat-up truck under the moon and stars had been an unplanned tryst that created an amazing gift.

Mindy had left for college two weeks later and Creed had enlisted into the military. It had only seemed right that they would be each other's first, but she hadn't anticipated that the condom would fail. What young couple did think of such things?

"Anyway, I would totally approve of you having smash." Jane slurped up her Coke through a straw, smiling widely.

"I don't have smashes."

"Do you even know what the word means?" Jane lifted her pierced brow—the piercing she snuck and got when she was seventeen and then a few months later a fist-sized tattoo of a butterfly on the small of her back. She'd always been spirited, curious and ambitious. And had the biggest heart. At twelve she found an abandoned litter of kittens and fed them through a dropper and back to health. On her fourteenth birthday she raised donations for the local animal shelter. During her summers she visited nursing homes, worked babysitting jobs and volunteered at underprivileged camps.

"No. I don't know teen lingo and I was afraid to ask." Mindy picked up her can of diet Coke and stretched her gaze to the jet ski speeding by. People were out enjoying the beautiful day on the water. Once upon a time, Mindy and Branch would take Jane out on the boat on a day like this one, sail for hours, swim, and eat picnic lunches. Much had changed since then. Her only child was now an adult and starting college and Branch had moved in with his girlfriend before the ink was dry on the divorce papers.

Mindy wasn't bitter, but divorce never was an easy thing.

Her friends had been encouraging her to start dating again, but after seventeen years of being with one man, dating seemed more like jumping off a cliff than an act of fun. Her ex-husband certainly had no problem in that area. He'd decided a year ago that he'd rather be with his twenty-five-year old assistant, Sian, rather than his family. The urge to blame her for the disintegration of their marriage seemed a natural emotion, but if it hadn't been the vibrant, firm-assed Sian taking him away, it would have been the next twenty-something that came along who gave him some attention. Mindy knew this. Understood this. Her marriage with Branch had been over for years. Although he'd been a decent father, he'd always had one client, another appointment, or a need that kept him from coming home early.

Mindy had kept her focus on her daughter, while Branch had fixated on adding another place value to his bank account. No one could deny he'd created a reputable business from the ground up and that took time and work, but somewhere along the way he'd lost himself—lost his family.

"Smash means casual sex. A hook up. A fling, or whatever your generation calls that activity."

Mindy gave her daughter a raised brow. "I most definitely don't do that activity, and this is a conversation we shouldn't have."

"Mom," Jane simpered. "I'm eighteen. I already know about the birds and the bees. You deserve someone who can show you how beautiful you are, especially after Dad made the biggest mistake of his life and dumped you for Sian Infantile."

"Sweetheart, that's not very nice." Mindy had worked hard to be in a place where she could encourage peace with Branch, and Sian.

"You wouldn't be defending her if you were around her for more than five minutes. She uses 'like' after every word and calls Dad "Baby Love". It makes me sick."

"Your dad loves her, so you need to respect that. As for me, I'm not looking for anyone. I'm concentrating on finding myself."

Jane frowned. "In all seriousness, how are you since the divorce? It's been what…two months?"

"Six months."

"Sheesh."

"Honey, the divorce decree was just a piece of paper stating what I already knew. The marriage was over years ago. I'm okay. Really I am. Thank you for your concern but you don't have to worry."

"I think I do. You're running away." She reached for the bottle of sunscreen, flipped open the lid and poured the thick cream into her palm.

"I'm not running away!"

"That's what you would say to me." She applied the sunscreen to her legs.

"I haven't been to Cooper's Hawk in years. I grew up there. That's not running away."

"Mom?" Jane gave Mindy the I-know-you-better eye. "Is this because of the house?"

"You're heading to college and I would be here alone anyway. This house is way too big for one person." Mindy and Branch had agreed that she would stay in the house for one year and then she'd choose to put the home up for sale, and split the profit, or buy Branch out of his share. "Some Montana fresh air will help me decide what I need to do with my life." Mindy plucked at the frayed hem of her denim shorts. Since he'd asked for a divorce, she'd been asking herself the grueling question, *"Where will I go from here?"*

"I want you to be happy," Jane said.

"I know you do, and I will be. This is a hurdle I need to get over and it takes time, but it can happen."

"Does that mean you've decided to sell?"

"I haven't decided anything yet, but more than likely I will."

The sadness on her daughter's face only lasted a second. "I'm getting a text." She read the screen on her phone and smiled. "I've got to go. My squad is waiting." She jumped up, gave Mindy a tight hug, then pulled on the cover up over her bikini. "Love you." She started for the French doors.

"Wait. What time will you be home?"

"Don't wait up!"

"Jane Elizabeth!"

"Sorry. I'll be home around midnight. We're grabbing a pizza and watching a movie."

Mindy responded with, "I love you too," but the door was already shut.

Getting up from the lounger, she took the stone steps down to the wooden dock and sat at the edge. She dipped her feet into the warm water, swirling her toes in the murky blue depths, wishing she had all the answers to her problems.

What would she do with her life?

She married Branch when Jane was a baby and they'd been happy, but the honeymoon stage had lasted less than a year. While Mindy had been up to her ears in dirty diapers, midnight feedings and keeping the house—then a two-bedroom apartment—running, Branch's focus had been on building his reputation and clientele in the photography world. When he'd landed a shoot for a popular fashion lingerie company his business had taken off like a rocket. What should have been a lucky break turned out to be less time at home.

Mindy had maintained loyalty to her family through the years, running Jane to school and sports and supporting Branch in all his endeavors. All the while the gap grew wider and deeper until they couldn't find their way out of the man-made hole. It happened to a lot of couples. Over the years she'd lost count of friends who'd divorced because they no longer loved one another.

At times, she'd tried to stick a match to the flame by surprising Branch with new lingerie and buckets of chilled champagne, but at some point, she felt he had lost interest. She faulted herself for not realizing that when she'd suggested they have a child together five years ago and he gave her a hard "no" that he would never be the family man. By then he'd completely segregated himself from her and the dream of building a larger family had fizzled.

A year ago he'd taken her to her favorite restaurant for dinner and proceeded to tell her that he wanted a divorce. It was, but wasn't, a shock. She'd suspected for some time that he was seeing someone else, and it was almost a relief to finally hear the truth—to finally have him stop denying what she'd accused him of a handful of times. Jane, although sad that her parents would be divorcing, had almost seemed relieved too.

A house built on lies was no home.

If Mindy could have peered into a crystal ball to see what her future held, she would have taken a different path. Prepared better. Would have put away more money—got the college degree she so dearly wanted but had quit her junior year because being a mom, wife and college student had spread her too thin.

The day Jane started kindergarten, Mindy applied for a position as a figure skating coach and landed the job. She'd enjoyed coaching skaters at the nearby rink.

When the nights became lonely because Branch wasn't home, she started writing in a journal. The stories had exploded and a writer friend suggested she submit them to a local newspaper. The editor loved her articles about the trials and tribulations of motherhood so much that she gave Mindy a small spot on the front page of the daily paper. She wrote the column until sales started to decline and the newspaper closed.

From where she sat on the dock, with the soothing sounds of the water splashing the rocks and swirling around her ankles, she closed her eyes and imagined she was back in Cooper's Hawk. An image filled her mind. Pale blue eyes and a dimple-bracketed grin. Dark hair and silky waves she would tangle her fingers in. Large, callused hands caressing her sensitive skin. The intoxicating scent of leather and sandalwood, and the husky words whispered in her ear as she gave herself to the cowboy she'd never forgotten.

Cool water sprayed her face and she opened her eyes, watching as a speed boat passed. The couple waved at her and she waved back.

Standing, she looked at the house that appeared so regal with the white columns and stone siding. The architecture was beautiful indeed, but the house never seemed like home, not like the two story, white-sided farmhouse back at Sage Ranch. She missed the horses. The pygmy goats she'd raised for 4H. The sunrises and sunsets that never quite seemed the same outside of Montana.

What divorced woman needed a four-bedroom, three-bathroom, home with a lake for a backyard? The days of social gatherings, boat rides, swimming, and grill outs were over.

Selling was the best option.

Why wasn't she overcome with emotion? Wouldn't it be normal for her to shed a few tears? Feel an overwhelming sorrow? But she didn't. She felt numb.

She'd call the real estate agent in the morning.

She'd thought about her next journey most of the day, debating if going back to Cooper's Hawk for a while was the best option. What she wouldn't give to have the slow pace and comfort of the small town. More so, she'd love to meet that girl again, the wild and carefree Mindy who loved challenges, dirty boots, Daisy Dukes, and a simpler life.

There was a chance she could find herself. She needed to go back to the place where she'd been more herself than she ever had been. Call it running away or not, Cooper's Hawk could be described as an elixir.

There was only one obstacle to this profound decision.

Creed Hawke.

Meeting on the kindergarten playground when they'd both grabbed the last available swing, he'd offered for her to go first and from that point on they'd been best friends…until the summer after graduation when he'd kissed her. They'd kissed before, a brushing on the cheek or on the forehead, but this time his lips had lingered, exploring and passionate. Before she knew it, they were in the back of his truck taking things to a new level. She'd been a naïve eighteen-year old, but in his arms, she'd become wild and fervent.

But things had changed after that night. Turned awkward. They'd been too young to understand how to handle the leap they'd taken together.

Two weeks later she left for California.

Creed and Branch were polar opposites. He'd been everything she needed at the time to get over the heartbreak she'd left in Cooper's Hawk. He had been charming and loved to tell stories, not all were true, and he didn't seem to mind that she had a baby.

Her love for Creed had been mind-consuming, like fireworks and freshly baked brownies, so the easy, uncomplicated love she felt for Branch had been a welcome difference. His smooth appeal, charming good looks and his ability to make her forget her past life in a small town all made her say "yes" when he asked her to marry him two months into their whirlwind relationship.

Yet, over the years she'd thought about Creed, wondered what he was doing. Was he happy? Did he think of her too? Were there any regrets remaining between them from that one night so long ago?

Where was he now? In Cooper's Hawk? She doubted he'd gone back.

Though he wasn't the reason why she needed to go back home.

That country girl with smears of dirt on her cheeks, goat fur on her jacket, wearing short shorts and dusty cowgirl boots remained inside of her. The ambitious girl who'd started figure skating as a hobby at five and by eight was competing and winning awards existed. Thankfully she had Creed, Sage Ranch, and skating that got her through the pain and grief of losing her mom when she was ten. A lot had happened that year. Creed had asked her to marry him during a tornado. Her dad, Rusty Sage, had started drinking. And Creed's mom, Abby, had become more like a second mom to Mindy.

Retracing her way up the steps, she grabbed the pop cans and her cell from the patio and stepped through the French doors into the kitchen where she spent a lot of her time creating culinary masterpieces. The space with grey stained-glass cabinets, matching Italian stone backsplash, stainless steel professional appliances, and large butcher's block island surrounded by special order barstools seemed extravagant in the wake of a divorce and no income coming in.

A row of large glass canisters filled with Jane and Branch's favorite candy lined the granite counter, alongside a bowl of fresh fruit and a stack of photography magazines that Branch forgot to change the address for.

Grabbing a piece of licorice from the candy jar, she popped it into her mouth then picked up the magazines and dropped them into the trash on her way to grab the crystal vase filled with dried flowers sitting on the table—the round pedestal table had once been filled with their family, laughing and sharing stories over breakfast. The polished wood was marked with Jane's stick figure family and math equations. Everything in the house had been touched with love.

This chapter of their lives had come to an end.

Dumping the flowers she'd received from a friend two weeks ago, she washed the vase with extra vigor and set it in the drainer to dry.

Asking Alexa to play her favorite station, she turned up the volume louder than usual and shimmied her hips to the upbeat tune of an ACDC song right into the wine closet where she picked out a bottle of Moscato. Opening it, she poured herself a tall glass and sipped while she took out the makings for a salad from the refrigerator. Like most evenings these days, she planned a quiet one alone with her wine and a chick flick on the flat screen…

Until she heard a harmonious knock on the door.

Her friend and neighbor, Linsey, stood on the other side of the glass door, holding up a bottle of wine and smiling from one fringed earring to the other.

"Great minds think alike," Mindy said after she let her friend in. "I just popped open a Poli Grappa di Moscato. Come in and help me finish off the bottle."

"Oh, the good stuff." Linsey breezed in like a breath of fresh air. Her sheer purple ankle length dress billowed around her legs. The stacks of bangles clanked from both wrists as she placed the unopened bottle of red on the counter.

"It's the last of the stash Branch and I brought back from our trip to that vineyard two years ago."

"The one you enjoyed alone because he stayed on his phone most of the time?"

"Exactly." Moaning, Mindy poured her friend a glass. "Hungry?"

"Always."

"I'm making a salad and I saw that the movie *Under the Tuscan Sun* is playing. It seems rather fitting." Mindy reached for a knife from the magnetic strip and chopped lettuce and tomato.

"Honey, what did we say about watching movies that justify your hurt?"

"Why do you think I'm still hurt?" She whacked a cucumber with the knife.

"Oh, just a silly thought…" Linsey smiled and peaked over Mindy's shoulder as she added olives, mushrooms and parmesan crisps to the bowl. "What am I going to do about eating when you leave?"

"I suggest you take a cooking class. That's how I learned. I got tired of burning water." She tossed the salad, poured in a drizzle of vinaigrette and set the bowl between two plates at the bar.

"I don't think there's any help for this woman, Mindy. Can't teach an old dog new tricks."

"You're only sixty. Far from old." Taking a seat on the stool, Mindy sipped her wine. "I'm glad you came over."

"I saw Jane leave with her friends so I thought you might like some company. This could very well be the last time you and I get to hang out."

"I'm only visiting Montana, not another planet. Come and visit."

"Forgive me for being a little emotional." Linsey grabbed a napkin from the crystal holder and blotted her eyes dramatically. "You were there for me when I had the cancer scare and Pete died. I've known Jane since she had pig tails and now she's going to college and you're leaving." She sniffed loudly. "I can't handle the changes."

Mindy patted her friend's hand. "More reason for you to come visit. Any time."

Stabbing a piece of lettuce with her fork, Linsey popped it into her mouth. "Homemade dressing?"

"Of course."

"Branch was a dimwit. He's going to regret that he ever let you go."

"There's more to keeping a marriage alive than good food."

"Yes, sex too."

"Now remind me. What is sex again?"

Linsey blinked. "What? Exactly how long, my friend?"

"Long enough that I no longer worry about wearing the sexy silk and lace."

"I'm sorry, sweetie." Linsey laughed.

"What's funny?"

"I think you should have a warning label because when you finally do end the dry spell you're going to explode like a geyser."

"Cheers to that." Mindy lifted her glass and Linsey tapped it with her own.

"How are you doing with Jane leaving?"

"It's bittersweet to watch her go off alone into the big world, but I have to be brave." Feeling an attack of tears coming on, Mindy managed to control the urge. She busied herself spooning salad onto her plate.

"Have you decided what you'll do with the house?" Linsey forked a piece of tomato.

"I think it's best I sell. This place is too big for me."

"Oh boy."

"What?" Mindy poured herself more wine.

"You'll be staying in Cooper's Hawk."

"No…maybe. I don't know yet. I don't think so though. I just know I need a break from here."

"Understandable." Linsey nodded. "Have you and Branch had a chance to speak since the divorce was final?"

Tucking a strand of hair behind her ear, Mindy pushed an olive around her plate. "Yes, we spoke a few days ago about Jane and if she needed anything for school. He's moved in with Sian."

"That asshole," Linsey ground out through clenched teeth.

"Although I've used that very sentiment a few times, I've come to realize that he wasn't the only one who destroyed our marriage. I saw the train wreck coming and instead of reacting I ignored the signs."

"Lord knows Pete and I had our fair share of problems before he passed, but at least we had great make up sex. I hope whatever you're looking for you'll find a man who has a big—"

"Linsey!"

"Heart. That's what I was going to say. Get your head out of the gutter."

Chapter 2

"WHOA, GIRL. EASY does it." Creed patted the mare's neck as they carefully maneuvered the slippery rocks along the ridge of Trip Ease Mountain. The topography could be hazardous enough in pleasant weather but add the rain, and lack of light, the area became treacherous. This only made search and rescue efforts much more difficult.

Before he and his brother, Boone, took the horses out of the trailer and saddled them at the base of the mountain, they got all pertinent information from Sheriff Conley about the missing person. The thirty-year-old man's car had been left on the pull off and there was no sign of foul play, so they assumed he was still somewhere on Trip Ease. Creed and Boone were called in when geography was too difficult for locals to handle.

The Hawke brothers started a helicopter tour company, Cooper's Hawke Landing, and soon after they were asked to partner with local law to aid in search and rescue efforts. Since then their team had grown by seven more members, each skilled and trained in trailing and tracking, avalanche recovery, swift water and wildlands rescue, rappelling, and helping during wildfires. Each member had extensive training in medical and search and rescue operation, on top of the combined years spent in the military. They were a group made up of business owners, retired military, firefighters, and pilots. They were strong and powerful with one thing in common, to help others. Each came with their own skill—and each with their own personality as diverse as their professions.

They could cover the area of Trip Ease faster with horses than searchers could on foot.

"What did Conley say the missing man's name is?" Boone trailed a few feet behind on his mare.

"Terrance," Creed raised his voice over the rushing water below. "He's thirty, athletic and an accomplished hiker. He's also an emergency room nurse at the hospital. His wife is the one who called the Sheriff. Terrence had left a note saying that he was going on a hike up here and would be back early for an appointment. She'd worked night shift so she laid down and when she woke up a few hours later he still wasn't back. He'd missed his appointment. She called his cell, but the service out here is shitty, to say the least, so there hasn't been any contact with him."

"I hate to ask but we've been here before. Is there a chance that he's up to no good?"

Creed never liked asking that question, but it was important that any time he and his team members were on a mission and putting their lives at risk that it was for a good cause.

"Conley believes the man is out here. His wife believes he's within two miles of West Peak. That's the path he usually takes."

Knowing the mountain range like the back of his hand, Creed visualized the layout and features, focusing on spots where Terrence could be lost, or worse. Hikers were warned to never hike alone and stay within the designated public areas, and very seldom did they listen. That's why the SAR team was up on the mountain often.

"How often does he come out here?"

Creed shifted in the saddle. "The wife said two or three times a month. I don't think with all this rain we'll be able to track his path. Hopefully we'll find him hunkered down somewhere safe." They always went into a search and rescue mission looking for a live person. Most of the time people survived and that's what gave him satisfaction. To help someone. To bring them home.

After his contract in the Navy ended, and a short time on the rodeo circuit, he then came home to Cooper's Hawk, named after his great, great grandfather, Cooper Hawke. Creed now lived on the land that belonged to that same grandpa, Hawke Farm. His oldest brother, Hank, also a SAR, had moved above his bar, Pelican Hawk, a few years ago and Boone moved into the guest house on the farm's property for more privacy.

"You think he's still alive?" Boone asked as they steered toward West Peak.

"I think there's a good chance he is. He's young. In good condition. Trained in medical survival." Creed took the lead again as the trail narrowed and sandwiched between the ravine below and the rock wall.

The rain pummeled his hat, streamed off the rim and soaked his thick jacket and jeans. The temperature dropped as the sun set, which only made the situation more dire. The clock was ticking.

The only light would come from their flashlights soon.

"We're going to have to walk from here, Boone." The unstable path would be too dangerous for the horses. Sliding out of the saddle, Creed tied the reins on a tree limb and Boone did the same, and they continued the narrow, muddy path on foot.

"Shit, it's cold out here." Boone zipped his jacket.

Creed dragged his survival bag up further on his shoulder. "We've been through colder."

"That's for damn sure." He gave a dramatic shiver. "Makes me want to snuggle up with a warm, soft body."

"When do you need an excuse?"

"Speaking of, guess who I ran into yesterday."

"No clue." His words made a puff of fog.

"Penny Castle." The thirty-something, cute brunette was a teacher over at the middle school.

"Okay."

"What do you mean "okay'?" Boone groaned. "She's beautiful, smart, kind—"

"Then why don't you date her?"

"She doesn't want to date me, bro. She's had the hots for you since you divorced."

Creed didn't want to talk about his dating life—or the lack of—with anyone. "Who was the blonde I saw leaving the guest house last weekend?"

Boone chuckled proudly. "Vicki Barnes."

"Never heard of her." That didn't surprise Creed. His brother kept a rotating bed.

"Met her while I was out of town. She'd never been to Cooper's Hawk, so I invited her to come and visit. It turned into an overnight stay." He wriggled his brows.

"There's going to be an alignment of the stars when you finally find the one."

Boone snorted. "A man doesn't plant a garden to have one flower. He wants a variety."

Creed shook his head. "Mark my words."

They'd walked longer as the temperature continued to drop, and the rain still came down. Creed scrubbed the wetness from his face and whiskers, but it didn't help. As soon as he wiped it off more water gathered.

"Hell, we don't even know if this is the way he came," Boone complained.

"Hush!"

"Fine, ass—"

"Shh! Did you hear that?"

They'd stopped walking and listened. "It sounded like someone yelling. Wait. There it is again."

"It's that way." Creed took off on the trail. His boots slipped on the mud but somehow, he managed to stay upright. They reached the ridge that was marked by a safety sign urging hikers to stay off the unstable cliff. Beyond was a one-hundred-foot drop into the gorge. "Hello?"

"Down here! Help me, please!" came a weak voice.

Creed slowly stepped past the safety point which caused more rock to crumble.

"Come back, bro. That ain't going to work," Boone warned.

Lowering to his knees, Creed stretched out onto his stomach and pulled his way closer to the edge of the cliff. He pulled his flashlight from his belt and shone the light below. The man had fallen onto a ledge twenty feet down. "He's here," he informed Boone. "Terrence?"

"Y-yes. That's me."

"I'm Creed Hawke with Landing Search and Rescue. How hurt are you?"

"I broke my leg. A compound fracture. Some cuts and bruises. Probably a concussion," the man's voice quavered. "I've lost a lot of blood and I'm close to hypothermia. I've been down here for a w-while. M-my wife will be worried."

"Stay calm. We're going to get you out. I'll be right back."

"No. Don't leave! Please don't leave." His tortured moan traveled up the side of the bank.

"Listen, Terrence." Creed remained calm. He understood how being hurt and trapped could scare even the bravest person. "I know you must be worried, but my brother is here with me and we make it our job to help people. We will get you home to your wife. We just need to make sure anything and everything we do is done safely so we have to go slow."

"Okay. Okay." His teeth were chattering. "I can do this, but if I don't make it—"

"Terrence, you'll make it out. Hold tight." Creed crawled off the rock, stood and headed to his pack that he'd dropped on the path.

"What are you doing?" Boone asked. "That cliff is about to crumble."

"I'm going down after him." Creed took his rope, harness, carabiners, and leather gloves from the pack. He slid his knife into his boot in case things went awry.

"That's going to be almost impossible in this rain."

Creed dragged on his gloves. "What choice do we have?" Finding a sturdy tree, he began securing the aramid rope around the base and at the other end he tied a stopper knot. "When I get down there, I'll hook him up in the harness and you can help pull him up."

"Wait, Creed. We could send him down rain gear, warmers and water. It'll work until the weather lets up some."

"He's lost a lot of blood. Radio the medics and have them meet us at the base of the trail." He patted his brother's shoulder. "We have to get him out of there. This situation will only get worse and we can't wait for Mother Nature to appease us. You ready?"

Boone nodded. "I'll take care of things on my end.

"That's what I'm counting on. I know you have my back." Creed crawled back out on the rock and dropped his rope over, hearing it land below. He gave a prayer then positioned himself on the edge and rolled over, keeping his center of gravity close to the wall.

Holding the rope in a tight grip, he repeated the mantra *Stay low, go slow.*

"You okay?" Boone called out.

"I'm fine."

Facing the wall, he planted his feet shoulder-width apart and slowly walked several steps, but the unstable rock crumbled, twisting the rope, sending Creed sideways and hitting the wall. "Humph." His breath rustled out of his lungs. He grabbed the rope snugger in his gloved grip, pressing his boots against the rock to keep from hitting the solid wall again. Pebbles fell around him like a rock shower. He needed to move as quick as possible.

What seemed like hours had only been fifteen minutes when Creed's boots finally touched ground below. His arms were tired, his knuckles ached, but the relief of making it down took some of the pressure off his shoulders.

Terrence was lying in a twisted posture, obviously with his leg broken. Creed was glad he'd brought the harness with him.

"Thank God you found me." The man was close to tears.

They weren't out of the woods yet. "I'm going to get you to safety but it's important for you to listen to what I tell you to do. Is it your leg that's only broken?"

"Yes. I think so. A few cuts here and there but nothing major."

Creed grabbed the flashlight from his belt and made a quick evaluation of Terrence's condition. His ripped clothes had a faint staining of blood, but the rain had washed most of it away. His hiking shorts exposed his injured left leg that he'd wrapped in a makeshift bandage made from a red handkerchief. He was lucky to be alive because two inches one way and he would have landed in the ravine. Creed was grateful the man remained calm. Panicked rescues could lead to more injuries. He'd come out of a few missions with black eyes.

"Can you handle being lifted up?"

"Yes. I can handle it. I want the hell off this rock," Terrence rasped, shivering from the cold.

Creed removed his jacket and helped the man pull it on. "Have you repelled before?"

"Yes. A couple of times."

"Good, then you know how this works. I'll get the harness on you and we'll lift you up since you can't use your leg. It's going to hurt like hell."

Terrence nodded. "Let's do it."

As careful as he could, Creed secured the harness. "You ready?"

The man gave a weak nod. "As ready as I'll ever be."

"Ready, Boone," Creed said into his radio.

"Roger that," Boone answered.

The rope jerked and Terrence gasped in pain. "You okay?" Creed asked.

"I'll be fine once I'm up there."

Boone lifted him higher and higher, inch by inch. Slow and steady. More rock fell onto the lip.

Once Terrence reached safety, Creed breathed a sigh of relief and sat down on the edge of the rock. He then realized the rain had finally stopped. Staring out into the darkness, the moonlight brushed the tops of the trees making them look like a painting. It was quiet here on the mountain. He could have stayed there longer but when the evac rope struck his shoulder, he gathered himself and climbed up the side of the rock wall.

The adrenaline rush of saving a life only lasted the amount of time it took Creed to get home and walk through the front door. His mother had called and left a message telling him that his daughter had snuck out of the house during the night.

Fourteen-year-old Livvy Hawke jumped up from the couch and screamed, "You can't do this! It's unfair!"

"I can and I'm doing it." Creed Hawke did his best to remain calm although his daughter liked to push the limits of his patience far too many times.

"It's my phone! Not yours. You can't take it!"

"Really? Does that mean you'll be taking over the payment?"

Her face turned red and she fisted her hands at her sides. "I'm going to go live with Mom," she threatened.

If he had a dime for every time he heard this threat he'd be a rich man. He knew, and so did she, that going to live with her mom wasn't an option. Melody left Cooper's Hawk when Livvy was two and had only come to visit a few times since. As far as Creed knew, his ex was living in New York, or Hollywood or Chicago, following her dreams that didn't include being weighed down by a family.

When she'd first told him that she was leaving, he'd been hurt, not for himself but for Livvy. She was young, still needed her mom, but even more so now as a teen, as changes were taking place in her body that he couldn't possibly understand. For that reason alone he'd been a little more understanding, forgiving, until she started acting like she was an adult in a kid's body. He'd been warned by other parents that the day would come when teen-hood struck like a ferocious demon being uncaged.

"You'll have plenty of time to think about your future because you're grounded. No TV, no phone, and no friends for two weeks."

"You can't take my friends from me." She'd lost some of the anger in her tone as her punishment started to become real.

"Would you like for two weeks to turn into a month?" Creed narrowed his gaze on her, feeling his patience slip some. He was doing his best—had always done what he thought was best, but even parents were human and had limits. "You should have thought twice before you snuck out of the house."

"You don't understand. You never understand." She stomped her foot.

"What's there to understand? You didn't have permission to leave the house. You know the rules when I'm at work. Your grandmother was worried sick."

"When are you not at work?" She crossed her arms over her chest and gave him the stubborn Hawke expression.

He took a deep breath and let it escape through his teeth. He couldn't argue because no doubt, he worked more than he should. "It doesn't change the fact that you disobeyed the rules. You made your choice."

"I hate you!" She stamped her foot and puffed out her bottom lip like she would do when she was a toddler.

"Join the club." Although her words struck him straight in the center of his chest, he remained relaxed and didn't allow her to ruffle his feathers. These days it felt like she was doing everything and anything to push his buttons. He understood it couldn't be easy for a teenager to not have her mom around. Hell, things weren't any easier on him. Creed had thought he was doing a pretty good job at parenting until she turned thirteen and things spun upside down. "Then you won't mind if you go upstairs and spend some time in your bedroom."

"Fine!" She turned on her heels and stomped up the stairs. He could hear her feet pounding the hardwood floor and then the slamming of the door.

"Holy Sheets. What's all the racket?"

Creed greeted his ma with a weak smile. "The same routine, Ma."

"You know she's right."

"That I don't have the right to take her phone?" He strolled into the kitchen, grabbed a water bottle from the refrigerator and downed half of it in one gulp.

"No, you have the right to discipline her. I was referring to you working all the time." Abby folded her arms over her chest and looked at him above her square glasses, the way she did when he was in trouble as a child. "Have you even calculated how many hours you've worked this week alone?"

"Bills don't pay themselves and this farm, Sage Ranch and Cooper's Hawke Landing won't run themselves." He whipped off his Stetson and dropped it onto the counter.

"Yeah, and your daughter won't raise herself either."

Leave it to his ma to rip off the bandage. "At least she has you here with her." Although he appreciated everything she did for him and Livvy, sometimes he wished he could ignore her logical thinking.

"But she wants her father more." Abby sidestepped him, opened the refrigerator and took out a carton of eggs and package of bacon.

"Have you listened to her lately? I think I'm the last person she wants to be around." He finished his water and smashed the bottle, dropping it into the trashcan on his way to sit down at the small round table. Damn, he was tired. After saving the man off Trip Ease, he then was called out to search for a missing teenager who was separated from her group of friends. The SAR team spent all night searching until finally a call came in that she'd wandered back into her campsite completely unaware that she'd been the target of a missing person's search. The eighteen-year-old had huddled up in a cave to get stoned and fell asleep for the night.

"Those are just words. I always said we should spend more time watching actions instead of listening to words. You hungry?"

"Yeah, I could eat." He swiped his hand down his whiskered jaw. He needed a good scrub, a shave, and a couple days of sleep. Two of those he could manage but sleep wasn't in his near future because he had to stop over at Sage Ranch sometime that morning.

"Did she tell you where she snuck out to last night?" Abby broke an eggshell and dropped the contents into a frying pan.

"We didn't get that far," he grumbled.

"Hmm."

"What's that supposed to mean?" He stared at his ma's back.

She swiveled, wooden spoon pointing at him. "You two never get to the truth, or the core issue. When was the last time you two had a father to daughter talk? Just went out and had some fun?"

He opened his mouth, but nothing came. He had no answer. "Look, I know I'm not what she needs—"

"That's not what I'm saying." She slid the egg onto a plate, added a piece of toast and took the plate to him. She sat down across from him. "What I'm saying is that I know a thing or two about parenting and it's hard. We try to balance things, but it doesn't always work, especially when we're trying to run a household and hold down a job. That child is hurt, and you need to figure out why. Find the time."

He forked up a piece of egg, shoved it into his mouth then nodded. "I see your point."

The back door came flying open. Hank strolled in, swiped off his black Stetson and stuck it on the L hook. He, Boone and Creed were all about the same height and weight but Hank kept his hair high and tight, and he was missing a few fingers from his left hand from his days as an Explosive Ordinance Disposal Specialist in the Army. He came home, battled a case of PTSD, then opened Pelican Hawke. When he wasn't at the bar, Hank was working the land at the family farm and volunteering at Hawke Landing. Turning forty in May, he was looking more and more like their father, Damon Hawke. He'd been their superhero, taught his boys everything about the land and unfortunately had passed away too soon.

"I smell some good cooking." Hank pushed out his stomach and rubbed the pouch theatrically.

Creed was glad for the distraction.

Abby stood and gave Hank a hug. "Hungry, son?"

"I could eat a horse." He pulled out the chair across from Creed. "But not that new mare you just bought, bro. I could use her bones as toothpicks. I swear she hissed at me when I got close to her this morning. She refused to eat too. What did the vet say about her health?"

"Doc won't be out until later to check her over. I'll bet it's more psychosomatic than physical. That bastard who owned her before abused her." When it had come to Creed's attention that the horse was being abused, he talked the previous owner into selling the mare for a hefty price. That's one thing Creed couldn't tolerate…the abuse of an animal. "Don't give up on her, Hank. You watch and see. She's got it in her to make a damn good asset on the farm."

Abby set a full plate in front of Hank. "Thanks, Ma." He plowed through the eggs and bacon, downed it with his coffee, then licked his fingers. "What are your plans today?" He directed his curious, Hawke-renowned-blue eyes on Creed.

"I have to stop over at Sage Ranch and do a couple things. I'll be back this afternoon. I need to get moving." He pushed the chair back and stood.

"Not so fast, son." Abby had made another plate and handed it to him. "Go feed your daughter."

There was no use in arguing. Grabbing his hat and shoving it on his head, he took the plate and headed upstairs. At Livvy's closed door, he knocked, and pretty much what he had expected, she yelled, "Go away!"

"I have breakfast for you."

A few long seconds passed. "What is it?"

"Eggs, bacon and toast."

"Do you forget everything? I'm a pescatarian."

"A pesca-what?"

"Pescatarian. I don't eat meat except for fish."

"Since when?"

"A month ago."

With a shrug, he grabbed the slice of bacon off the plate and shoved it into his mouth. "It's now a pescatarian plate," he said around his mouth full. "Unless you don't eat eggs either."

Ten seconds lapsed until finally the lock clicked and the door came open. She slanted her gaze through the three-inch crack and shot invisible torpedoes at him. "I eat eggs. And this doesn't mean I've forgiven you," she muttered, opened the door wide and grabbed the plate.

"I didn't think so, but can I come in?"

She went to the bed and sat cross legged on the colorful blanket. Music played from the speaker on her shelf and a book was open on her nightstand. He picked it up and read the cover. "This any good?"

"If you like books about teen girls who are being imprisoned in their home. It's right up your alley."

"Okay then." He set the book aside and sat down on the end of the bed. "Why did you sneak out?"

"It doesn't matter." She scooped up egg onto her toast.

"It matters."

"Does that mean you'll consider giving me my phone back?" She paused with the fork in the air.

"No. You'll still be disciplined." Her frown returned. "But why would you risk getting into trouble?"

She set her plate to the side and clasped her hands in her lap. "You wouldn't understand."

"Try me."

With a nibble at the corner of her lips, she finally said, "I needed to see Alex."

The fourteen-year-old was Livvy's best friend since kindergarten. Creed liked the kid and he had good parents, but that didn't mean his daughter could sneak out to see him. Feeling a familiar stab in the center of his chest, Creed rubbed his forehead. He understood friendships and the importance of them. "Alex couldn't come to the house? Did he sneak out too?"

In that instant he saw her wall come back up. "No, Alex doesn't have to sneak out because he doesn't have prison guards as parents." She grabbed her Air pods, stuck them in her ears and closed her eyes, signifying the end of the conversation.

"Good talk," he said and got up, leaving the room. He took the front stairs and stepped outside, inhaling a combination of freshly mowed grass, pine trees and hay.

Leaning over the porch rail, he stared out into the vastness of Hawke Farm. Once upon a time they owned two hundred acres of prime land until their father fell on hard times and sold all but forty to Rusty Sage next door. Damon Hawke had always wanted to buy back the property, had promised his sons that he would, but years had passed and then it was too late.

The sound of cattle mooing caught on the breeze. Horses grazed the field inside the white picket fence. The pounding of hammers hitting nails came from the men fixing the leak in the barn roof. Farm business as usual.

What Creed could use was a long ride to clear his head. He had some time to spare. Some people took medicine for their ailments, but he rode to keep himself healthy.

Taking the worn path to the stables, there he saddled up Miss Daisy, climbed on, and led her through the south gate. Once they were in the wide-open field, he clicked his tongue to command her into a trot.

The weather was nice, still cool from the sun hiding behind the clouds. He rode along the fence that marked the property line between Hawke Farm and Sage Ranch. Further on he came to the ramshackle barn that was being held up by a couple of rusty nails and a few splinters. Rusty and Creed had talked about tearing down the death trap, should have happened years ago, but every time it came to do the project, Creed felt a knock in his ribs. The barn, or rather what was left of it, had history for him.

This was where he and Mindy had hunkered down during a tornado and he'd made a promise to never let anything happen to her. He knew that day—that very moment—he'd love Mindy Sage for the rest of his life.

He'd also been young and dumb.

She'd left Cooper's Hawk for college and he'd signed up for the Navy. Many times over the years he'd wanted to contact her, just to say…what? *How's the weather? Do you still like to run barefoot in the rain? Do you remember me?*

His chuckle reverberated through the quiet.

He guessed he could have asked Rusty about Mindy at any time, but Creed didn't need to know the details. Not really. Didn't want to know. Hell, truth was he didn't want to hear about how happy she was with another man. That could make him seem bitter, and maybe he was, but scraping open old wounds didn't sound like much fun.

Scanning his gaze over the mountains in the distance, he loved the beauty of this spot. In fact, he and Mindy had come out here often, climbed trees, built forts, or just played chase. Sometimes he enjoyed catching her just to hug her.

He'd once dreamed of building a house right here in this very spot.

It wasn't too late.

In his head, those years seemed like ages ago. Yet in his heart they felt like yesterday. Spurred over Mindy leaving and finding solace at the bottom of a beer, one night he ran into Melody Rumor at a party and he fell into her soft, warm embrace. They'd had a few good times and then she'd hinted that she wanted to get hitched. South of his sterling silver belt buckle, the idea didn't seem so bad. He was leaving for boot camp and having someone back home did have its advantages. She'd known all the right moves, had made him forget Mindy, at least for a minute.

He'd lost his ever-loving mind and asked Mel to marry him, and the plans were locked into place. His brothers had warned him. His mother had warned him. He'd finally come to his senses when he woke up one morning and realized the only thing he and Mel had in common was the way she made him feel between the sheets.

Calling off the wedding, Mel had thrown a hurricane sized hissy fit and left town. He left for boot camp and spent the next few years proving his love for his country.

When he came home, he found that he wasn't quite ready to settle back down at Cooper's Hawk. He still had some roaming left in his blood and joined the rodeo circuit. He loved the eight second ride, even did well for himself by saving up some money and lining a shelf with shiny awards, but after a short period he started missing home. He split from the rodeo and headed back to Montana. Mel had been visiting her folks and one thing led to another and they found themselves back at square one.

And then she got pregnant.

Creed had done the right thing and asked her to marry him for the second time. He'd ignored his cold feet and put a ring on her finger.

From the start, he'd known for a relationship to work between him and Mel, they'd have to jump some serious hurdles. She had big dreams of becoming a star and it certainly wasn't going to happen in Cooper's Hawk. She wanted to rub elbows and party with socialites and the only party Creed was interested in involved a keg and roasted hot dogs. Mel wanted to travel and although he liked to explore some too, he had responsibilities. And soon they had the responsibility of a daughter.

Mel always said she liked cowboys, but she didn't like ones that got his hands dirty. She always complained how long he worked, how much he sweated, and the dirt under his nails after a hard day on the land.

Sometimes two people, even if they shared a child together, just couldn't work things out.

Maybe it was time he went on a date. There were some available women in Cooper's Hawk. For instance, Penny Castle had invited him over for dinner a few times. She'd even stopped over at the house one day and brought him cupcakes. He didn't have the heart to tell her that he didn't much care for cake.

Turning the horse to start back, his gaze naturally fell on the words engraved on the side of the big oak tree. *Mindy + Creed* wrapped in a heart. He'd done a lot of things back then that he couldn't see himself doing now.

Chapter 3

THERE WAS A big difference between perception and reality in figure skating. People believed it was an easy sport, but what Mindy had learned over the years, after lots of blood, sweat and tears were left on the ice, competitive skating required a fearlessness—both mentally and physically—that a lot of people didn't have.

In her younger years she'd learned triple loops without a care in the world. In her twenties, she'd understood the bravery behind tossing herself into the air and landing perfectly on her skates because if she didn't she would seriously injure herself. She could be off the ice for weeks or months, or worse, she could do permanent damage and she'd have to hang up her skates. She'd had a few scary scrapes with injuries but had been lucky, if one could call it luck.

There was an expiration date on the sport and now, in her late thirties, she understood how unbelievably insane it was to still get out on the ice and take risks, but just like being in love, a person must take chances or lose everything.

Throwing herself thoughtlessly into the air and hoping for the best didn't feel the same at thirty-seven that it did at twelve. The moves became harder and her bones resisted, especially those parts of her like her ankles and knees that had paid the price of hitting the ice.

But there was a lioness within Mindy that kept her from giving up what she loved, what made her happy.

Listening to the blades of her skates slide against the ice was music to her ears. Her body moved from muscle memory. She closed her eyes and counted the steps in her head. Opening them, she jumped into a single loop, came down steady on her skates to hear clapping off to the side.

"Bravo! Bravo!"

Her old coach and owner of the rink, Isabella, waved from the sidelines.

"I didn't know I had an audience." Mindy felt her cheeks warm. She hadn't skated in front of anyone, outside of her students, in years.

"You deserve one, my dear." Isabella was still as beautiful as ever. Her long, silver streaked hair was pulled back into a severe bun, showing off high cheekbones, olive complexion with only a trace of wrinkles. At five eight, she had a thin, athletic body and the leotard and skater's skirt complimented how shapely she still was at sixty.

"You're only being nice." Mindy opened the gate and walked in to sit down on the bench.

"I'm being truthful. Have you ever known me to be dishonest? You were my best student." Isabella sat down on the other end of the bench. Skaters came from all over Montana, and sometimes beyond, to have lessons with the Olympic medalist.

"You were the best coach. This place brings back so many memories." Mindy felt refreshed, better than she'd felt in a long time. "I'm so glad to see that you're still here too."

"What else would I do?" Although she wore a smile, Mindy could see the concern in Isabella's soft grey eyes. "How long are you staying in Cooper's Hawk?"

"I'm not sure."

"Watching you out on the ice, like the little girl who showed up here with such a strong attitude and full of determination, I too was taken back to a different time," she said with an accent from her German roots. She'd moved to Cooper's Hawk with her American husband when she was nineteen who she'd met during the Olympics.

"I love this place. I haven't been on the ice in months." She untied the strings of her worn skates and slipped out of them.

"That's a tragedy, my dear. People like you and me, we belong here." She clapped her hands together, much like she did when Mindy was younger and she'd made a mistake. "I have a proposition for you."

Putting on her flats, Mindy also grabbed her jacket and shrugged into it, covering her black leotard. "A proposition?"

"Come help here at the rink as a coach. I don't skate like I once did, not since the knee surgery a few years back. You would be perfect."

Mindy hadn't considered getting a job while in Cooper's Hawk. She'd planned on working on the ranch, but the offer was very tempting. "Do you have any students right now?"

"Five, but I know with you here there would be more."

"And the schedule would be flexible?"

"Sure. As much as you like, dear. We could discuss it later in more detail?"

Why wasn't Mindy jumping at the opportunity? She felt more alive on the ice than anywhere. "Let's do that. I'd love to coach."

"Great!" the older woman's eyes twinkled. "When did you get back?"

"A few days ago. I've been sticking around the house, reacclimating myself to ranch life. Working with the horses."

"How's your father doing? We used to run into each other often. Since Benny passed Rusty no longer comes to visit." Ben was Isabella's husband. When Mindy had heard the news of his passing she'd called and had spoken to Isabella. What she and Ben had shared had truly been a love story. The sadness remained in Isabella's gaze.

"Since Daddy's heart attack he's been different. I know it takes time to recover, but he seems, well, depressed. You know how he is. He's as stubborn as a goat and doesn't want help from anyone. When he was told he'd have to have surgery to repair the damage in his heart, and I then told him he'd have to come to California for the operation and stay with me while he recovered, I thought he was going to tell me he'd rather meet his maker. In the end, he conceded, and I do think he enjoyed visiting."

"You know, my Benny had suffered greatly when he got sick. He changed too. Illness is such a terrible thing for masculine men like my Benny and your father."

"He's definitely grumpy."

"Age with all the muscle aches and forgetfulness makes us into, how do my kids put it, sourpusses," she joked. "When I had my knee surgery, they all tried to make me sit down and relax like an old woman. They soon learned that age didn't make me old. They even suggested I sell the rink." She laughed. "They would have seen a sourpuss then."

"I couldn't imagine this place not being here in Cooper's Hawk. It's a part of the history."

"It's so nice to have you back in town." Isabella patted Mindy's hand. "I'm sure Rusty is happy too. He always kept me up to date on your achievements."

"I'm sure he mentioned the divorce?"

"Yes, yes, he did. I'm sorry. Just remember though, sometimes the heartbreak builds us into the person we need to be."

"Thank you, Isabella. Thank you for everything. When Mom passed away you were there for me. You helped me through, and I can never tell you enough how much it meant to me."

Tears filled Isabella's eyes. She sniffed and stood to pat her hair in nervous energy. "So then I'll be in touch soon, my dear."

Mindy left the rink feeling elated after a skate and a job opportunity.

Turning onto Sage Ranch later, a sense of home washed through Mindy.

Clicking off the AC and rolling the window down, she breathed in fresh, country air. She caught a salty combination of straw and cow manure and instead of being repulsed she smiled. What had she ever been thinking when she'd wanted Branch to move here with her? He would have gotten one whiff of poop and vomited.

Across the grass she saw Bo. The cowboy had been working Sage Ranch for as long as Mindy had been alive. Putting her car into park, she got out and met him halfway. She walked into his open arms for a tight hug.

"Well, well, well. Let me look at you," he said when she stepped out of his embrace. His leathered skin had more deep wrinkles and he'd lost weight. "You know things just ain't the same around here without you, Miss Mindy."

She couldn't remember one memory on Sage Ranch that didn't include the charming, happy-go-lucky Bo Walters. "It's been a long time. How's May?"

"Wifey is great, even better now that I'm only here a few days a week. If I'd known you were back in town I'd have come sooner."

"Daddy told me you weren't here as often."

"May wanted me to retire completely, but you know this old man needs something to keep his bones in shape."

"Will you tell her hello from me?"

"Sure thing, sweet girl. You know she'll want to see you. And I'm sure she'll make you one of her rhubarb pies that you used to ask for."

"I'll stop over one day, but she doesn't have to go to any trouble."

"No trouble for our favorite cowgirl."

She kissed his cheek and bid him farewell.

Starting for the car, she saw movement in the field and spotted a shirtless man near the fence. He was pounding a post into the ground. Each movement made the muscles of his broad back flex. The waist of his worn jeans settled low on his slender hips and his thick, long legs went on for miles. She couldn't deny that she'd missed cowboys, especially ones that looked this good.

There was something familiar about him…

The man dropped the hammer into the grass, swiped off his white Stetson and hooked it on the nearby post. He bent and reached for a water bottle from the ground and she saw his profile. Every bit of air trailed out of her lungs. Her knees wobbled. Sweat beaded between her breasts. Her heart played like a banjo.

She knew him!

The cowboy was none other than Creed Hawke.

What was *he* doing here?

Leaning against the driver's door, she watched him from the cover of the car, barely able to draw oxygen into her lungs. Her limbs tingled and the threat of passing out was real.

He dropped the bottle, grabbed the hammer and went back to pounding, unaware that he was the object of her heated stare.

Swallowing against the thickness in her throat, she laid her forehead against the cool metal of the car. *Get into control. Get into control. He's just a man.*

Lifting her head, she felt a swirl of heat through her.

God, he looked good.

Better than good.

His shoulders were broader, his back wider and his bottom firmer. He was all around bigger and stronger. Masculine. She felt a pool of desire in the pit of her stomach that awakened her nerve endings.

He turned and she squealed, jumping into the driver's seat and ducking down. She kept her gaze locked on him above the steering wheel. Age had been kind to him—unfairly kind. His bright blue eyes were radiant against his tanned skin. His handsome face had chiseled lines that made him look warrior-like. His sharp cheekbones and jaw were covered in dark whiskers, making him look dangerous, not scruffy. The thick waves of his hair touched his nape.

Thankfully, he didn't see her stalking him.

Once he returned his attention to the fence, she sat up in the seat, turning the AC on blast, and facing the vents her direction until she felt the tip of her nose grow cold. Unfortunately, the blast of air did nothing to ease the warmth between her thighs.

Her body and mind were at a war of sorts.

Tears welled in her eyes and she blinked them away, refusing to fall victim to her emotions.

The risk of seeing him had been there all along. Although she'd known the reunion wouldn't be easy, she needed to be strong. The days of being the girl who followed him around like a puppy were long gone. Sure, he looked good—very good—but her tastes had changed. Hadn't they?

A cocktail of hurt, anger and guilt took her body prisoner.

Lying to herself only made this harder.

She still cared for him. Still found him attractive and desirable. Not just physically, but those invisible parts of her that missed the times they'd shared. The joy he'd given her. The scab was torn away, allowing all the emotion to bleed through her.

He'd married and moved on. He could still be married and probably was.

In the end, he'd chosen a life with Melody Rumor.

Mindy had come back to Cooper's Hawk nineteen years ago to tell him about the child she carried. Scared and confused, she'd needed him. She wanted his assurance that everything would be okay. Instead, she'd learned that he and Melody were engaged to be married. She'd gone back and forth over the course of two days whether she'd tell him or not.

Then she'd decided to write him a letter and allow him to decide what he wanted. She left it in his truck that was parked at the factory where he'd worked at the time.

Mindy had confessed everything, from her pregnancy to loving him. She'd asked him to meet her at the ice rink if he wanted her and the baby—if he wanted a family.

Sometime while she was waiting for him, she'd fallen asleep in her car, only to wake later to a knock on the window. She'd jumped up in the seat, expecting to see Creed on the other side of the glass, but instead she found a scowling Melody who looked like she wanted to rip Mindy from limb to limb.

Creed's fiancée had come to tell Mindy that he wasn't coming.

Mindy had doubted Melody. After all, the two women had never gotten along, but she had pulled up text messages Creed had written to her. *"Mindy means nothing to me" "I'm glad she's gone" "I never want to see her again"*. Her heart had taken a terrible blow. The proof was in his words. He wanted nothing more to do with her. He especially couldn't want an unplanned baby.

Crushed, she left Cooper's Hawk three hours later and never looked back.

The secret could destroy lives.

Pressing on the gas, she drove up to the house, blinking away the tears that blurred her vision. The stabbing sensation of betrayal flooded her body and she wanted to run away, but she reminded herself that she was no longer afraid.

Mindy had known the time would come when she would have to face the truth. Maybe divulging the truth would help her move on.

Taking her phone from her purse, she pulled up a picture of Jane. She looked so much like Creed. From her wavy, disobedient hair. Eyes that were so pale they could be compared to a clear blue sky. And a smile that warmed hearts.

More tears fell to her cheeks and she brushed them away, focusing on the anger instead of the pain.

She really wanted to hate Creed. Mindy didn't want to feel the burden of guilt any longer. She wanted to break herself from the secret that bound her to him.

Leaning her forehead against the steering wheel, she felt the hairs at her nape lift. She would tell Creed about Jane and then allow him to decide what he wanted.

Look at the mess she'd become.

Married seventeen years to a man she never really knew. Her daughter never knew her biological father. And Mindy's heart was still full of love…for a man she could never have.

Over the years Creed had become the man she'd compared Branch to. When her husband had touched her, she'd feel a sense of void. Branch could never add up. He'd been in competition with her past and he never knew it. However, he did know that she'd never gotten over the pain and loss. She'd tried to be a good wife but bombed.

Lifting her head, she peered into the rearview mirror as if she could still see Creed. His bare torso only triggered a need inside her she should never have. His callused hands had left an invisible tattoo of his touch on her skin. There was still a lure, or magnetism, between them—at least for her.

Climbing from the car, she grabbed the grocery bags from the trunk and ran inside the house, bursting through the door of her childhood home. Dropping her purse and keys on the table, placing the groceries in the kitchen, she then went in search of some answers. "Daddy? Where are you? We need to talk. What in the world is *that* man doing on Sage Ranch? And why didn't you tell me he was back when I got here?"

She picked up speed in the hallway, determined. The heels of her cowgirl boots clicked loudly on the pockmarked wood floors as she made her way toward the office. She came to a dead stop in the open doorway and settled her heated glare on her daddy who sat behind the cluttered desk. He brought his narrowed chin up and cool, grey eyes targeted her. "What's all the fuss about?"

"Daddy? Didn't you hear me?" She crossed her arms and tilted her chin. Her father had aged, looking almost frail sitting at his desk. Growing up he'd been a powerful presence with his thick hair, pensive eyes, tall, broad shouldered stature. He'd always been kind, friendly, and then he'd lost a part of himself when Mindy's mama died. He'd turned to the bottle to get him through the days and she remembered how sad he had become. Thankfully, he'd stopped drinking—as much—after his heart attack.

He pushed a stack of papers into a folder, closed it then gave her his undivided attention. He finally smiled, but the expression didn't quite reach his eyes. "What was that?" Rusty Sage's eyes appeared paler against the backdrop of his weathered skin.

"What is *he* doing on this ranch?"

He swiveled in the chair. "I don't know. Who is *he* and what was *he* doing?"

"Creed. Looked like he was fixing a fence to me."

"Now, now. Don't get yourself all in a mess, girl. He's working." Rusty waved his gnarled hand.

"Why is *he* helping out?"

Her father showed his growing impatience by rubbing his wrinkled forehead. His eyes almost looked haunted. What was he not telling her? "Mindy, did you come all the way to Cooper's Hawk to grill me?"

Was that the way he saw it? "I'm only asking why Creed's working here? Daddy, you know—"

"Yes, I know," he said in a whispered tone. "I wanted to tell him but it's not my place."

She swallowed hard. "I'm sorry that I asked you not to."

He lifted his gaze, holding hers. "I told you how I felt. Won't do any good now," he muttered.

Lowering her gaze to gain her equilibrium, she asked, "Daddy, I don't think I should be judged—"

He lifted his hand, stopping her. "It's not my place to judge you, especially when I don't know all the details, but take it from an old man, clear the air."

"Is that why you hired him? Do you feel guilty?"

Rusty stood, wobbled, and gained his balance by holding the corner of the desk.

"Daddy, are you okay?" She went to his side to help him.

"I'm doing okay. No worrying. You're at Sage Ranch. You're home." He patted her shoulder and winked.

Although the conversation was far from over, she'd save it for later. "Come help me put away the groceries. I grabbed you a jar of those pickled sausages you love, and I have some news I want to share."

"I haven't had one of those good sausages in a long time." His eyes twinkled.

In the kitchen, Mindy opened the jar for him and he took one of the sausages out. This was the happiest she'd seen him since she'd come home. While he munched on the snack, she opened a tray of chicken, took down the cast iron pan from the cabinet and set it on the stove.

"What are you doing?" he asked.

"I'm making dinner."

"I always eat dinner over at the club on Cow Tuesday," he mumbled.

"Tonight you don't have to go anywhere. I'm cooking and we're eating healthy."

"I like eating unhealthy," he grumbled. The bear had returned.

"You only like eating that way because it's easy. The market in Cooper's Hawk now has a great selection of lean meats, nuts, and other clean items. Here, try this." She handed him a plastic container.

"What's this?" He held it at arm's length to read the label.

"It's hummus. Don't knock it until you try it. And I'll also make us roasted cauliflower."

His nose wrinkled and he pushed the container far away from him. "I don't want to try something that I can barely pronounce, and I don't like cauliflower. I'm not a rabbit."

"Rabbits like carrots not cauliflower. Be open minded."

He looked concerned. "It's steak and potato night at the club. The cook always prepares mine perfectly with a baked potato full of butter and bacon." He rubbed his stomach.

"You can miss steak and potato night for one evening. Anyway, we are celebrating that I got a job." She sprinkled the chicken liberally with seasoning, poured on soup from a can and placed it into the prewarmed pan to sear it.

"A job? What about helping here? Learning the ropes."

"I will. I wasn't looking for a job, but I was at the ice rink and ran into Isabella. She asked if I would help out coaching the kids." Mindy felt proud of herself, until she saw her father's disapproval.

His shoulder's slumped. "If that's what you want. You know I don't like chicken though."

"I'm making the meal that mama used to make with a few healthy tweaks." She washed her hands and dried them of on a towel. "You know, the casserole with mushrooms and onions? I'm adding asparagus—"

"Humph. Onions give me heartburn and asparagus turns my pee green."

"Don't be a booger."

"I'm going to starve to death."

"Daddy, are you intentionally giving me a hard time?"

He huffed a sigh, shrugged a shoulder, then left the room.

Breathing in a calming breath, she busied herself cutting up vegetables and thinking about Creed.

How dare he work here at Sage Ranch.

This was her home and he shouldn't be here.

Why didn't Daddy tell me?

Setting the knife aside, she dropped the veggies in with the chicken and placed the pan in the oven.

She didn't come to Cooper's Hawk to feel bad.

Last night she'd tossed and turned. She guessed she knew why.

Going up the stairs into her childhood bedroom, she was met with the decorations of a teenager. The posters on the wall and the pink blanket screamed youth.

Ripping the pictures off the wall, she shoved them into a cardboard box.

Opening her closet, she dragged out her wooden chest and opened the lid. Inside she found memories that she no longer needed—or wanted. Movie tickets. Letters. Pictures…all connecting her to Creed. Had she ever had her own existence?

Why did she need to keep this stuff?

She didn't.

Grabbing armfuls of the items, she dumped them into the box. She came to a picture of her mother and stopped. "Oh, mama. I wish you were here."

Swallowing back emotion, she took the photo and stuck in on the mirror of her dresser. She looked so much like her mama.

"I hope you're still watching over me," Mindy whispered.

Swiping away tears, she grabbed up the box and took it outside.

It was time she got rid of the past. This would prove to herself that she was over Creed.

In the firepit, she started a fire and once the blaze was hot, she dropped the posters in and watched them incinerate. A part of her childhood was up in smoke.

That didn't feel so bad.

She picked up a shirt, shook it out and suffered an internal kick to her ribs. The jersey had belonged to Creed. He'd given it to her the night they'd made love because she was cold.

"I hope you're not thinking of putting *that* in the burn pile."

Her body stilled. Her heart jumped inside her chest. She'd know the thick, husky tone from anywhere. Dragging in a labored breath, she turned and felt the dirt cave from under her bare feet.

Creed had his hat lowered on his forehead, but it didn't hide the faded denim color of his gaze that caught the rays of the sun. His worn, dirty jeans sat low on his hips and the large silver belt buckle glistened, drawing her attention to his crotch. She gulped and jerked her gaze upward, onto a safer region, but his wide chest wasn't much safer. He was now wearing a shirt and the tight-fitting black cotton stretched across his broad shoulders. She remembered earlier how good his sweat-slicked torso had looked as he pounded the fence post. His cocky smirk took her down memory lane of those long summer nights on a mountain trail, loud country music playing from the truck radio, and barefoot races in tall grass after a downpour. The moonlight streaming down as he undressed her, awakening her body to his touch, taking her with such gentle, kindness that ruined her for other men.

Warmth spread through her.

She suddenly felt self-conscious. She'd changed, but he hadn't—no, he had, but he'd gotten better over time. In uneasiness, she wrung the jersey between shaking hands imagining that it was his neck.

Chapter 4

"MAYBE YOU SHOULD give her the phone back."

"She's getting to you, Ma. You're caving. She has a way of blinking those innocent eyes and hypnotizing us to her ways." Creed poured himself a thermos of coffee, tightened the lid, and stuck it under his arm. "Rules are in place for a reason. She broke them."

"If I remember correctly, you and your brothers always said to me, "rules are made to be broken", or at least that seemed the run of things with you boys growing up."

"I thought you said girls are easier to raise than boys," he reminded her.

She held up her hands in defense. "I didn't say that. I wouldn't have anything to compare it to. Anyway, Livvy needs a mother."

"She has you."

"I can't stay here forever, Creed. I love Livvy, and you, but I'd like to do some traveling before I get too old."

He narrowed his gaze. "I never heard you talk like this before. Is there something you'd like to confess?" He'd suspected for some time that she had someone she was trying to impress. She came home one day with a new hairstyle, new color, and a manicure. Not that she wasn't allowed to pamper herself, but for as long as he could remember, he'd never seen his mom with polished nails.

She dropped the towel she'd been drying dishes with and shrugged. "When there's something you need to know I'll tell you."

"Oh, I see. You can give your opinion about my love life but yours is top secret? Why don't you give this much heat to Hank and Boone about their relationship status? They're both single."

"Because they don't have kids, a daughter, who needs a female role model."

"Ma, let's not have this discussion now. Please." The last thing he needed was the added pressure of asking someone out right now. In his twenties he had no qualms about asking a woman out, but dates never seemed to get beyond the first. They were either too chatty. Too needy. Too something or other. Hell, who was he kidding? He was just too damn particular. In his thirties, as he matured, he got too busy with Livvy and work, and didn't have the time for dating. Now as forty approached, he realized most of his friends were married and dating wasn't nearly as easy. "I need to get going. I'm stopping off at Sage Ranch then heading to parent teacher conferences with Livvy's teacher. Maybe you can coax Liv into coming down to eat dinner." He kissed his mom on the forehead. "Sorry that my brothers and I were tyrants. I'm having trouble with one teen and you had three boys. Lord, you deserve sainthood."

"Don't worry about Livvy. We'll be fine."

His daughter seemed to listen more to his mother than she did to him. At times he felt like he was a visitor in his own home—in his own relationship with Livvy. He thought about this as he climbed behind the wheel of his truck, started the engine and let it idle. Maybe his Ma was right, it had come to the point where he needed to do this alone, without her assistance. He couldn't deny he'd used his Ma as a buffer on more than one occasion and Livvy knew this.

When had he become the bad guy?

He had no clue what a girl—or woman—needed. He hadn't been on a date in so long he'd forgotten how to. If his parenting skills had any relation to his ability of making a woman happy, he was out of luck.

He was still thinking of the dating/marriage thing when he drove onto Sage Ranch and climbed from his truck. He gave a look around before he headed to fix the fencing he'd been meaning to get to for a few weeks. His other intention had been to hire new hands to take up some of the slack around the property.

The sun beat down hot. He dragged off his shirt and hung it on the post as he worked to pound the post into the ground. A hard day's job always did his body good.

Thirsty, he dropped the hammer, grabbed a water bottle and drank the cool liquid, then wiped is hand across his face.

Picking the hammer back up, he started hammering, but the hair on his neck lifted. He got that queasy feeling that he was being watched. Jerking a gaze around, he spotted the silver BMW sitting on the lane, but he didn't see anyone behind the wheel.

Squinting, he wondered who in the hell came around these parts in a luxury car?

Shrugging, he went back to work and once he finished, he strolled back to the barn where he found Bo finishing his chores.

"Evenin', Bo."

"Good to see you, Creed. Any luck finding hands?"

"No, but I have a few ideas. How are you, buddy?"

"Fine. I'll miss this place but I'm getting old. Time to close the curtain."

"Never old, my friend, just finely seasoned. Were you able to switch out the grain for the cattle?"

The other man blinked. "No, I didn't. I forgot. I'll do that." He took the saddle he was polishing and laid it aside.

Creed didn't want to make it his business to remind someone that they were slacking but he'd noticed Bo seemed preoccupied lately. "Don't worry. The feed store will put the new grain on the next delivery. Are you sure all is okay?"

There was a long thoughtful hesitation. "I haven't told anyone but Rusty, but our oldest son, Gavin, has been having some trouble finding a job. May's been sick with worry over him, you know, since he came back from Iraq. Now is probably the best time for me to retire and take care of my family business."

"Have Gavin call me. He's a good guy and I need a few good men around here that I can rely on."

Bo's eyes widened. "Really? That would be very generous."

"You're a good man, Bo. Rusty and I both appreciate all the years you've dedicated to Sage Ranch. Helping your son out is the least we can do."

"Thank you. I'll tell him to call you."

"I see Rusty has a visitor."

"You didn't know?" Bo's tan faded.

"Know what?"

"I guess I assumed you knew." Bo swiped a hand over his thin jaw. "Remember a few years back, we were at that welcome home party for Adam Case? We were sitting around the fire, drank a little too much whiskey, and I asked you what your biggest regret was in life?"

Yeah, he remembered the party. His old buddy Adam had come back from his military contract early, injured when an IED exploded and left him without a leg. Adam had a wife and kid and although they were happy to have him home, he sensed there was a lot of concern. A man never knew what life would be like when he came back from across the pond, but losing a limb had its own barrel of issues. "Hell, beats me. I was pretty upset to see my buddy hurt."

"You said you regretted not chasing after *her*." The corner of Bo's mouth twitched.

"Her?" Creed didn't need to search his memory. He could play dumb, but the man's gaze nailed him in accusation. That could be a problem with drinking, loose lipped confessions never helped anyone.

"Do you need to clean out the cobwebs?"

No denying, he'd been hurt when she left but, in his gut, he'd known it had been the best thing for all of them. "A lapse of reasoning on my part."

"Oh? What if I told you she was back in Cooper's Hawk?"

Creed chuckled and swiped a hand down his whiskered jaw. He looked across the hay strewn floor of the barn and caught the grave expression on Bo's face.

Huh?

Creed was ready to throttle the man if he was lying.

"Nothin' to joke about." Creed muttered the words.

"She's been back a few days. The BMW is hers."

The loud mooing of a cow right outside the barn mingled with the heavy beating of Creed's heart in his ears. A vivid image developed inside his head of her, his first love. His first kiss. His first…everything. At ten she'd been his best friend. At sixteen she'd become a woman overnight and stole his heart. At eighteen he'd finally worked up the nerve to make a move, but instead of treading slowly, he'd jumped off the proverbial cliff and wound up making an effing mess of things. Big time.

He never understood why he'd become the tongue-tied, wet-behind-the ears, foolish idiot when it had come to talking about his feelings for her. For a long time she'd been one of the boys, until she woke up one day and had blossomed in all the right places then she'd been the target of all the boys' interest. She'd always been beautiful, but she'd grown curves. Breasts. And she'd learned to work magic with her dark eyes.

At eighteen, and not nearly as mature as he thought he'd been at the time, he'd been embarrassed at the strong reaction of his body each time she was near. If the wind caught her scent, he grew hard. If she brushed against him, he would lose his head.

He shoved his shaking hands in his front pockets. Even now, he lost himself thinking about her. "If you're lying, I'll hang you by your toes—"

Bo swung his palms up. "Hey, I like to joke about a lot of things, but even I have a line I won't cross. Your past is one of them. I just wanted to warn you."

Mindy.

Mindy.

Mindy.

She was home.

His chest became heavier and his gut twisted. His jeans stretched. He was a dumbass.

Anger sliced through him. Why the hell was she back? She left Cooper's Hawk—and him—in her dust years ago and didn't look back.

Creed stepped out of the barn and looked around the green pasture. Why couldn't he get air into his lungs? It was as if he had a ton of bricks laying on his chest. Why did his boots feel a size too large and his boxers a size too small?

Damn. Mindy was home.

His Mindy.

The biggest heart break in his life had been the day she told him she needed to get out of Cooper's Hawk and she was leaving for California. Not once had she asked him to come along. He wouldn't have because he'd signed up for the military but being asked would have at least proven to him that she cared.

He strolled up to his truck and pressed out the tension in his forehead with his thumb and forefinger as he wrapped his head around the idea that the girl who broke his heart was here…at Sage Ranch. Driving a BMW.

This shouldn't come as a great big surprise. Not really. After all, this was her childhood home.

He rubbed his eyes and muttered a curse word.

Mindy.

Mindy.

"Mindy," he huffed out. He couldn't think clearly. Hell, he couldn't breathe. Clenching his hands into fists, he felt his knuckles ache and loosened the grip.

How many times had he dreamed of what could have been if he had told her how much he cared for her? How she made him feel? How many times had he wished he'd done things differently? If he had though, he wouldn't have Livvy. Some paths needed to happen although unplanned.

"She's only back for a visit. She'll leave and things will go back to the way they were," he muttered to himself. Back to what way? His lonely existence?

Better than being near a woman who'd stamped on him then kicked him to the curb.

In the meantime, how could he dodge her?

Cooper's Hawk, population of six hundred, could be a pretty hard place to keep from seeing someone, at least anyone that didn't live under a rock.

Opening the driver's door, he climbed in, turned the key and pressed on the gas pedal causing the door to slam shut. The tires kicked up rocks and dirt, and he coughed against the dust cloud that drifted through the open windows. Once he could manage to inhale again, he continued the narrow gravel lane toward the main road. He glanced in the rearview mirror, seeing the farmhouse in the distance. Something triggered inside him, like a dam wall cracking. When had he become weak? A coward? He had nothing to run away from. This was *his* town. His place. He wasn't the one who slept with her then walked—no ran—away.

Whether he liked it or not, he'd have to face her—had to prove to himself and to her that he no longer cared for her. No longer craved her more than his next breath. Hell, he'd been a stupid kid who'd allowed his brains to settle behind his zipper. Who the hell knew who they wanted to spend their life with when they're ten? So what that they'd exchanged some playful vows in a barn during a tornado when they were snot-nosed kids who'd been out catching frogs. Years had passed. They weren't the same people.

Damn.

Slamming his foot on the brake, he slid to a stop, causing the back to veer.

He needed to man up.

Jerking the steering wheel, he made a quick U-turn in the grass and peeled out. The rubber finally caught traction, causing a loud crunching sound of rocks that caught the attention of the cattle in the field. They watched him, chewing cud. He felt about as ridiculous as they looked.

The back of the truck shimmied and he straightened the steering wheel and skillfully pulled back into the long gravel driveway, headed toward the old farmhouse that felt more like metal to magnet. He parked next to the sleek, silver BMW with Cali plates. "Well, well, well…" She certainly did have expensive tastes. The girl he remembered was into horses for transportation not pricey cars that were unfitting in redneck valley.

This brought him some relief. Exactly. She wasn't the girl he knew back in the day when they're biggest concern was not getting caught after toilet papering principal Hahn's front yard. In fact, he'd guarantee she had physically changed. With a BMW palate, she probably had collagen infused cheeks and lips and big, fake tits. He didn't mind the latter, he wouldn't lie, but he preferred his women real.

"Shit!"

He needed to get it through his thick skull that sitting there moping in his truck wasn't tapping into the bravery he had a minute back. He was acting like a full-blown idiot. He needed to stomp right up to the door, knock and pretend nothing was cockeyed except for the welcome sign hanging on the red door.

Once his worn boots hit rocks, he strolled up the broken stones of the walkway, took the steps to the porch two at a time, and straight up to the door. His hand was suspended in the air ready to knock when he caught a strong scent in the air. He sniffed. *Smoke. Fire.* And it was close. There was a no-burn order in the area so who would be stupid enough to go against the rule?

Jumping off the side of the porch, he saw the plume of grey smoke coming from behind the house.

Agitated, he rounded the corner and almost got knocked off his feet by the vision in front of him. There she was.

His heart was beating fast enough to jump right out of his chest. He could only stand there and stare.

This didn't look like her, but it was her.

The Mindy he'd loved had been blonde with light highlights, tanned body, and a smooth smile that was a hook to his internal fish.

She'd been cute, bright eyed and fancy free. A sweet girl hidden under a layer of dangerous sass that had been his undoing.

She bent over, sticking her firm bottom up high and his mouth salivated.

His body hardened so fast it hurt to breathe.

Once she stood, he concentrated on her timeless beauty. Her dark blonde hair was cut to her shoulders, angled longer in the front. One bright blonde highlight framed her face.

The spaghetti strap to the white cami slipped down her shoulder, leading his gaze downward to the outline of her small, firm breasts. That answered his question. No implants.

She lifted her chin. Her thin brows curved over surprised eyes, then she blinked twice.

Lord, although she'd changed some, she was still the tall, leggy beauty that could rock a pair of Daisy Dukes like no other.

She shook out whatever she was holding and he groaned. He recognized the shirt as his football jersey that he gave her to wear after "that one night". He never got it back. Hell, he wanted it back.

"I hope you're not adding that to the burn pile."

He'd caught her by surprise because her deep brown eyes nailed him with a combination of disbelief and something else, something he couldn't quite pin. The ends of her hair brushed her exposed skin in the skimpy top that dipped low, showing off the tops of creamy mounds. She was barefoot and her toes were curled in the grass. He crawled his gaze up on those amazing, knock out legs and onto her frown.

She dragged a tendril of hair behind her ear and he saw a helix piercing and a row of three diamond studs down the other ear lobe. Her lush lips were now drawn into a straight, irritated line that matched her death stare.

He snarled.

She moaned.

Seconds ticked by in awkward silence. Someone needed to make a move or they could have a staring contest for hours. He knew because they had a few as kids.

Clearing his throat, he pushed back the rim of his hat and smiled. "You look different." Hard to believe this was the same girl who could spit a watermelon seed farther than any guy and ride a horse faster too. Her eyes widened and he caught a glimpse of the pigtailed, freckled face girl. And that had left Creed feeling things he'd never experienced before. A mixture of jealousy for the time he'd lost and appreciation that maybe the country girl remained.

Slow down, bro. The girl he once knew was lost that night when he'd allowed his need to get in the way in the back of his truck and destroyed their friendship.

"Great way to welcome me back," she whispered.

"That's not my job." Guilt wavered inside him. Why? He didn't owe her a damn thing. Holy smokes, and why did he feel a teasing throbbing below his belt? Nope. Nope. Nope. He couldn't do this again. He clenched his teeth and took a step forward, but she shook her head, holding up a hand to pause him.

"Stay still."

"Why?"

"Because I can't promise I won't punch you."

He chuckled but he could see she wasn't laughing, not in the slightest. "And I can't promise that I won't take you over my knee and swat your tight bottom. How dare you come back," he snarled.

"How *dare* I come back?" She crossed her arms over her flat stomach and laughed. "Wow. I didn't know I needed your permission before I came home, to *my* ranch, to see my daddy. You always did have an overexaggerated imagination, Creed Hawke. I see you haven't changed one bit." Her pert nose wrinkled. "Still thinking the world evolves around you I see."

She was the spitfire he knew back when. That certainly hadn't changed.

Several thoughts slip-slided around inside his whirling head. *Her* ranch? So, Rusty didn't tell her that he'd sold most of the ranch to Creed three months ago. Sum'bitch. He knew better than to keep something as serious as the possession of a homestead under wraps. Mindy could explode and he didn't want to be the target. Creed had figured her father would tell her.

"Mindy—"

"Creed? What are you doing here?" There was a squeak to her voice. "Why are you hanging out at Sage Ranch? Don't you have anything better to do, or at least stay on your own territory?"

Now wasn't the time to burst her bubble.

He angled his head toward the burn pit. "The fire. There's a no-burn order in place." There was also a tightness in his throat. Pulling himself out of his reverie, he marched over to grab the garden hose off the hook and squeezed the nozzle, extinguishing the now raging flames, splattering her with water in the process.

"Hey! Wait! It's a contained fire."

"Doesn't matter. You know how fast a fire can get out of control around these parts." He dropped the hose. "You could be fined for this," he growled.

"Oh really?" She drew the words out through those plush, kissable lips. Her dark eyes glowered. "By whom?" She tilted her shapely hip. "You always did have a bigger bark than bite."

"Not me, sweetheart. Sheriff Conley."

"That old hoot?"

"No, his son."

"Same difference. Just because you have pounded a couple fence posts on the property doesn't give you the right to boss me around."

"Are you testing me?"

"Now why would I want to do a thing like that, Creedy?" She arched a high brow. What had he been thinking? She was more beautiful than ever. Sexier than ever. He liked her new confidence and the small tattoo of a cross on the inside of her wrist.

"I haven't been called Creedy in a long time and I'd like to keep it that way."

"Hmm," she moaned deep in her throat. "Old habits die hard."

"You didn't answer me about the shirt." He strolled over and looked down into the box. An invisible fist rammed into his stomach. She was going to burn the pictures taken of them together. The memories they'd shared. Like they were nothing but trash. Anger slipped through him.

"You can have it back."

She threw the shirt and he caught it against his chest. "What are you doing here?"

"I thought we were passed that. I'm visiting. Is there a fine for that too?" She looked down her nose at him.

Acid rushed in his blood while desire assaulted his body. They were no longer the same two people. Life had changed for them both. He'd moved on and she couldn't affect him the same way she once did. "Not unless you're committing a crime, like burning and putting *my* town at risk."

She giggled and he wasn't sure what he'd said that was so humorous. "If I remember correctly you sure didn't have any trouble breaking the law back when we were kids. How many times did you sneak off with Mr. Delaware's eggs? Or all the times we toilet papered Mr. Hahn's trees."

This was exactly what he'd been trying to tell Livvy. No matter how many years passed, the past always had a way of coming back. This time, it came and smacked him hard across the face. "I've grown up since then. We both have." He allowed his gaze to travel downward on her slender body. What was she now? Thirty-seven? Thirty-eight? She didn't look a day over thirty, but something in those pensive eyes told him she'd been hurt a time or two which made her wiser. Lord, he understood completely.

What had she been up to?

He didn't need to know. He couldn't slide back into caring for her—couldn't let her see the journey he'd traveled to forget her. "So you're visiting. Does that mean you'll be leaving soon?" He swiped off his hat and pounded it against his thigh. The temperature had risen, and his clothes felt too tight. It was that damn fire he'd put out. Unfortunately, he still had a blaze inside his body.

One corner of her lips quirked. "Wow, is this the welcome home party? Cooper's Hawk has really gone downhill with their welcomes."

He chuckled, not allowing her to ruffle his feathers any more than she already had just by seeing her. "I'm sure you'd think so. We're probably too hillbilly for the likes of someone that drives that Beemer in the driveway. But I see you found those cowgirl shorts." He narrowed his gaze on the faded denim a little longer than he should have.

She inhaled deeply. "You don't know me."

"And you don't know me! Not that it matters. Abide by the law while you're in town," he said.

"As if I'm a law breaker. Are you done threatening me?" Her lips tightened.

"Sweetheart, I don't make threats. Don't think you can waltz back into this town and start stirring up trouble. Times have changed."

"Do you call your wife sweetheart too or just those you've screwed and forgotten?"

"My mistake. Maybe I should call you Mrs. Newland," he growled. Anger swished through his blood like dragon's breath.

A flash of awareness washed over her expression but disappeared once the screen door came rattling open.

"I thought I heard voices out here." Rusty interrupted the heated battle. He looked from each of them and chuckled. "I see you two are still pickling each other's gardens. Come inside and have dinner, Creed. Mindy's making a chicken dish in celebration."

Her mouth fell open and some of her tan disappeared. "He can't stay."

"I can't?" Creed smirked.

"He can't?" Rusty muttered.

"Yeah, I'm sure you're busy building fences." Her bottom lip trembled.

Who did she think she was? In town less than a week and already trying to tell him what to do. The hell with that. "In fact, I do have some time." He grinned, feeling vindicated when she bared her teeth. Why did it feel so good to see her feathers ruffled?

She turned on her bare feet and stomped inside, but not before he got another good look at her long legs and firm bottom encased in pocketless denim. He felt his lungs slam into his stomach. Maybe he should leave. Hit the road while the gettin' was good. He didn't need the chaos added to his already full plate.

"Come on, Creed. Let's get in there before she burns our food out of spite." Rusty's laughter mingled with the crickets chirping in the distance.

Stepping through the doorway, he inhaled savory home cooking and his stomach growled. The Mindy he knew couldn't boil a pot of water let alone make something delicious.

Placing his hat on the eagle hook by the door, he swiped his boots off on the spiked welcome rug and glanced over at Mindy who was standing at the stove stirring a pot. It didn't look like water. Rusty was grabbing beer from the refrigerator.

"Want one?"

Yeah, he did. "I'd better have a bottle of water if that's okay." Creed reminded himself that he had to be at Livvy's school later that evening. He didn't think showing up with alcohol on his breath was a good way to enter the parent teacher conference.

"How's your mother?" Rusty handed Creed a water.

He only caught the last few words of the question because he'd been ogling Mindy who was noisily pounding a wooden spoon against the edge of the pot. She was angry. Whoo-wee. He could feel her anger clear across the room. Well, at least they were both on the same page then. "Huh?"

"The family? How are they?" Rusty guzzled half the bottle of beer.

"They're good. Real good." He couldn't actually admit that his daughter was rebelling, and his mother was giving him a hard time about moving on.

"That's good to hear. I heard there was a fire over at Carson's Creek. I bet it was a doozy. Was there any damage to the bridge?"

"Took us a few hours to contain the blaze but we managed to get it in control." He stepped over to the sink, scrubbed his hands with soap and water then asked, "Can I help with anything?"

"Yeah, leave," she whispered.

He laughed. "I don't mind sticking around." He shook the excess water from his hands and used a paper towel to wipe them dry.

"Suit yourself, but don't blame me if I burn your food." She bent over and took out the casserole dish. "Ouch!" She hurried to set the dish down and tore off the mitt to blow on her finger.

Every logical part of him screamed for him to stay away, but another part of him urged him to take a step forward. "What'd you do?"

"It's nothing."

He could see that it was something by the way she was holding her hand. "Let me look." Taking the initiative, he reached for her hand. The thumping of her fast pulse beat against his thumb. Her nails were short and neat, painted with polish the color of pearl. Her skin was as soft as silk. There was a slash of redness and the starting of a blister on her finger. He heard her hiss of breath at the same time she jerked her hand away.

"I said I'm fine. Dinner's ready."

"Suit yourself," he said smartly and joined Rusty at the table. "Did you get that new head of cattle?"

"Last week."

"How about the wood for the new barn?"

"Wait. What new barn?" Mindy asked as she set the steaming casserole dish in the center of the table.

"It's nothing," Rusty said.

Feeling her gaze on him, Creed did his best not to look her way. The last thing he wanted was to get in the middle of whatever the father and daughter had going on. Creed wasn't sure why Rusty was keeping the details of Sage Ranch a secret, but he also understood Mindy hadn't shown any concern about the land for a long time.

With an agitated sigh, she went back to the stove and came back with bowls of green beans, cauliflower and rolls then took a seat across from Creed. She shook out a cloth napkin and laid it across her lap. "So you're working here now?"

He looked up from his plate and realized she was speaking to him. He glanced over at Rusty and received no help. "A few times a week," Creed answered, grabbing himself a piece of chicken smothered in vegetables. His mouth salivated. Although he'd grabbed a sandwich earlier, he could still eat.

"Isn't that just cozy," she muttered, pulled off a piece of bread and popped it into her mouth, all the while keeping her inquisitive gaze on him.

"So this is a celebration dinner?" Creed asked around a mouthful of chicken.

When she didn't answer, Rusty said, "She's working at the ice rink. Coaching."

"Congratulations." His heart betrayed his head. Why did he feel elated and angry all at once?

"It's temporary," she pushed out.

Although the chicken was moist, he had a hard time swallowing and sent it down with a gulp of water. "So you still skate?" He remembered how she'd dedicated every evening to skating. He always loved watching her on ice.

She didn't even look at him when she said, "Of course. Is that hard to believe?"

"I didn't mean—"

"Don't mind her," Rusty sniffed. "She's just sour over that bastard husband—"

"Ex-husband," she added, blotting the corners of her mouth with the napkin.

"Ex-husband left her for some teeny bopper."

Mindy looked uncomfortable. Her cheeks flushed. "Hardly a teen, Daddy."

"Told her not to marry him in the first place but did she ever listen to me?" Rusty groaned and speared a piece of cauliflower, staring at it like it was alien.

"That's none of *his* business."

"Yeah, it really isn't." Creed could literally see the tension building.

"It's time you came back to the ranch. This is your legacy here, Minnow." Rusty dropped the vegetable back onto his plate. "I won't live forever."

"Daddy, don't say that. You have plenty of time—"

"That's the problem with the younger generation. They think they have all the time in the world. Foolish. You'll go back to California soon enough."

"Maybe you should stop drinking," she snapped.

As if this triggered something inside him, his expression changed as he pushed back his chair and stood. "If you'll excuse me, I have somewhere to be." He strolled from the kitchen.

The fork dinged loudly on the plate when Mindy dropped it.

Her shoulders slumped. "If you'll excuse me I have somewhere I need to be too." She stood and dropped her napkin on the table.

Creed watched her leave the room, feeling his chest tighten. He shouldn't care, but he did. So her husband—ex-husband—had cheated. Creed couldn't wrap his head around that truth. Who in their right mind would want another woman when they had Mindy? Who could kiss another pair of lips when they had hers to kiss every day? It was all too difficult to understand.

He looked across the barely touched feast on the table, shrugged, then spooned up more chicken and green beans. No reason for any of it to go to waste.

Chapter 5

MINDY DROPPED THE horse brush into the bucket and stretched her back. She'd been working chores for the last few hours and she'd forgotten how laborious it could be.

"Hi, Mindy! Good to see you out here."

"Mornin', Bo. I noticed that one of the horses is getting a supplement to her feed. Why is that?"

"Vet diagnosed her with an ulcer so she's being supplemented with an edible clay. She's eating better. Feeling better. Aren't you girl?" Bo rubbed the neck of the horse.

"What do you think of Creed Hawke working here?" She watched several expressions flicker across his face.

"Been here for almost three months now."

"I was shocked." She followed him inside. "Do you mind if I ask if you were hurt? I noticed you're limping."

He grabbed a shovel from the corner. "Don't mind at all." He patted his thigh. "I tripped at home over my dog, Susie, and broke my leg. The son-of-a-gun hasn't healed completely."

"I'm glad you're still here at Sage Ranch."

"I won't be much longer."

"Why?" She crossed her arms over her chest. "Is that because Creed is working here?"

"No, but he's hiring a few new hands and it's best this old coot does what he should have done a couple of years ago."

"*Daddy* hired them?" Had she heard wrong?

"Rusty didn't hire them. Creed did." Bo shoveled up dirty straw off the floor and dropped it into the wheel barrel.

Several seconds floated by as she absorbed what he was saying. "Creed hired them. Why?"

"Yes, ma'am. Don't look so astonished, girl. Creed's a good man. He didn't push me out. He's doing some good changes around here."

"What's going on, Bo?" She removed her gloves and laid them on the workbench. She'd suspected from the start that they were all hiding something from her.

He lifted his gaze from the floor. "Mindy—"

"Is there something I need to know?"

He blew out a long breath and shrugged. "I mind my own business and I'd like to keep it that way." He went back to mucking the stall.

"We've known each other for a long time. What am I missing?"

He paused in shoveling. "Mindy, you haven't been here in a long time. Best I can tell you is talk to your Pa." He turned his back to her, signaling the end of the discussion.

Realizing the discomfort of the hand, she didn't pressure him. He wouldn't give her any information anyway.

She went in search of her daddy and found him standing in the center of a circle of hands.

When he saw her, he stopped talking.

Stepping up to the group of men, they all greeted her with a nod. Her father shifted from one dusty boot to another.

"Go on and get back to work," Rusty commanded and the men dispersed.

"I'd like to speak to you, Daddy."

"I'm headed to take care of some business." He turned and strolled toward his truck parked along the grass.

She caught up to him as he opened the driver's door. "Since when did Creed take over the running of this ranch?"

"What do you mean?" He slid behind the wheel.

"Hiring hands. Making decisions regarding the livestock. I don't know a lot about ranching but how does a hand take over unless he's boss?"

He narrowed his grey gaze on her. "You're right, you don't know much about ranching so stick to what you know."

"I know enough that I can sniff out bull crap when I smell it. What's going on around here that you're not telling me?"

"If you were so good with sniffing out bull crap then why didn't you sniff out that your husband was having an affair? Or that he was a self-absorbed jerk from the very beginning? I'd say you need to worry about your personal life before you start worrying about what's going on here."

"I do have my personal life in order."

"Really? Could have fooled me," he huffed.

"What's that supposed to mean?"

The wrinkles around his eyes and mouth softened some. "Listen, I'm glad you're here, but I don't need you to start nagging me about the running of this place. For nineteen years you haven't cared about Sage Ranch. Are you sure you care now?"

She took a step away from the door as he started the engine.

He pulled away and she stood there for the longest time, long after the dust cloud faded. A cold grip held her.

Mindy had other ways of finding out important information.

Following the worn path up to the house, she stepped inside and made her way down the hall and into the office, closing the door behind her and locking it. The place was a cluttered mess with stacks of papers and files on the desk, on the chair and an overflowing trash can. Scooping up the pile on the chair, she laid them on the desk and sat down, scooting the chair closer. Most of the paperwork were paid invoices, but at the bottom she found an envelope marked "Deed".

Lifting the flap, she took out the thick document and unfolded it, skimming the words, "Deed of sale" "Transferred to Creed Hawke" "Sold". Her heart sunk. Oh no! What had her father done? Why did he sell the ranch to Creed?

How could he do this?

How could Daddy not tell me?

Staring at the legal document until her temples ached, anger scoured through her. Why didn't either one of them mention this? How was this possible? Why would her father sell the land?

Taking the envelope with her, she stomped outside and got into her car. The tires sent dirt flying as she pressed on the gas pedal and spun out toward the road. Pulling over next to the barn, she waved one of the younger hands over. He shyly stepped up next to the driver's door, resituating his Stetson at least a dozen times before he finally gave her a smile.

"Hi there, uh….?"

"Grady."

"I'm Mindy." She forced a smile on her lips. "Do you know where Creed would be right now? Is he here?"

"No, ma'am. He's not here too often. I'd guess he's at Hawke Landing."

"Where would I find Hawke Landing?"

Grady told her, she thanked him and pulled onto the road. The drive took long enough for her blood to boil even more. She wanted to throttle Creed.

By the time she walked through the door at Cooper's Hawke Landing, she had rehearsed a dozen times what she'd say to him. She stomped up to the receptionist desk and the pretty blonde with pale blue eyes behind wide rimmed glasses lifted her gaze from the computer. A millisecond later she smiled. "Mindy Sage? Is that you? Of course it's you!" The woman stood and reached over the counter to drag Mindy in for a tight hug.

When she was finally released from toned arms, Mindy scanned the woman's face and then it struck her… "Willow? Oh my gosh. You look amazing."

"I'm fifty pounds lighter. And now a blonde." She twirled one of the dyed strands around her knuckle.

"I'm sorry I didn't recognize you—"

Willow waved a hand and laughed. "Honey, if you'd have recognized me, I would have been disappointed. I left the shy, timid Willow back in high school where she belonged. Anyway, what brings you to Landing? Do you have an appointment? I don't remember seeing your name." She searched through the open planner on her desk. "Hmm. Nope. You're not on here."

"I came to speak to Creed." She thrummed her fingers on the desk.

"Oh…I'm sorry. He's booked today. Can I add you for another day?" Willow sat back down and reached for a pen from the butterfly holder. In a click of a second, she'd gone from friendly to all business.

Mindy leaned over the counter slightly, looking down at the planner, thinking quick. "He said I could stop by any time." She hated lying but she wasn't leaving until she had a long, thorough discussion with the new owner of Sage Ranch.

"He did?" Her groomed brows scrunched slightly. "He's up to his eyeballs in trouble today, Mindy. What with working on the heli and trying to get it up and running before his next scheduled flight. Then we had a missing person up on the mountain—"

"Oh, I understand." Mindy glanced around the small office space, stalling for time. Then she remembered… "Hey, whatever happened to Vance Neil? Remember him? He was your senior prom date, right?" Willow had the biggest crush on Vance, although he didn't know she existed. Mindy couldn't understand what Willow had seen in the rude twerp, but with a little convincing from Mindy, Vance agreed to take Willow to the dance.

"He's married with three kids and bald—" her brows snapped together. "Hey, wait. I see what you're doing." She tapped the end of the pen against the planner and sighed. "You're calling in a favor, aren't you?"

"No, not really. Just recalling how we were such good friends back in the day." Seeing the softening lines of Willow's face, Mindy could practically see the chains of resistance breaking in the woman.

"I can also recall how hot you and Creed used to be. What a waste. I would have staked my front teeth on you two getting hitched." Willow shrugged. "I guess I was wrong, just like I had been wrong about Vance. Because you were always so nice, I'm going to let you pass, but if I get fired—"

"I won't tell him. I'll say that I didn't see you if he asks."

"Fine. He's in the hangar, but I'll warn you, the bear is out of hibernation."

Smiling, Mindy took off toward the door that read "private".

The hangar held two helicopters. One was disassembled with two wide shouldered men bent close. Her cowgirl boots thudded the polished cement floor as she strolled to where the Hawke men were discussing something about an airframe and transmission. She cleared her throat which brought the youngest Hawke's attention up from the engine.

A smile appeared on Boone's handsome face. He elbowed Creed who brought his tight jaw up looking at her like he could have bit nails in half with his teeth. Both wore stained white T-shirts that fit their torsos like a second skin. That was a lot of testosterone for one room.

"Well, hell. Do my eyes deceive me? Is that really Minnow coming my way?" Boone whistled through his teeth.

Mindy blinked. The last time she saw him he was a scrawny kid with a bushy head of hair, acne on his face, and a dusting of dark fine hair on his upper lip. He'd grown up and looked a lot like Creed, with less vinegar in his veins. She could practically feel Creed simmering in his anger.

"Hi, Boone—"

Mindy squeaked when he wrapped his arms around her waist and swept her off her feet, swinging her in a full circle. The deed was crushed between them, momentarily forgotten in the happy reunion. She'd always liked Boone—always enjoyed his infectious personality. Of all the Hawke clan he was the easiest going. Of course, she hadn't seen him in so long.

Once he set her back down, she fixed the straps of her top then giggled at his excitement. At least she knew she had one friend left in Cooper's Hawk.

"Hope I didn't get any grease on you," Boone said.

"I'm not wearing my Sunday best so don't worry." She couldn't get over how much the man had changed…and looked like Creed and Hank. They all had dark wavy hair, broad jaws, pensive eyes, and were tall in stature.

"Girl, California has been good to you." Boone slipped his gaze down her then whistled.

Beyond his shoulder she saw Creed's frown. She felt a flush crawl up her neck and into her face, and certainly must have turned red. The brooding glare he had on her didn't help with the awkwardness.

"Boone, what are you up to these days?"

"About six-foot three last I checked." He winked.

The Hawke men had good genes. "Sorry I'm interrupting, but I need to speak to Creed."

"We're working here," he said gruffly, pulling a dirty white cloth out of his back pocket and wiping his hands. His biceps stretched the knit of the T-shirt as he tossed the rag onto a work bench. Fumbling inside of a red box, noisily slinging tools, he seemed to be doing his best not to look her direction. She skimmed his broad back wondering how much more the cotton could take before it ripped. The loose-fitting jeans had large holes in the knees and more near the front pockets. He had a smear of grease down his cheek and a lock of hair had fallen over his forehead making him appear younger.

A grim set came over his lips. "We're booked for today. Make an appointment."

"I need to speak to you now." Nervously, she tugged at the hem of her shirt that suddenly seemed too tight. Her breasts tingled and her nipples scrunched. A breeze rolled in through the hangar door and blew over her, easing some of the fire in her core.

"Do ya?" He snapped up a thick brow, one corner of his lips lifted as if he found her demand amusing. "Sure, let me take a moment to speak to you instead of fixing the heli that we need running by afternoon."

Boone looked from Mindy to Creed then back at her with an apologetic shrug. "You two can chat. I'll keep working. I'm smarter than Creed anyway."

He didn't show even a sliver of tension relief at his brother's joke. Instead, he growled, dropped the tool on a nearby table, and muttered, "I have five minutes to spare."

"Wish me luck," Mindy mouthed to Boone who gave her a thumb's up.

She followed Creed through the door and out into the warm sunshine. She thought they would talk there, but instead he kept walking across the concrete lot in such a fast pace that she had to jog to keep up with him.

They stepped up to a door that read, "Office".

He shot a look at her over his shoulder, frowning from ear to ear. "I'll open it for you so you don't break a nail." He jerked open the glass door.

Mindy smiled. What he meant as a burn she let slide. "You're real cute. And so is the frown." Why was he so damn angry? Like he had the right! She strode in first and was met with a blast of cold air from the AC that was whirring from a window. The room was clean with two large desks, a computer, a row of file cabinets against one wall, and a water container in the corner. She didn't see any pictures, no personal effects.

He strolled over to the farthest desk and dropped down into the worn, ripped black chair that gave a loud whine of resistance at his weight. Once he was settled, she sashayed her way to his desk, not allowing his heated gaze to ruffle her feathers.

"Tell me what the hell couldn't wait." He swiped a hand down his whiskered jaw.

Slamming the crumpled deed down onto the desk, she tilted a hip and watched several unreadable expressions flitter over his handsome face. He shifted uncomfortably and she wondered if the chair would hold up. Then he caught her off guard when he huffed a gruff laugh. "Still snooping I see."

"It seems it's about the only way I can find out the things I have a right to know." She glared down her nose at him.

"Communication never was your strongest suit," he growled.

"I'm sure there's an angle to that comment but right now I really don't care. What I want to know is how you stole Sage Ranch out from underneath my daddy?" She drilled him with what she hoped was an evil stare.

"Stole?" His baritone laughter made her nipples tingle. "I've never stole a damn thing in my life, outside of a cookie now and then." His eyes turned a dangerous color.

"Stop stalling, Creedy. I want to know why in the hell you are on this deed." She leaned over the desk, planting her palms on the mahogany wood.

"Look, you don't have the right to storm in here and demand anything from me. Take it up with Rusty." He refolded the deed then held it up for her.

Mindy didn't take it, instead continued to stare at him. "Whether you like it or not I'm not leaving until I have some answers." When he didn't respond, she kept right on talking, "I always wondered why you hung around Sage Ranch. You used to tell me how much you wanted to stay there. You were different around Daddy, as if you couldn't try hard enough to get him to like you. Well, now it looks like you finally gained his appreciation. Was this the plan all along?"

"Enough."

"No, it's *not* enough because I need to hear the truth from *you*. You won't be satisfied until you have taken everything away from the Sage's, will you?" She wasn't sure where the words came from but once she opened the gates, she couldn't stop the flood. Years of hurt and anger had been stored inside of her.

"I won't say it again," he said flatly, almost dangerously.

Mindy wasn't the type to back down. Maybe she needed answers to all the questions of the past and present. "Damnit, Creed. Give me answers. Something! Why? How?"

He jumped up so fast the chair hit the wall, knocking a glass off a file cabinet and crashing to the floor, but neither paid any attention. He rounded the desk in two long strides which brought him in front of her. His teeth were bared. His eyes were charged with an unspoken fury, and his hands were gripped into fists. She'd never seen this side of him before. He didn't scare her, had never been scared when they fought, but she was frightened of the whirlwind of emotions increasing inside her. She couldn't trust what she'd say to him when her emotions were on high.

Taking several steps, the backs of her legs struck the flowered chair and she froze as he followed her, staring down at her with pent up emotion.

"You crossed a line, Mindy," he whispered.

"And so have you." She wished she could control the shaking in her limbs.

"You want answers?" he said in a low, dangerous murmur. "I'd like some fucking answers too. How about we start with why you left Cooper's Hawk? No goodbye. No kiss my ass. You just picked up and left." His gaze seethed with anger.

"You knew I was leaving. You were leaving too."

"My God, must we beat around the bush?"

She slammed her head back onto her shoulder to look up at him. She wasn't short at five eight, but he was still much taller. Broader. Angrier, and yet, she didn't feel any fright. "I-I thought I was doing us both a favor." Her knees quivered. "I thought I knew you as well as I knew myself but turns out I knew nothing about you."

"You're the only one that probably ever knew me," he said the words so softly, but they contradicted the blue inferno in his eyes.

How could he upend her so easily? She had every right to be outraged. Creed and her daddy had kept the situation with Sage Ranch a secret.

A splash of guilt washed over her. She had secrets too.

Why couldn't she manage to keep her head on straight when she was near him? Why did the old emotions come charging in and threatening to turn her into the woman who thought he hung the moon?

Hurt made her want to bring out the big guns. "If I knew you so well then why couldn't I foresee that what we shared in the back of your truck would change you?"

His nostrils fared and he looked like he was searching deep for lost patience.

Chapter 6

CREED FORCED AIR into his lungs and exhaled noisily. He heard Mindy's words but was he hearing right? How dare she come flouncing in here, into his life, and demanding that he open himself up to her. "That's entertaining. You were the one who walked away, sweetheart. Not me."

"Things changed after we slept together. I guess you got what you wanted, and it was time to move on to the next one." Once the word parted her lips, she realized how ridiculous they sounded. Creed had never been a player, not with her or anyone. He'd always been respectful. Why couldn't she just admit that she'd felt rejected when things had gone back to what felt like "friends" only after they slept together.

He blinked. "You're really saying stupid shit now. What the hell are you talking about? I was a damn kid, Mindy. So were you. I'm sorry that I was an awkward kid who had no clue how to act after he'd slept with his best friend."

"So then what? Was I supposed to give you time? My God, I'd already spent most of my life up until that point following you around like I was your shadow. Maybe I'd hoped..."

"Hoped what?"

"You knew how much I cared for you. I made my feelings clear. I wanted—hoped—you'd treat me like a woman instead of a best friend."

Her words burnt his ears. "We were best friends. Are you suggesting that I mistreated you? I saved your ass how many times? Didn't that prove I cared?"

"Saved my ass? How?" She chuckled but it lacked humor.

"How about the time you jumped off the bridge into the creek? Do you think I wanted to jump too? I had no choice but to follow because I was afraid you'd drown."

She squinted. "I didn't drown. I knew what I was doing. I wanted to swim."

"Obviously you didn't down. You're missing the point. How about the time you climbed into the bull pen and that old fat bull thought you were the red flag. Or how about the time I beat Bobby Sager up because he touched your—"

"I do get the point! You were always there for me." As if the realization of her own words struck her, her eyes widened, and she dropped her arms to her sides. Her bottom lip trembled. "Just don't throw those times up in my face. I never asked for you to take on the job as my bodyguard."

"You're a real piece of work, you know that? No matter what I say you're going to peck me to the bone like a vulture on roadkill. Don't blame me because you went in search of a whole new world in California. You got what you wanted, and life here went on without you. Are you seeing that you no longer have a place here?"

Hurt filled her eyes. "What happened to the nice Creedy?"

"Maybe he went out the door with the nice Mindy," he growled. "Then again, when were you ever thinking of my feelings?"

"Really? That's a riot! You talk about the times you were there for me but who was there every time you decided to do something stupid that could have gotten us into trouble?"

"You're so annoying. I see that hasn't changed."

"You're still an asshole. And like all asses you're a bigger one now than ever."

"Oh, that's just funny. Coming from the woman who had her nose so high in the air she'd drown in a rainstorm. Check out my BMW. Ooh ooh. Check out my pretty diamond. Oh oh." He mocked her tone, lifting his hand and waving his fingers.

Her mouth fell open, but he sparked her fiery spirit. "The car was a present from my ex who had a large guilty conscious. The ring, as you so cruelly point out, belonged to my mom. It was her engagement ring from my father and the only piece of jewelry she owned."

He felt a kick to his gut. *I am an asshole.* "Mindy—"

"Jackass."

Smiling, he shrugged. "Controlling."

She smirked. "Bitter."

"Childish."

"How does a man become so full of himself?"

"Probably the same way a woman thinks every man owes her something."

"Do men gather in groups to brainstorm these ridiculous, sexist comebacks? When a man gets a little upset with a woman, he negatively points out her strength or accuses her of needing something from a man. Do you make index cards with these crazy points? I don't need anything from a man." Her face shifted from anger to something else far more dangerous.

"And women are any better? You all blame the male gender for everything. If we communicate too much, we're weak. If we don't communicate enough, we're closed off. If you ask us a question and we don't answer it perfectly then we've become the enemy. Can a man ever be good enough to make a woman happy?" he seethed.

"I'd love to answer yes, but I'm guessing no."

"Don't come in here busting my balls. You don't have the right. When you left Cooper's Hawk you gave up every right to expect anything from me." He shoved his hands to his hips.

"I guess I should be grateful that I was smart enough to give up on that childhood dream. Where would we be now? Melody was much more your speed any way. Glad it only took you a couple weeks to get over what we shared."

The mention of his ex made the hair on his neck lift. He took a step back and tore his hand through his hair. He wasn't sure how much she knew about Melody. That was a train wreck he wasn't willing to unveil with her, not right now.

With slumped shoulders, he took another step back. "When I came home from the rodeo circuit your dad and I became friends. He offered me a job and I worked at Sage Ranch while still helping run Hawke Farm. I needed to raise the money for this place. There's something you're right about. I always loved the ranch and respected your father. Year after year passed, I stuck around, even after I opened Hawke Landing. After Rusty's heart attack he'd changed, mentally and physically. You had to see that for yourself. He started talking about his fear of losing the ranch. And financially, he was drowning after the medical bills came rolling in and a few business decisions turned ugly. He came to me one day and said he was tired, wanted to retire. He asked if I was interested in running Sage Ranch. Your name did come up, but he believed you wouldn't come home.

You were too busy." He blew out a long breath and rubbed his forehead. "I couldn't stand to see him sell the place to a stranger. It's true, I had a personal stake in this too. A lot of Sage Ranch used to belong to my family. It had always been my father's intention to get back what rightly belonged to the Hawkes."

"I remember. Our fathers were friends until the transfer of land."

"Dad could barely look at himself, let alone Rusty. Not that he was the enemy, but he was a reminder of Dad's failure. Rusty felt like the property should be back in the hands of the Hawke family. He made me a fair offer and I couldn't refuse. Didn't want to refuse. The house with a few surrounding acres still belongs to your family. Why he didn't speak to you first, or share the news, is something you'll need to ask him. I've told you my side of things." He picked up the deed and shoved it toward her.

With hesitancy, she took it, causing the shoulder strap of her shirt to fall down her shoulder. His attention was drawn to her necklace. Taking the space between them in two strides, he lifted the familiar looking metal ring. "What's this?"

"It's the makeshift ring you gave me during the tornado."

He jerked his chin up. His breath was stuck between his lungs and disbelief. "You had it made into a necklace?"

She nodded. "The only time I take it off is when I'm skating."

Dropping the necklace, he felt his chest tighten. "Why?"

"Do you really need to ask why?" She held his gaze.

His stability came crashing down. He needed his space. "Five minutes is up. If you're finished grilling me, I need to get back to work."

Without a word, she stepped passed him and started for the door.

"Mindy?" He caught her at the threshold. She looked back at him. "You said I wanted Sage Ranch all along. No. That's wrong. I wanted you," he said quietly.

Without a response, she left.

He watched her through the window, the soft sway of her hips and the stubborn pride of her stiff back. He'd almost told her too much. There would have been no honor in telling her how he'd convinced Rusty to keep the house and surrounding property for her and her family. Creed knew in his heart that no matter how many miles were between her and Cooper's Hawk a part of her remained there, and with Sage Ranch. This was her home. He saw the hurt in her eyes when he'd told her she didn't have a place here any longer. What he hoped would happen, she would prove him wrong.

He dropped into the chair, leaned his head back and closed his eyes. What he was realizing, the more he tried to convince himself that he no longer cared for Mindy the more he understood he'd never stopped. He'd still jump into water after her or beat the hell out a man if he hurt her or took liberties. Hell, he'd hunt down her ex and throat punch him if necessary.

Why hadn't Creed gone after her?

Instead, he'd buried his feelings at the bottom of a whiskey bottle and tried forgetting Mindy by holding another woman.

Melody had been a mistake, one that had replicated itself too many times.

Pushing up from the chair, he strolled from the office and back into the hangar, still reeling from the rift he'd exchanged with Mindy.

"That good, huh?" Boone joked.

Creed gave him a disgruntled look. "Just what I need, another female busting my balls."

His brother's laughter echoed off the walls. "Good to see that things haven't changed between you two."

"Between Mindy and me?" He sniffed. "Everything's changed." Creed reached for the wrench and went back to the heli.

"Yeah? Could have fooled me. If I got too close, I was afraid I would have been scorched from the blaze."

The tool slipped and hit Creed's hand. "Shit!" He jerked back in pain.

"I think you need a longer break, bro. Anger's only going to slow us down. We've been at this for hours." Boone had always been the most logical one.

"I need to get it done," Creed muttered.

"Sure, but not at the risk of breaking something."

Realizing his brother was right, Creed sat down on a stack of crates and reached for his now warm water to down it in one gulp.

Boone opened the refrigerator and grabbed an energy drink. "Why's she mad? She's not one to get a hair crossway without reason. So what'd you do?"

"She just found out I bought Sage Ranch."

His brother paused with his bottle mid-air. "What? She's just now finding out?"

"The property belonged to us anyway. The house and surrounding acreage still belongs to Rusty."

"You mean it belongs to you, right bro?" Boone pulled over a swivel chair and dropped into the cushion.

"I've told you, it belongs to all of us. I'm still waiting for you to start paying back your share," Creed growled.

"Should have thought about that before you signed the deed without consulting with Hank and me first."

"Hell, what choice did I have? I couldn't bear the thought of the place being sold to just anyone. It's not that I needed it—"

"No," Boone muttered.

"But I wanted it. Dad wanted it returned."

"Did you explain that to Mindy?"

"As much as I thought I should. I have one hundred sixty-seven things on my plate. I don't need another woman to appease. Livvy hates me and mom blames me. I can't win for losing."

Boone chuckled and stretched his legs. "Did they mention the terrible teens in all those parenting classes you went to back in the day?"

"I'm glad you find this a joking matter." Creed gave a fake laugh and stood, crushing his plastic bottle.

"What is your plan this time, bro?"

"My plan? For what?"

"Are you going to let Mindy slip through your fingers again?" Boone stood and yawned.

"I didn't let her slip through my fingers the first time. She left."

"Since you're playing dumb, I'll have to spell it out for you. Mindy didn't leave. She went off to college just as you were leaving for the military. Remember the jackass you became when she left? She's home now and I didn't see a ring on her finger. Isn't it about time you got over yourself and found out what could have been?"

"Let's get back to work." Creed ignored Boone.

Chapter 7

WALKING UP THE flower lined pathway and stepping up onto the porch adorned with a row of white rockers, Mindy felt like she had jetted back to the little girl with pigtails and big dreams. The last time she'd been at Hawke Farm she was sitting on the steps eating a slice of watermelon and listening to Creed go on and on about enlisting into the Navy, just like his father had done. Townsfolk had thought Creed would take a different path. He'd been offered a handful of full scholarships to play football which wasn't too bad for a small-town boy.

She looked at the step and could almost see her younger self and Creed sitting there together and the time he'd dared her to spit a watermelon seed as far as she could. Just as any nice girl would do when faced with a challenge, she spit that seed so far it landed in poor Cooter's eyeball. That hound dog spent most of his days lounging, never hurting anyone. So she'd felt lousy when he had to wear a plastic shield around his neck for weeks so he wouldn't scratch at his sore eye. Thankfully, he didn't lose it.

Turning back to the door, she looked at the word "Welcome" carved into the wood sign, pretty sure it didn't include her.

Truthfully, she realized she should turn and leave. The less she was around Creed the better. After their heated argument at Landing she couldn't be sure what the next face to face meeting would hold.

Yet, after a long discussion with her daddy, she realized the deed was done. Much of the Sage Ranch was gone. However, when she thought of giving up the horses and the goats she wanted to cry. Where did this change leave her? She understood her daddy's need to retire, he wanted to live his life, but it hurt her that he didn't think to speak to her first.

If she planned on staying in Cooper's Hawk she and Creed would have to come to some sort of understanding.

Knocking lightly, she waited.

"Come in," came the husky rich voice of the man who had haunted her every thought over the last few days. This time she'd left her proverbial guns at home and came with a peace flag. But would he want to see her?

Looking at the doorknob like it was a dirty bomb, she breathed in deeply, digging deep for bravery. She prayed she could control her emotions and not allow Creed to conjure up the wickedness within her. Stepping inside, she was met with a pleasant combination of vanilla, leather and masculinity. Closing the door, she couldn't see much. The curtains were drawn on the windows and so it took her a few seconds for her eyes to adjust. She scanned the dimly lit room and found him sitting on the sofa, his legs stretched out and hooked on the coffee table and the TV tuned to a sports channel. He didn't even look away from the football game.

"You were supposed to be here an hour ago," Creed complained.

"Sorry, am I interrupting?"

He jumped up from the sofa and turned on the lamp. The golden light filled the space, exposing his surprised expression. "Yes…I mean, no. I thought you were Boone. He was supposed to come by." A man like Creed wasn't caught off guard too often. Did he think he needed to gear up for round two?

She waved her invisible peace flag through a smile. He looked good, always did. His wavy dark hair looked like he'd just woken up from a hard night's sleep. He'd recently shaven but he had a new layer of whiskers. His broad shoulders stretched the knit of the long-sleeved, checked button down. Creed could easily be described as dangerously masculine, sexy and brooding. All those physical characteristics were great, but his eyes…she'd always been a sucker for those denim blues.

But she hadn't come to admire his good looks.

She'd come to find resolution. To find even ground.

"Let me turn this off." After clicking off the TV, he replaced the remote in the basket on the table. "I didn't expect you. Are you angry with me again?"

"No, that's not why I came." She tucked a strand of hair behind her ear. "I came to apologize." She laughed at his surprised expression.

"You? Apologize? What's the catch?"

Oh, there was certainly a catch, not that she knew what that looked like. She needed to prepare herself, and him. "Don't make this harder than it has to be."

He reshaped his expression into indifference. "Fine. I accept it."

"Can I have a seat?"

"Sure."

She took a seat on a worn, flowered chair, crossed her legs, as he sat back down on the sofa. Her every intention had been to stay professional, keep this on a business level, but the way his perceptive gaze seemed to search her soul sent professionalism out the window. They had too much history between them to forget.

"You were angry. I get it."

"I was. It was a shock to learn what Daddy had done." She plucked at a loose thread on her best sundress. "But that doesn't excuse my behavior for storming into your work and venting. I reacted impulsively." Her throat constricted.

"Does that hurt?"

"What?"

"To admit you're wrong. You look like it hurts."

"Maybe I was wrong that you and I could have a talk." She stood.

"Come on. Sit back down. I'll keep my pestering to a limit. I promise."

Sitting back down, she clasped her hands in her lap. "I'd appreciate that." He had the upper hand in this and she didn't like it.

"Did you finally have a heart to heart with Rusty?"

"I don't think heart to heart would surmise the conversation, but yes, we did have a discussion." She felt a surge of impatience. "I can't, and won't, say that I understand why he didn't speak to me first, but crying over spilled milk won't do any of us any good. I'd like to speak to you about a proposition."

"I'm not selling the land back to you," he blurted.

"That's not what I'm wanting."

"Then what?"

The next part was hard to say. "Whether you realize it or not I love Sage Ranch. It has always been my home. Truthfully, I don't want to run Sage Ranch. I only want to buy back a portion of the land."

"That's not possible."

"Why not? I'm only wanting to be able to ride horses along the west ridge, where the old barn is. You know that's my favorite place on the property."

"Mindy, you're welcome to ride anywhere on the ranch." He scooted to the edge of the cushion.

"It's not the same. It will no longer belong to the Sage family. What if I wanted to build a house along the ridge?"

"Do you?"

"Maybe."

"Save your breath. I'm not selling."

"You're being ridiculous."

"Your sweet facade is slipping."

"And you said you'd keep the pestering to a limit. You are refusing to consider my offer."

"That's right. I am."

She laid her hands on the arms of the chair, squeezing. "What will you do with all the land? You have this farm and now most of Sage Ranch. I'm only asking for twenty acres. You'll barely miss it."

"Twenty acres? You talk as if that's nothing."

"Okay. I'll compromise. Ten."

"Forget it."

"Won't you think about it?"

"To sell to you so you can build a house? I thought you were going back to California?"

"I never said that would happen."

"I'm not interested in selling prime land to someone who never showed interest in it for over nineteen years."

"You're really being unfair."

"Call it what you like. Just so you know, I want to build a place on that plot of land, and now that it's mine, I can."

"You're only saying that to bother me." She couldn't believe her ears.

"Dad! Where's grandma?"

Mindy jumped at the voice. A beautiful teen stepped into the room from the hallway. Her dark curly hair bounced around her heart shaped face. The teen lost her confidence in the surprise at finding Mindy sitting in the living room.

Blue, curious eyes settled on her.

With an apologetic, shy smile the girl shifted her gaze onto Creed. A flush crawled over her cheeks. "I didn't know you weren't alone."

Mindy slid to the edge of the chair, feeling a heavy pounding of realization in her chest. She stared at the pretty girl as thickness lodged in her throat. She'd know Creed's child anywhere and she should because the child looked so much like Jane.

"Livvy, I'd like for you to meet an old friend of mine. This is Mindy Sage," Creed offered. "She's Rusty's daughter."

"Hi," Livvy gave a bashful wave.

Mindy stood shakily. She could feel Creed's curious gaze on her as she absorbed meeting his daughter—his other daughter. "Hi. Livvy is such a pretty name."

"Thank you," Livvy answered. "It's short for Olivia."

"You look like your father."

The teen looked from Creed and back to Mindy several swipes. "I guess." She shifted in her flip flops. "Where's grandma, Dad?"

"She's running errands. Do you need something?" Creed stood, hooking his thumbs in his front pockets.

"I just need to ask her something." The teen glanced down at the floor for a quick second.

"Can I help?" Creed asked.

"You don't know how to make cookies."

"I know how to make cookies. Maybe I can help?" Mindy offered. The girl looked so much like Jane that Mindy wanted to hug her. She blinked back moisture in her eyes, feeling caught in a swirl of emotion. The weight of guilt grew like a boulder in her chest.

Livvy blinked, hesitating. "I don't have a recipe."

"That's okay. We don't need one."

"Well, if you want…"

"I love baking. It's one of my favorite things to do, besides figure skating, of course."

"You ice skate?" Appreciation spread over Livvy's face.

"I started when I was younger than you. Are you thirteen? Fourteen?"

She gave a shaky nod. "Fourteen."

"I'll understand if you want to wait for your grandma—"

"No. Well, I'd like your help. Unless you don't want to."

"I won't ever turn down a chance to bake cookies. What's your favorite?" Mindy rounded the coffee table and she and Livvy started for the kitchen.

"Chocolate chip."

"Do you want to make chocolate chip? Or were you wanting to try peanut butter or oatmeal? We can even try snickerdoodle."

"You can make all those?"

Mindy laughed. "Yes. My daughter and I would spend hours in the kitchen baking."

"What's her name?"

"Jane. She's eighteen and she started her freshman year in college."

After an awkward hesitation, the teen shrugged. "Grandma usually makes everything."

"I have a recipe for a special chocolate cookie if you'd like to try. They're my daughter's favorites."

"What do we need to make them?" Livvy slipped off the rubber band she had around her wrist and pulled her thick hair into a high messy bun. The action made Mindy stare for a long moment. Remembering how her daughter did the same before she'd bake. "Are you okay?"

"Yes, yes. I'm fine." She listed the ingredients they'd need while Livvy went into the pantry to retrieve them.

She came back carrying an armload of ingredients and set them on the cutting board island.

"Looks like we have everything we need." Mindy looked over the items. "Would you happen to have an extra rubber band for my hair?"

"Sure. I'll grab you one." The teen raced up the back stairs.

Mindy preheated the oven then grabbed milk and butter from the refrigerator. Hanging from a turtle magnet was a picture of a Creed holding Livvy when she was a baby. Mindy's heart pounded against her ribcage. She could barely breathe and tears filled her eyes.

"Can I help with anything?"

Alarmed by the voice behind her, she swiveled and met the curious gaze of Creed who was standing in the doorway. She forced air into her lungs, hoping he didn't see straight through her. "The picture…you look very happy. I didn't know you had a child…a daughter."

"You haven't been to Cooper's Hawk in a long time," he answered softly.

"Dad! You can't be in here. We're making surprise cookies," Livvy said when she returned, shooing her father back out into the living room. "Found one." She handed over the elastic.

Hair up, hands washed, aprons on, they started on the cookies.

Livvy measured the dry ingredients into the mixing bowl, "I know who you are."

Mindy looked at the teen's profile. "You do?"

She gave a jerky nod. "You're in the picture that my dad keeps in his drawer." She tucked her bottom lip in as she fixated on folding the wet ingredients into the dry.

Livvy's divulgence made Mindy suck in a breath. Creed kept a picture of her. A tingling sensation skipped through her. "Your dad and I, well, we used to be very close."

"We used to be also," Livvy admitted.

"You're not anymore?" Mindy cleared the dirty measuring spoons from the workspace and placed them into the dishwasher.

The long hesitation warned Mindy that Livvy might refuse to answer.

"He works a lot. And he doesn't understand girls. How were you close to him when he doesn't get us at all?"

Mindy smiled. "Believe it or not, your dad was my best friend. He was about the only one who did get me. I don't think you're the only teenager who thinks that their parents don't understand what they're going through. When my Jane was your age, she told me all the time that I didn't know what it was like to be a teen."

"Really? You seem very nice."

"Thank you. I too used to tell my dad all the time that he didn't appreciate how girls ticked."

"My grandma lives here with us. She has since my mom left."

"Do you see her often?"

"She's an actress," Livvy said with exaggerated enthusiasm. "She's on TV. She works a lot too and says she can't get away right now. She told me she wants me to come stay with her soon in New York City."

"How long has it been since she visited?"

"A couple of years."

"I'm sure she misses you. A lot. But I know your grandma very well and she's an amazing woman." Mindy buttered the cookie sheet. "Let's roll the dough into balls. Like this." She showed Livvy how.

"So you don't have a mom either?"

"She died when I was ten." Mindy concentrated on rolling the dough between her palms.

"Can I tell you a secret?"

"You can tell me anything." Mindy gave the teen a comforting smile.

"I forget what my mom smells like. She always wore the same perfume from a pretty bottle. I wish I knew what it was called."

"Sometimes I forget what my mama looked like, smelled like too…and the sound of her voice. I do remember the song she sang, Twinkle, Twinkle Little Star, to me every night at bedtime. I miss her every day."

"I miss mine too, although my mom didn't die. She left. Dad says she is an actress at heart. I think she just didn't love me enough." Livvy rolled the tip of her finger through spilled flour on the counter.

"Oh, honey. I'm sure she loves you dearly. Sometimes…well, sometimes a parent has a difficult time showing how much they care for one reason or another. After Mom passed, my dad had a hard time for a while." She didn't know how much to share with the teen but remembering how she felt at fourteen she only wanted people to be truthful.

"Dad's that way too. I think sometimes he hates having me." The words seemed to suck the oxygen right out of the room.

Mindy wanted to hug her—wanted to tell the young girl—going on young lady—that everything would be alright. "I'm sure that's not true." Mindy's chest twisted. No child should ever feel unwanted or unloved. "I felt the same way about my father too, but I was wrong."

"Is the pan ready to go in?"

"Yes."

Once the pan was in, Livvy said, "Dad won't even let me wear makeup. All the girls at school are allowed," she huffed. "He treats me like a baby."

Mindy had these same arguments with her father, and with Jane. "You're a beautiful girl and he probably thinks you don't need any."

"He doesn't understand anything. He especially doesn't understand Alex." A sparkle came to her eyes.

"Alex? Is that your boyfriend?"

Livvy's face softened some and her cheeks flushed. "No. He's my friend. We've been friends since we were kids and we like the same things. Basketball. Kickball. I think Dad would like it if I didn't have any friends."

"I bet Alex is a nice boy." Mindy needed to tread carefully. She didn't want to make anything more difficult between Livvy and Creed. Mindy understood how difficult teen years could be for kids and parents both. Jane had gone through a similar stage where she was lying and skipping school with friends. Thankfully, they'd survived the rebellious years.

"He's always taking my phone. If I breath too loud he'll take it."

Mindy decided not to point out the exaggeration. "I'm sure that can be upsetting. What do you like to do for fun? Outside of texting and socializing on the phone? I know you said basketball and kickball."

"I like to read too. And draw, but I'm not good at it."

"I found figure skating and I immediately loved it, but I'd fall all the time. Then I was in competitions. I'll be coaching at the local ice rink."

"You're that good?"

Mindy laughed. "I think I can hold my own."

"I'm sorry, I didn't mean to make it sound rude. I'm always being told that I don't have a filter, whatever that means."

"You're fine. I haven't dedicated myself to the sport as much as I once did because I had other things vying for my attention but it's important that we find what we love and hold onto it."

"Thank you for helping me make cookies."

"If you need help with anything, I'll be around."

~~~~
~~~~

Creed looked across the space of the porch steps at Mindy where she sat with the slit in the skirt of the dress parted, showing off tanned thigh. She played with the necklace and stared into the night sky.

He dragged his gaze back to her face where she took a long drawl from the bottle of beer. Something jerked inside him— something powerful and amazing. He inhaled sharply and took in the smell of freshly baked cookies. He appreciated that she'd offered to help Livvy.

"Just like old times." She winked and set the bottle on the top step.

"Thank you," he said

"For what?" Her gaze met his for a good three heartbeats before she turned away.

"For helping Livvy. I'm sure she'd rather have you in the kitchen with her than me," he muttered, feeling the weight of disappointment on his shoulders. He didn't choose to have things so chaotic between them, but he didn't seem to have the capability to stop the train from speeding out of control.

"I did feel some tension."

"Hell, you sure it wasn't a tsunami? I feel like I'm caught up and can't get out. She hates me." He sighed and scraped a palm down his jaw.

"She doesn't *hate* you. She's a teen who is unsure about life and wants to be valued and loved." She stretched her legs and the hem raised a few inches higher above her knee.

"Oh, so she talked to you?"

"She did."

Why did he feel a jab of envy? As Livvy's father he couldn't get her to talk but Mindy knew her for less than fifteen minutes and she had become a chatter box. "What am I doing wrong?"

"Fourteen is a hard age. Things are always changing—with their body and peer pressure."

"You survived parenthood. Any suggestions?" Did he sense some hesitation in her?

"Jane is wonderful and kind, but she wasn't always so sweet. In fact there were a few times I'd lock myself in the bathroom and cry until I couldn't see straight." She pulled off her sandals and set them to the side.

"Oh, so then we're not on an island?"

She smiled. "Nope. Happens to most parents of teens. It gets better. I promise. That is unless you screw up majorly and Livvy runs away and joins the circus."

He felt an invisible punch in his gut. "Circus? Is that even possible?"

"Jane used to threaten me almost every single day. She watched a movie where a teen boy ran away from home and joined. Thankfully, she didn't see the plan through. Unfortunately, she'd said some rather rotten things during that time. I wasn't at my best either."

"Where was your husband?" That word 'husband' burned his tongue and anger tumbled down his spine. Who had she married? He flicked at the corner of the label on the bottle hoping she gave him a window into her life after she left Cooper's Hawk.

"Well…" She swiped the palms of her hands together and sighed. "He was building his career. In his defense, he certainly has made a name for himself but somewhere along the line he'd given up a lot to gain clientele."

"Did he cheat?"

"Yeah, he did. With his assistant."

"One of those, huh?"

"I wish them the best. I don't hate him I just don't want him, thankfully."

"You sound like you're handling things like a trooper." He respected that, although for the life of him he couldn't see why a man—any man—who had a woman like Mindy Sage would want, or even look, at another woman. She had the brightest smile and eyes, and certainly was one of the smartest women he'd ever met. Her ex must be a real idiot.

"It took me some time to get here. I'd be lying if I said I'd handled the divorce like a champ. Okay, enough about my sad, sad past. From what Livvy said, Melody hasn't visited in a long time." She turned slightly, facing him, lifting her hair off her neck.

The bull frogs sounded in the distance and the crickets tweeted. It was a nice, comfortable night. He felt the tension leave his muscles as they sat there together, drinking a beer.

"So she told you, huh? Livvy doesn't usually talk about her mom to anyone especially anything negative. You must have left a lasting impression."

"Your daughter is amazing."

"I wish her mother thought so. I'm not saying Mel doesn't love Livvy, but she took off years ago to follow a dream of becoming an actress in Hollywood and she never came back."

"I'm sorry."

"It was bound to happen."

"So, big question. Why haven't you remarried?"

He laughed then chugged the rest of the beer. "Who'd want this old bear?"

"You can't tell me that you don't have a line of women in Cooper's Hawk who'd love to take your last name. What happened to all those followers of the football running back that stole so many young hearts?"

"Those young hearts are now women with logical heads on their shoulders."

"You're being modest."

"Seriously, I was grounded after my daughter came. I guess that's the best way to describe things." Although the word grounded was a bit exaggerated. "I've dated some but Livvy and I are a package deal."

She brought the beer to her lips, sipped, then set the bottle between her legs. "Kids change us. Make us better." Something flashed over her face, as if she blocked her emotions from showing. "Jane made me a mommy and it's the best job ever."

"About the property. I've been thinking over your proposition."

She smiled. "Really?"

"Don't get excited. I didn't say I would agree." He hated to see her frown, but he needed to be truthful. "Have you spoken with Rusty about what you want?"

"He doesn't see my commitment, I guess."

"Okay, but have you listened to his side of things. Maybe he's right."

"You keep asking me but honestly I don't need his permission." Her voice was as fragile as frozen lace and through the sliver of light from the moon and stars he could see the heat in her irises. "I'd like for him to sign over the rest of Sage Ranch to me."

"And?"

"It's in deliberation." Her sigh seemed like a muffled cry.

"You really haven't given any of us reason to believe you truly want the house and land."

She propped her elbow on the step and pressed her cheek against her palm. "He should have never sold it to you, at least not before he spoke to me first."

He blinked. "We've accomplished that already. Just so we're clear, how long since you visited last?" He knew the icy blast would come but it came much quicker than he expected.

Her pink tinted lips twisted. "Of course you're on his side on this."

"I'm on no one's side," he confirmed. "I own my share. I have nothing at stake here. I'm only telling you what you need to hear."

She dropped her hand away from her face, astonishment causing her eyes to widen. "Shouldn't you be working less instead of more? Can you handle this farm and Sage Ranch?"

"I have it covered."

"Oh do you? Livvy told me you work all the time."

"That's a low blow," he muttered.

"What is it you're worried about when it comes to me and the ranch?"

"That you'll leave or not take care of it, not the way it deserves. But that's your choice. Do what you need to do."

"I need to prove to Daddy that I can handle my share."

"Better start crackin'."

Agitated, she took the space between them in two sashays, then tilted her hip. He lifted his gaze up her amazing legs, firm breasts, passed the stubborn tilt of her chin to her glazed gaze. "What can I do to prove my good intentions?"

He chuckled. "Why do you want this so badly?"

"I want to keep my home. Isn't that enough? I want Jane to have this place to call home one day, hopefully."

Standing, his thigh brushed hers, causing a raid of sensations to gallop through him. Staring down at her bright eyes surrounded by thick, dark lashes, he denied the urge to sweep her up in his arms and remind her of that one night so long ago. It would come, eventually. He needed to know if she still tasted like ripe strawberries.

"It's more than a plot of land, sweetheart."

"What do you mean?"

"What happened to that girl who was invested?"

She drew back slightly, several seconds drifted by, and she said on a wistful sigh, "How can I prove that I am when you and Daddy can't even tell me the truth?"

He gave a jerky shrug and scratched his temple with his thumbnail. "How have I kept the truth?"

She crossed her arms. "I don't know."

"That's what I thought."

"What would you like me to do, Creedy?"

He tore a hand through his hair. "It's not up to me."

"Come on, let's not kid ourselves. If I stay how much longer can we deny the tug that draws us together?"

"Who says I'm denying it? Maybe I'm just waiting for you to stop."

"That almost sounds like a challenge, and you know me and challenges," she said in a soft tone that dipped in and teased his desire.

"Take it however you want. I'm not making any promises that I'll sell you a portion of the ranch. So if you're trying to use that sexy body to get me to do what you want then you're wasting your time."

She gritted her teeth and he knew he'd struck a chord. It wasn't his aspiration to piss her off, but he seemed good at it.

"You have a lot of gull, Creed James Hawke!"

"I have a lot of gull? Really? I think it's interesting how you suddenly want to fit in here in Cooper's Hawk like nineteen years haven't passed."

She crossed her arms and he could see the tremble in her bottom lip. "I'm about sick and tired of hearing you throw that up in my face! I might have moved away but it sure as hell didn't take you long to move on. You and Melody married before the stain of our lovemaking was washed away from your truck bed."

He could see the simmering anger in her irises, but that didn't deter him. "Why would you care?" He leaned in a few inches. Her eyes widened slightly.

"Forget it! It's no use." She turned, but he grabbed her elbow and turned her back around.

"No, I won't forget it! You don't have the right to spew off words in anger then run away. If you plan on sticking around, we're going to have to find some peace. You left, Mindy. What did you expect from me?"

"I didn't expect you to screw the first girl that came along."

"And I didn't expect that you'd leave. If you cared why didn't you come back?"

She squinted. "I did come back, Creed. Five months after I left, I came back." Her voice faded as he saw tears fill her eyes.

"What? You're lying." He realized he still held her in his grasp, and he dropped his hand to his side.

"What would I gain by lying?" There was a seesawing of emotion in her voice.

"Why did you come back?" he practically growled the words.

"I left you a letter. In your truck."

"What letter?"

"Stop, Creed! You know what letter I'm referring to."

He rubbed his jaw. "This is like pulling teeth. I never received a letter from you. I want to know what it said and why you came back."

She lowered her eyes and when she looked back up at him all emotion was gone. The strong Mindy had returned. "It doesn't even matter anymore."

"Don't even try that. You're not getting off so easy. Why. Did. You. Come back? Answer me," he demanded.

Trails of moisture glistened on her cheeks. "I-I came back to see you. To speak to you. In the letter I wrote to you, I asked that you come see me. I waited in the parking lot of the ice rink for hours. Then Melody showed up. She was visibly upset that I was back. I knew then it was too late."

His breath came out on a hiss. "What was too late?" he whispered.

Her gaze met his and a surge of energy passed between them. "Too late for us."

He sucked in a tempered breath and it took him a long time to process what she had told him. "I had no clue you had come back. Melody didn't tell me."

"It doesn't matter, Creed. She was your fiancée. I can't blame her for being concerned."

"We didn't get married."

She blinked. "You said that you two did."

"Later, we did, but not that summer." He rubbed his forehead, feeling a throbbing coming on. "I backed out. I couldn't marry her then. I left for the Navy and when I came back, I joined the rodeo circuit. It wasn't until later, when I came home that things started up again. She got pregnant with Livvy and I wanted to do the right thing, so I asked her to marry me. From the get-go I knew it wouldn't last but I didn't want to risk that she'd walk away with my child."

She swiped her knuckles across her face to remove the tears. "I-I thought you two married. All this time—"

"It doesn't change the fact that you got married too, Mindy. A year after you left. After that I asked Rusty to never mention your name to me again."

"Creed, I need to tell you—"

Headlights flashing across the house made them both look toward the driveway.

"That's Ma."

Abby walked up the sidewalk and came to a stop and blinked as if she'd seen a ghost. "Mindy, is that you?"

"Yes, Abby. It's me." Mindy still had some shakiness to her tone.

"I heard you were back. I'm so glad to see you." She dragged Mindy in for a tight hug. She sank against the woman, fighting back tears. Abby had been like a second mother to Mindy.

"It's been too long," She pulled back. "We shouldn't allow so much time to pass before we see each other."

"I agree." Abby patted her shoulder.

"Ma, will you stay with Livvy in the morning? I need to take Mindy somewhere at sunrise."

His mother looked from each of them, a broad smile on her lips. "Of course. What's the plan?"

"It's a surprise." Creed grinned when Mindy looked at him with a narrow eye.

"Shouldn't you ask my opinion before you make plans?"

"I'll leave you two kids alone." Abby backed away and started for the house. "Again, it was nice seeing you Mindy. Don't be a stranger."

By now, Mindy had her arms crossed defensively over her chest.

"Come on, Mindy. The girl I used to know would be up for any surprise."

"I'm a few years older and a lot wiser," she recited.

"Trust me. What I want to show you, you'll want to see." Suddenly this meant more to him than he could explain.

"I don't."

"Then don't but at least do this for me."

Several seconds passed and he thought she'd deny him this chance. Then finally she dropped her arms to her sides in submission and nodded. "Fine."

"Be ready by five A.M. Dress comfortably."

Chapter 8

MINDY AWOKE TO the sound of her annoying phone alarm.

Blinking against the shadows in her room, she fumbled for the dismiss button and rolled back over, then remembered Creed would be there soon.

Jumping up, she shimmied out of the sheets and her jammies and fumbled for the clothes she'd laid out at the end of the bed. Within minutes she was dressed, a beanie pulled over her head, and her boots on. Her phone lit up from the nightstand.

Grabbing it, she read the text from Creed.

"I'm in the driveway."

Barely able to keep her anticipation down, she typed, *"On my way."*

Tiptoeing downstairs, skipping over the three stairs that squeaked, she quietly went to the front door. She pulled it open and there he stood, the cowboy she'd spent most of the night dreaming about—just like in the past. He slipped his gaze down her from neck to the tips of her boots and back up to hold her stare. "Ready?"

"Sure. Where are we going?" she whispered.

"Are you sneaking out?"

"Old habits die hard." She closed the door behind her. "Now, where are we going?"

"You always ask too many questions." Creed grabbed her hand and practically dragged her down the sidewalk toward his silver Chevy Silverado. She dug her heels in. "What are you doing?"

"We're going for a ride."

"Wait. How do you know I'm interested in taking a ride with you?" She wanted to, but she didn't want him to think that she wasn't still upset with him.

"Mindy, what changed from last night until this morning?" His gaze held hers.

Dreams. Tons of dreams about you. Me wearing a white dress and you in a tux.

She couldn't tell him this.

His expression softened and his eyes bore into her. "Have patience."

Lifting a brow, she smiled. "I'll try."

"You're going to enjoy what I'm about to show you."

"I've heard those words before." Her brows wagged.

His deep smile turned his dimples into pools. "Not that I'm opposed to your mind being in the gutter, but that wasn't what I was referring to." He reached over with his free hand and lifted a misbehaving tendril of hair off her cheek. She felt the warm caress of his touch all the way into her bones. He made her weak and she disliked how much control he had over her. Hated that even now, well beyond her teenage years, she still felt like that young girl under his spell.

"Tell me where you want me to go," she whispered.

"It's a surprise."

"Just tell me."

"Ugh, Minnow."

"Maybe this is a bad idea."

"Why?"

As much as she searched for a reason, she couldn't find even one little white lie. "Okay, but this better be worth it." She hid her smile.

He opened the passenger door for her. She climbed up into the seat, inhaling the mixture of leather and coffee.

"Grab the cup with the letter S on the lid. Three sugars and four creams, right?"

Flattered that he remembered, she picked up the cup and peeled back the plastic lid, inhaling the amazing scent of vanilla. He even included the flavoring that she loved.

He touched her waist and she jerked, spilling some of the coffee over the rim and onto her hand. He pulled the seatbelt over her torso, smiling. "Creed, I can do that for myself." She took the strap from him and clicked the metal into place.

"Sorry. I guess I still feel the need to protect you." His words were like chocolate for the soul. Not that she needed a man's protection, but truth was, on occasion she'd like to have a man protect her or make her feel special. Branch not once had thought of helping her with her seatbelt, or even something as simple as helping wash the dishes after dinner. Creed opened the glove compartment, took out a napkin and laid it on her lap. "I'd clean you myself, but I might have to kiss you too."

She swallowed a moan.

His eyes were twinkling in mischief as he stepped back, slammed the door and she took the amount of time for him to round the back of the truck and climb into the driver's side to gain control of her unruly body parts. With shaky fingers, she used the napkin and wiped the coffee away.

Sliding the gear into reverse, he shifted to look over his shoulder to back out and she caught his clean, soap scent. She liked it, a little too much. Squeezing her inner thighs, she counted to ten, forcing her nerves to behave.

Once they were on the main road, she stared through the window into the lingering darkness. "Feels like old times when you and I would sneak out at dark. What were we thinking?"

"I'm sure this is a cliché answer, but things are different now. People are different. We can't sleep with our doors unlocked and invite strangers into our homes any longer. I wouldn't want Livvy doing the same things we did."

"It's always different for our kids than it was for us." She turned in the seat to look at his profile. "Why'd you marry her, Creedy? Why in the world did you marry Melody? I understand you wanted to be a father to your daughter, but she wasn't the girl for you."

Whistling through his teeth, he tapped his fingers on the steering wheel. "Let's just jump right into that hot pot, why don't we."

"If I'm going to be hanging out with you, we need to clear the air on some things."

"I wish I knew the answer."

"I'm angry with you. For a lot of things, but still, thank you for the coffee."

Shadows played over his features. He huffed a low chuckle and he turned left heading away from the farm. "Melody seemed to be the best opportunity to take my mind off things." The eerie quietness of his tone made her curious.

"You call that an answer?" She gave her head a jerky shake.

"It's all that I got."

"But you married her." She wouldn't let him off the hook. "Marriage isn't meant to be shared with someone who simply takes your "mind off things'."

He gave a tight shrug. "Yeah, I married her."

"Why didn't you two marry the first time?" Now that the ball started rolling, she had a dozen questions.

"I wasn't ready for marriage, with her or anyone."

Mindy slanted her gaze to the window, hiding the tears that developed in her eyes. If he'd known about their baby would he and Mindy have married? What would their life together look like? Could they have weathered the storms that couple's face? As far as she saw things, if she and Branch made it as long as they had, without communicating—without sex—she and Creed would have had a fighting chance.

Time was such a wasted thing.

A familiar pain settled in her chest, right over her heart. She'd mourned not only the end of her and Creed's relationship, but each milestone Jane had reached that he'd missed out on. She drew up one knee, laid her chin on it and looked across the seat, attempting to figure things through his profile. "I'm sorry things didn't work out with Melody. I do mean that."

"You sure?" He glanced over at her. "You certainly bring it up enough with that throaty, angry sound in your voice."

"I do mean it. Not for you as much as for Livvy. Single parents raise children all the time, but Livvy knows she could see her mom, if only…"

"Mel would get her head on straight," he grumbled. "What about you and your ex? Why did you marry him?"

"I loved him." She did love him at one time, as much as she could.

He brought his hand up and rubbed his whiskered jaw. "I guess that makes sense."

There were so many things she could add. That she never loved anyone as much as she loved Creed. No one ever made her laugh more. Or as angry as he could. That she'd never wanted to share all her hopes, dreams, fears, and wishes with Branch as much as she wanted to share with Creed. Divulging all those thoughts would only open a pandora's box. She'd then have to tell him that

Branch had been a good stepfather—as good as he knew how to be. They'd shared some good times, all revolving around Jane.

"He was an idiot for cheating," Creed mumbled. "Just sayin'." His tone sounded different, deeper and huskier. He leaned in and turned up the radio. The popular country song vibrated the speakers. Was this his way of saying that the discussion was over?

She reached over and turned down the volume. "The cheating was secondary to the fact that our relationship had been over for years. We just kept moving like robots. Each day beginning and ending, flowing together. When Jane got older and spent more time independently from us, the scary truth of how far we'd fallen away from one another was hard to ignore. I think I knew all along he was cheating before he admitted his unfaithfulness. I was just as much at fault because I chose to overlook the blaring truth."

"What's she like?"

"Jane?" Mindy's heart bubbled up with love and pride. Tears blurred her vision. "She's amazing. Smart. Bright. Athletic. Spunky. I could go on and on." Her smile came automatically. "She's at Columbia U studying zoology. She wants to work with wild animals."

"She sounds amazing."

"Oh, she is. I'm so proud of her."

"Of course with a mama like you she couldn't be anything but remarkable. What does she think of you coming back to Cooper's Hawk?"

Mindy looked through the window at the faint blue streak appearing in the sky as the sun flirted with the morning. "She's okay with me being here. She's far more mature than most kids her age."

"Does she look like you, or her father?"

Just like you. "Like her father." She lowered her leg and pressed the back of her head against the seat. "She has my attitude." The conversation stung her soul. What had she done? She'd prevented Creed from knowing his daughter. Over the years she'd been honest with Jane, to a certain point. When they talked about Creed, Mindy would be as detailed as possible, but Jane had never asked to meet Creed.

"You were the only one who ever really knew me, Mindy." His words came so low, so softly that she almost thought she imagined them.

"Creed, we were kids."

"Is that what you believe? We were kids so we didn't know each other?"

Swallowing against the constriction building in her throat, she blew out a long breath. "I'm not saying that—or maybe I am. What if you and I hadn't, you know, had sex?" She had Jane and Mindy could never be more grateful. "If we'd truly known each other why couldn't we communicate better?"

"I was a young and dumb cowboy. I look back and think how stupid I was to not tell you how I felt." His nostrils flared and his grip tightened on the steering wheel tuning his knuckles white.

"There's no better time than like the present."

"You wouldn't want to hear." There was a truthfulness to his voice that made the hair on the back of her neck lift. He switched on his turn signal and they turned left onto a narrow road.

She sat up in the seat. "We're headed to Hawke Landing. Or are we headed to the place where we made love?"

"Would that be a problem?"

"If you brought me out here so that we can take a tumble down memory lane—"

"Don't worry. Not interested," he teased her.

"Good because I'm not interested either. You're not my type any longer."

What had been meant as a burn didn't work. He laughed. "So what's your type now? Cheaters?"

"That's unfair."

"Is it?"

Opening her mouth, the comeback was lost on her tongue. "Me divulging horror stories about my marriage doesn't allow you to use them as leverage."

"And using your anger as a defense every time we start to talk about feelings and the past isn't fair either."

He had a point. "Old habits and all."

"So what man is your type now?"

"A man who knows how to work his—"

He jerked his chin up, causing the truck to swerve.

"Brain." She laughed. "Now who has their head in the gutter?" She liked teasing him.

"There's the old Mindy I remember so well."

"The Creed I remember could dish it but couldn't take it."

He snorted and chuckled. "Is this your way of deflecting the serious questions?"

"And what serious question was that?" She pulled off her hat and finger combed her hair. Things were easing right back into normal between them.

"Your type of man. You dated Jedd Brown once, didn't you?"

He remembered that? She certainly had forgotten. "Once for about five minutes."

With another snort, he said, "He's living with Jedediah Moss now. Has been for five years."

"Jedd and Jedediah? I had no clue…"

"No one did. They're great fellows. They run the local antique shop."

"That would explain a lot about the time Jedd and I went to a party at Darcy Clever's house and we played spin the bottle. I broke up with him that night because he wouldn't even sit next to me. I thought he hated me. He had the nicest hair."

"Nah, he didn't hate you. No one hated you."

"Except for Melody Rumor." Mindy rolled her eyes. She slipped off her boots and placed her bare feet up on the dash. Would he ask her to remove her feet off his pristine dash? He didn't say a word just gave her a wide grin.

"Maybe this would be a good time to tell me what was in the letter you wrote me," he urged.

No, definitely not the right time. "I wonder where that letter went." She tapped her fingers on her thigh.

He darted a glance her direction. "No clue."

"Come on, Creed. Melody took it. That's how she knew where I was waiting. She was so angry. I thought she would blow her top."

"What did she say?"

"Not a lot, never did. Except she did show me some interesting text messages you two had exchanged. Like just how happy you were that I left. That you wanted nothing to do with me ever again."

"Mindy—"

"Please don't defend her."

"I didn't plan to. I wanted to tell you that I never sent any messages about you to Mel. Not even when she and I were married. Any time your name came up it turned into an argument."

"Again, it appears that Melody controlled us like finger puppets." She allowed her shoulders to slump under the information. If Melody took the letter that meant she had to know about Jane. Why didn't she tell Creed? What would she have gained by not telling him? "Melody got what she wanted."

"Did she? You might think that was me, but it wasn't."

"We should stop talking about her because it might make me want to jump out of this truck and walk home." Feeling a chill she wrapped her arms around her waist.

"Are you cold?" Creed reached into the backseat and handed her the beige Carhartt coat that smelled like a heady mixture of leather, animal fur and the outdoors. "That should keep you warm."

She wanted to deny his offer, but truth was she felt a chill. Any talk of Melody made her sick, especially now that Mindy knew the truth. Sliding her arms inside the coat, she pulled it up around her chest and snuggled deeper into the sheep fur lining, finding pleasure at the scent wrapping around her. She felt a warm, tingling sensation spread through her and she realized it was the feeling of happiness, and it surprised her. Mindy loved her daughter, had grown to love California and her friends, but she found something here in Cooper's Hawk that didn't compare to anything else around the world. The fresh, country air, the rich history, the wonderful scenery like the one outside of the truck now.

And then there was Creed.

To deny how he made her feel would only be lying to herself. The connection between them remained and grew stronger each time they were together. They could toss inflammatory insults at each other and a second later he would do something kind and big-hearted, like offering his coat because he knew she was cold. These acts of thoughtfulness were what drew her to him. Yet, what would happen if he knew about Jane? Would he forgive her? Could he?

Chapter 9

KEEPING HIS EYES on the road ahead was a challenge with the beauty sitting next to him. Mindy was relaxed back in the seat, her boots off and her bare feet pressed against the dashboard. He wasn't much into feet, but she had nice toes with bright pink painted toenails. She tapped her toes to the beat of the music and stared through the side window.

He didn't like talking about Melody with her. Or Branch. He felt a mixture of jealousy and humiliation when those two names crept up into the conversation.

What right did Creed have to feel jealousy? He too had a child with another woman.

Maybe those feelings stemmed from the life he'd wanted with Mindy. A family. A house on the west property.

It was too late…

Or was it?

He stole glances between her and the road ahead, slowing the truck so he could stare a little longer.

What the hell had he done?

He'd allowed her to slip through his fingers.

Why hadn't he chased after her?

Because he'd been so wrapped up in his immaturity that he'd been incapable of seeing outside his own pleasure bubble. He'd made the mistake of believing she'd always be around. That wasn't the case.

He inhaled deeply, trying to make heads or tails of his emotions. The task was almost impossible.

Creed bereaved the loss of time they could have had together. The life they could have shared here in Cooper's Hawk. She wanted him to sell her back a portion of Sage Ranch, but what he wanted was for them to share it together.

And there it was.

A part of him still believed they could be together.

Since she'd come back, he'd noticed that the dark circles under her eyes were fading, the hollowness of her skin was now sun kissed. The light was returning in her eyes. That's what this place did for people. She couldn't deny that this place was where she belonged.

He rubbed his brow and sighed. What if he could have Mindy as his wife? The attraction remained. The desire was stronger than ever.

Creed didn't just have himself to think about. His daughter mattered, what she wanted mattered. Although she probably didn't think he cared. He loved her and wanted her to be happy.

Looking up into the sky, the sun was starting to come up. This was his favorite time of day when the light pushed through the darkness. When a new day was at his fingertips. He'd been around the world and he'd never seen a better sunrise than those here in Montana. It took his breath away no matter how often he watched.

He turned into the cracked asphalt lot of Hawke Landing but instead of pulling in front of the building, he continued the dirt lane that took them through the field of purple wildflowers and closer to the mountain. The truck rocked back and forth, and he slowed to ease over the bumpy landscape.

Mindy dropped her feet and sat up straight. "Why are we here?"

"You'll see." He tamped down her curiosity as he drove the truck along the mountain side until they came to a pull off next to a row of tall trees.

"Let's get out." He grabbed a flashlight from the glove compartment and a blanket from the backseat.

He met her at the front of the truck, grabbed her hand and led ger toward the trees.

"Slow down," she said.

"We have to hurry. We don't want to miss this."

He clicked on a flashlight and shone the light ahead of them as they followed a worn, rocky path he'd walked a hundred times.

Creed still held her hand and she didn't make a move to pull away from him. It felt nice to thread his fingers around hers, palms pressing to each other, as if they were more than just the history they'd shared.

"How far do we have to walk?"

"Patience," he muttered.

Her breathing was labored as they continued up the incline. "I didn't realize I was in such bad shape."

"It's the air. We're almost there."

The path branched off and they steered left, then pushed through a line of trees. This took them into a small clearing.

"No one comes here." He laid the blanket over the large, flat rock where he'd come and sit for hours. "Have a seat. Then watch."

The fluid orange of the sun peaked up from the horizon. The rays crawled across the sky, slowly. It first appeared like a blaze and soon became an awe-inspiring golden ball bidding farewell to the darkness and hello to the new day. The view went for miles and if they looked closely, they could see Cooper's Hawk, Sage Ranch and the Farm in the distance.

"This is wonderful, Creed," she said, still watching Mother Nature's show.

They sat on the rock at the edge of the cliff, holding hands, like they were kids again and feeling the excitement of what was to come. The feelings and desires rolling through him weren't that of a child though.

"No words to describe it, is there?" The sun was now up and lighting the pale blue sky.

"It's amazing. It's like I could reach up and touch the sky."

"I told you it was worth the effort. I come up here as often as I can." He squeezed her hand tighter.

She lifted her chin to look over at him. A piece of her hair had fallen over her cheek and without a thought he reached and slipped the tendril behind her ear. Her mouth curved into a smile and her eyes were like windows into her soul. Had she felt the surge of electric that passed through them?

Her hand came up and she wrapped her slender fingers around his wrist, staring at him with a host of emotions that he couldn't quite read. "You shouldn't touch me like that, Creed."

"Why? You said yourself that there's something left between us."

She lifted her chin slightly. "That's why you shouldn't. You and I always had a problem with being impulsive and we're not those dream-filled kids any longer. We're adults with responsibilities. We can't just think of ourselves and satisfying a need." Her deep brown eyes burrowed into him.

"Won't you ever give love a shot again? Will you allow responsibility and excuses to keep you from being happy?"

"Are you asking for personal reasons?"

"Well I'm not asking for another man," he huffed.

Several seconds floated by. "My divorce was only final six months ago."

"But you said yourself the marriage was over long ago."

The tip of her tongue came out to sweep along the plush curve of her bottom lip. He wanted to help her with that, but he held himself steady. He swallowed the urgency to kiss her, flooded with all the other desires he'd felt since she'd arrived in town. The bond between them came in pulsating waves of need and urgency and growing stronger by the minute. An undying ache lingered in him, from guilt to wanting her back in his life. How had it happened so suddenly?

He knew the reason. The love had never left.

It was like a fire that had been left blazing all these years.

She swallowed audibly. "What are we doing, Creed? We've been here and done this before and look where it got us? Do you even understand the depth of sadness and hurt I've endured?" Tears filled her eyes.

Pain swept through him. "And you don't think I've felt my own pain? Do you think it was my choice that we'd spend so long apart?"

"For a man who speaks about pain you certainly couldn't prove it by how long it took you to find someone to fill the void."

He squeezed his eyes tightly shut, wishing he could erase all the baggage. When he opened his eyes he saw one tear slip down her cheek. He swiped it away with a fingertip. "You have to forgive me at some point, just as I have to forgive you."

"Forgive me?" Her bottom lip trembled.

"You did leave, Mindy."

She breathed in, all vulnerability gone. "I came back."

"I hear that, but why? If it was for me why didn't you speak to me? I had no clue you were in town." He swiped off his hat and pounded it against his thigh.

"You're right." Her voice shook. "I should have. I didn't know what to do though. I didn't want to ruin what I thought was your happiness with Melody."

Confusion filled his head. What the hell? "Are you that daft? Do you think a couple of months could rid me of my feelings? Or even nineteen years. I loved you, Mindy. I might have been an idiot but that doesn't mean I didn't love you. When you left I told myself that it'd get better. That you and I weren't meant to be. Hell, I might have even had myself convinced for a while, but the second you came waltzing back into Cooper's Hawk I knew I'd been lying to myself. I might not deserve to have you as a lover, but damnit I want you as my friend. Can't we find some stable ground to build *us* again?"

"Creed…," she whispered, bowing her head.

"Mindy?" he said on an exhale of breath.

"There's a lot you don't understand."

"Do you believe I chose not to come see you when you came back?"

Hurt filled her eyes. "All these years I believed you chose not to show up."

She did that little move again, the tip of her tongue swept over her bottom lip. He growled as he tried to keep himself in check, but he couldn't hold back any longer. He pulled her into him and lowered his mouth over hers, reveling in the way her soft lips felt under his searching touch. She tasted like fresh strawberries and smelled like heaven. He thrust deeper, exploring her with his tongue. She made a throaty moan as if she was submitting to the whirlwind of emotions. He wrapped his arm around her waist bringing her closer. She still wore his coat and it was an intrusion on their intimacy.

He intensified the kiss, seeking something in her that he couldn't quite understand but it was more than needing satisfaction.

Her fingers dug into his arms, clinging to him, and then she moved her hands upward until they wrapped around the back of his neck. He could feel her ease into his arms, submitting to the desire she could no longer hide, and he could no longer ignore. Flashes of bright light warmed his blood, settling into his loins that were now gorged with need.

Burying his fingers in her hair, he held her head as he kissed her cheeks, her ears, nibbling the row of diamond studs. She leaned her head back onto one shoulder, giving him access to the length of her neck. He kissed the silken skin, drawing his tongue over her.

The flashlight dropped forgotten to the ground and he clutched the back of the coat, pulling her in. Her hands slipped from his neck and he dragged the thick material lower to bind her wrists. He lowered his mouth to the open neckline of the shirt, feeling her pulse thumping under his lips as he kissed the hollow between her collarbones.

My God. She smelled and tasted so good.

He undid one button then another until the tops of her firm breasts were exposed to his attention. He kissed the firm mounds, then suckled them. Her moans deepened and there on the rock on an edge of a cliff they found each other again.

"Creed…" came his name on a moan.

"Sweet, sweet, Mindy," he groaned against the cleft of her breasts.

"We. Must. Stop."

Stewing in his need, it took him a good five seconds to wrap his head around what she'd said. He lifted his chin, looking at her. Her eyes were glossy, and her cheeks were flushed. Her lips were rosy and moist from his kisses. "Stop?"

"Yes. I'm not ready. We're not ready." If this was the truth, then why did her enticing eyes tell him something different. He wasted no more time and pulled away, releasing her.

"Damn. Things got carried away." He heard the unsteadiness in his voice.

"For both of us." She hurried to button her shirt.

"I was thinking with something other than my brain. I haven't done that in a while. Got so carried away I forgot the consequences," he admitted.

She reached up and wiped her finger across his lip. "You're wearing my lip tint." Her smile was shaky, but at least she was smiling.

"We better get off this cliff. I have something else I'd like to show you."

Chapter 10

MINDY WATCHED CREED open the doors to the metal barn that sat next to the Hawke Landing building. He glanced back at her, looking like the young Creed again. His smile made his eyes sparkle.

She wasn't sure there was an underlying meaning to that look, but it unraveled her senses. Still reeling from the intense kiss they'd exchanged on the cliff, it wouldn't take much to melt her into a puddle at this point. Why had she stopped him? She'd wanted him, more than she could ever admit, but fear lingered in her. How could she get closer to him without telling him the truth? How could she do that to him?

Mindy had wanted to tell him. The time had come. The longer she was here in Cooper's Hawk the stakes grew higher.

What if he never forgave her?

I loved you.

Those words played on a reel inside her head.

Creed stepped into the building while she watched with uncertainty.

As much as she hated how cold he'd been after they'd made love at eighteen, she also realized he was young and so was she. They weren't ready. She'd made mistakes too. Angry and hurt she'd left without saying goodbye to spite him but a tiny part of her had believed—wished—he'd come after her. Make things right between them. But he hadn't.

He'd taken accountability. He'd acknowledged his stupidity.

So should she.

If only she'd known that he loved her back then—loved her like a woman needed to be loved and not just as a friend. Her life would have taken on a different path. She'd loved him with all her heart and that would have never changed.

He'd truly loved her. He said so himself. But he'd loved the old Mindy. The young, perky girl who thought she had life by the horns. Before she'd betrayed the man who owned her heart.

Could he still love her?

Care for her?

Want her in his life?

Lord help her, she wanted him to want her.

But the secret between them was like a mine field.

The look on his face when he divulged his feelings flashed through her mind. He had looked tormented. Hurt.

Over the years she'd pushed her feelings for him aside. Reminded herself each day that if they were meant to be, they would have been. When she'd lost her mama she'd been scared, sad and fearful of what life would bring. She'd buried herself in figure skating and Creed had been there for her. Perception was twenty-twenty and clearly losing him had invoked many of the same feelings she'd felt when she had to grieve her mama. Grief was grief, and unfortunately, she'd never been good at finding closure. Branch had blamed her time and again that she didn't give one hundred percent of herself in their marriage. Damn, he'd been right. She hadn't given herself fully.

"Mindy?"

Pulling herself from her thoughts, she saw Creed motioning for her to come over. A little wobbly, she managed to walk the distance across the hay strewn floor to where he stood in front of a horse stall. Inside she saw a beautiful chestnut mare. "She's magnificent." Mindy reached through the slats of the door to pet the horse's nose.

"Her name is Maggie," Creed told her.

"I like that…Maggie. It's like Maggie Blue." When she was little her daddy had bought her a mare and she named her after her aunt Maggie. She'd been the best horse and Mindy would often sleep in the barn to be close. Unfortunately, she'd died from a ruptured aorta a few years later.

"You should like it. I named her after her mother."

The air trickled from her lungs. "What? She's a descendant of Maggie Blue? How? We didn't keep any of her foals."

He unlatched the gate and opened it. "I was able to trace the foals, thanks to Rusty who never throws away any documentation. Fortunately, I was able to buy her from her previous owner. She's one of the best members of the search and rescue team." He platted her neck. "Aren't you, girl?"

She nuzzled her nose against his chest as if to show affection. "That's exactly what Maggie Blue used to do."

"What do you think of her?"

"I think she's wonderful."

"I thought you would."

"It's amazing that you have her now, Creed." Tears brimmed her eyes. What was wrong with her? Why was she crying so much?

"I'm not completely bad." He smiled.

"I never thought you were."

The radio buzzed from his belt. "Creed? You there?"

He pressed the button. "Yes, Willow?"

"We just got a call from Sheriff Conley about a missing child."

"I'm coming in now." He shoved the radio back into his belt. "I need to get inside."

Mindy wasn't sure what he wanted her to do, so she started for the truck.

He chuckled and took her hand. "Come with me."

"Okay." She had to practically run to keep up with his long strides. He held the glass door open for her that led into the office lobby. Willow was sitting at the receptionist desk and she stood when she saw Creed. Today she wore a pretty blue dress that complimented her skin tone and beautiful eyes.

"What do you have, Willow?" Creed hung his hat on a hook just inside the door.

"A missing female child." Willow acknowledged Mindy with a quick smile. "Twelve years old. Her name's Bailey Kenney. She was with family camping along Rock Ridge. Mom and Dad woke up this morning and she was gone from her tent. Her cell was left behind. They last saw her at around one A.M. last night."

"Did she run away?" Creed asked.

"Sheriff says that the parents say she'd never run away."

"Who's on call?"

"Boone has a heli tour at ten. Hank and Ruger are on call."

"Call all members. We'll need them. We have a kid missing and we need as many hands on deck as we can get. I'm saddling up the horse and heading out in five. Let Sheriff Conley know."

"I'll do that right away." Willow was already on the phone.

In all the years Mindy had known Creed she'd never seen him so assertive. Concerned.

She followed him down a narrow hall and through the third door onto the right. She stood in the doorway of the room that reminded her of a college dorm. He moved around the space filled with two sets of bunk beds and a row of lockers. He opened one and took out a large, green duffel bag and another smaller bag, and tossed them the few feet over onto the bottom bed. From inside he took out a stack of folded clothes then dragged off his button-down shirt.

He pulled on a long-sleeved black shirt fit him like a second skin. Several bright patches lined the sleeves and his name was embroidered on the front. An emblem that read Landing Search and Rescue covered the back. When he reached for the belt buckle, she quickly turned her back to him. His chuckle echoed off the empty walls.

"Not sure why that's necessary when you've seen it before," he teased.

"That was a long time ago."

There was that taunting laugh again. She heard the rustling of material and the squeaking of bed springs.

"It's safe. I'm dressed."

Turning, she found him sitting on the bed pulling on work boots. He stood and pulled on a tan leather belt with tools in the pockets. Swiping the keys off the bed he tossed them to her. She caught them and looked down at them curiously.

"You can drive on home," he said as he put his clothes back into the locker and slammed the door.

"What about you? How will you get home later?"

"I'll be a while."

"Creed...I—"

"What?" He took the length between them in three strides.

"Can I come?" she found herself asking.

His brows scrunched. "Come with me to find the missing girl?"

"Yes."

"No."

"But why?"

"We're wasting valuable time." He grabbed a jacket off the hook on the wall.

"Then just say yes."

"Why?"

"Do you always ask why?"

"Yes."

"Why can't I go?"

He looked her from top to bottom. "I'm not going for a ride. I'm going on a search and rescue mission. Rock Ridge can be dangerous."

"We used to ride up there all the time. I promise if I get up there and things get too bad, I'll turn around and come back."

He rubbed his forehead then stomped over to another locker and grabbed several things. "Here. You'll need these." He handed her a pair of gloves. "And wear that hat you had on earlier."

She reached in and took it out of the coat pocket.

Chapter 11

UP IN THE mountain seemed like another world.

If a person didn't like peace and quiet, they could go crazy on some of the paths along the rocky ridge. Although he hadn't wanted to bring Mindy along on the mission, he was glad to have her company. He would never have allowed her to come if there was ever any chance she'd be in danger. An extra pair of eyes and ears couldn't hurt. If he had to take an unsafe area of the mountain, he would send her back or make her stay put until he came back to get her. She was right, they used to ride in the mountains all the time, probably when they were too young to be out on their own.

Although the temperature was around fifty, she wasn't complaining, but then again, she still wore his heavy jacket that seemed to fit her three sizes too big. She had the hat on and the ends of her hair bounced along her shoulders. He'd saddled up Maggie for her because she was the most experienced horse they used. The horse would keep her safe.

Creed reminded himself that he needed to stay focused on finding the little girl, not admiring the spunk of the woman riding next to him. He couldn't seem to keep his mind from replaying the kiss they'd shared earlier. He'd wanted more—craved more. Even now when he was in rescue mission mode, he still had an energy rushing through him. It certainly wasn't the normal spiked adrenaline of helping someone in need.

A man knew when he was connected to a woman and he sure as hell knew he and Mindy had a connection. He wasn't strong enough to cut it loose.

They had to be on their toes on the narrow path of the trail.

Loose rocks shifted.

Tree branches had fallen onto the path.

Every little sound echoed off the rock wall.

A silence fell between them—a comfortable silence.

They'd been riding for at least an hour when his radio buzzed. His brother's voice came over the speaker. "Creed?"

He reached for the radio and pressed the button. "Yeah?"

"Any luck?" Boone asked.

"No. How about on your side?"

"No. Hank and Ruger are staying on the trail but I'm heading back for the tour."

"Over and out." He jammed the radio back into the leather pocket, cursing under his breath.

"You okay?" Mindy asked.

"The longer she's out there, alone, the likelier it is that she won't survive." He didn't care that he was showing weakness. Over the years he'd realized vulnerability didn't lessen his manhood. Being a father had changed him. When Livvy was younger he'd let her use him as a model for manicures, pedicures and make up. Honestly, he didn't like it one bit, but he couldn't tell his daughter no. But she'd helped him grow, to allow himself some humiliation.

"What you do—what your team does—is a heroic thing," Mindy said. "She'll be found, Creed. I bet she'd hiding in one of the caves right now, waiting for someone to come find her. Remember that time we rode up here, hitched the horses to a tree at the base of a trail and walked about a mile? We lost track of time and couldn't find our way back. We huddled down in that cave to wait out the rain. Eventually we managed to find the right trail. Actually, you found the right one. I was just a scared kid following you."

"Yeah, I remember. I also thought your dad was going to wring my neck. When I got home Ma threatened to ground me for life." He smiled at the memory. "I think we did a few crazier stunts after that but luckily Ma never found out."

"Whose idea was it to sneak out all those times?"

He lifted his chin and smirked. "You can't blame it all on me, Minnow. You were all for it." He resituated his hat on his head, feeling guilt slice through him. He couldn't count the number of times he'd come down hard on Livvy for the same things he'd done in the past. Maybe it was time he rethought some of the punishment.

"I know that look. What is it?"

"I'm thinking of Livvy. She reminds me a lot of myself."

"Yeah, she does. She has spirit and that's a good thing. Remember what our parents used to tell us. One day we'd have our own kids and they'd pay us back for all that we'd done. You were a feisty kid, Creed. What would you expect from your own child?"

"Damn," he pushed out with an exhale. "Maybe I've gotten too used to looking at things from inside a box. No daddy wants his daughter to grow up, but I guess I've had my head stuck in the sand for a long time. She's becoming a young lady at the flip of a switch. Got any pointers for me so I don't screw this up and risk losing her to the circus?"

Her smile made his heart flip. "I can tell you a few of the mistakes my own daddy made when I was a kid. The tighter his rules became the more I rebelled. The more lack of trust he gave me the more I didn't care if I broke his trust. I know it's hard to watch our kids grow up, mature, become their own person, but the harder we make that for them the more likely we'll regret it later. Give Livvy some space. Listen to what she's telling you. She's a good girl. This Alex fellow, I'd say he's good for her, just like you were good for me. Imagine if our parents told us we couldn't see each other. Would we have defied them? Probably so."

"Alex," he hissed. "That scares me. He also reminds me of myself at that age. Don't forget, I know what teen boys think about and it ain't all innocent."

"Oh? You mean all those times we spent sleeping up in your treehouse or skinny dipping in the lake you had less than pure thoughts?" She gave a theatrical sigh.

"Yes. No reason to lie. You would've punched me if you knew what my thoughts were."

"You kept your hands to yourself. You deserved a reward I guess." She chuckled.

"I was afraid of Rusty. I knew better than to piss him off."

"What changed your mind when we were eighteen?"

He looked across the short distance and caught her curious gaze. "Because I knew if he threatened to hurt me, I could tell him how much I loved you and planned to marry you."

Chapter 12

"MARRY ME?" MINDY tightened her grip on the leather reins. The hair on the back of her nape lifted and her inner thighs trembled. "You planned on marrying me, Creedy?"

He kept his attention on the view from the path along the rocky ridge. "Don't act so shocked. I told you how I felt."

"No you didn't."

He jerked his gaze toward her, his lips were thin. "What if I had? Would that have changed things?"

Biting her bottom lip, she wrapped her thoughts around his question. "Believe it or not, I wanted to stay, but I needed to go. Looking back at my childhood I can't think of any memory that didn't include you, outside of figure skating of course. I pathetically followed you around. I depended upon you far too much."

"You make that sound like a bad thing," he huffed.

"No, it's not a bad thing but sometimes distance helps a person put things into perspective." The soft jostling of the horse as she moved along the narrow path relaxed Mindy. She hadn't been riding in far too long. Sure, she went riding back in California, but nothing compared to riding in the mountains.

"Perspective, huh? Is nineteen years long enough to get things into perspective?"

She opened her mouth to tell him the truth but now wasn't the time. He needed to stay focused on finding the teen girl.

They rode on and hope was dwindling until she saw something hanging off a tree. "What's that, Creed?"

He led the horse closer and reached down to grab the piece of torn, red cloth. "She's been here. Sheriff Conley said she was wearing a red shirt." He held up the scrap piece of material.

Maggie pranced back and forth, whinnying. "Look, another piece there too. And more up ahead."

"Bailey left us a trail."

"She's close, Creed. Maggie senses her."

"Let's go!" He took the lead on the path. Rocks crumbled under the hooves of the horses but they were steady. "Be careful back there."

"I'm going slow." Mindy feared for the young girl. What if she came through the narrow passage during the night, lost her footing and…?

Mindy couldn't finish the thought.

The poor girl must have been so scared.

"Allow Maggie to go at her own pace. She's been out here numerous times. She knows the way of the land."

"Okay." Mindy wouldn't argue. She could see how it would take much longer on foot. They'd covered so much area.

"Bailey? Are you out here?" Creed yelled.

"Bailey!" Mindy joined him.

Finally Creed lifted a hand and pointed. "Is that a dog?"

Mindy searched ahead and saw brown fur. She craned her neck to get a better look and found the scruffy dog hiding in a bush. He stepped onto the path, shifting from front paw to paw, his ears perked. He backed up as if determining whether he could trust the intruders.

Creed climbed down from the saddle. "Stay." He patted his horse. "Come here, boy." Creed hunched down, holding out his hand as an offering for the dog to sniff.

The scruffy fellow lowered his ears some, swiping his gaze behind him and back to Creed until finally taking a leery step, then another, and whimpered.

"It's okay, fellow. I'm not going to hurt you."

Mindy climbed from her saddle and watched the scene before her in anticipation. "Did the little girl have a dog with her?" she asked in a soft voice.

"Not that I know of. Can you grab a piece of jerky out of the plastic bag in my duffel?"

"Yes." She unzipped his bag and searched through the items. Blanket, flashlight, water bottles, and finally found the bag. Taking out a piece of jerky, she took it to Creed.

"You want this, fellow?" He used the jerky to lure the hungry dog in.

Finally, after some bribing and coaxing, the dog gently took the jerky and gulped it down in one bite. "Poor boy's hungry," Mindy said.

"It appears so." Creed continued to offer the dog jerky until it was gone. He wasn't as timid now.

The dog lifted his ears again and pranced from paw to paw. He wagged his tail and darted back down the path.

"Wait!" But the dog continued. "Let's see if we can catch up to him. I have a feeling he's trying to tell us something."

They left the horses and hurried down the path.

"Bailey?"

A bark sounded.

They reached an opening into a cave and Creed grabbed his flashlight, switched it on and bent down to search inside the cold cavern. The dog guarded the opening. "It's okay, boy. I'm here to help. Do you know where she is?"

Mindy swallowed against the constriction in her throat as Creed crawled deeper into the cave. Seconds turned into minutes until finally she heard…

"I found her."

Creed came out carrying the girl in his arms. Her long curly hair was matted and leaves were entangled in the mass. Her eyes were closed. "Oh my God. Is she okay?"

He didn't answer. He laid her on the worn path and did a quick physical examination. Her pale color and the cuts on her face made Mindy's stomach twist. She watched in horror as Creed checked her pulse. "She has hypothermia. Her skin is freezing, but she's alive."

"I'll grab the blanket." Mindy ran back to the horses, rummaged inside his duffel bag and took out the thick blanket. She hurried back and laid the cover over the girl her, feeling her motherly instincts kicking into gear. "Does she still have a pulse?"

"It's weak. We need to get her as warm as possible then get her back to the start of the trail. Paramedics can pick her up there. They'd never make it back here."

The dog barked twice as if to ask how Bailey was doing.

Creed stood and walked a few feet to radio for assistance while Mindy rubbed the girl's hand.

"Bailey, you're going to be okay. You're in the care of someone who's going to get you help very soon," Mindy whispered to the poor girl.

"Mindy?"

She brought her gaze up, looking at Creed through unshed tears. "Yes?"

"I'm taking her on the horse as fast as I can. Every second counts. I need to get her help. Can you make it back okay alone? Maggie will take care of you."

"I'll be fine. Go on ahead," she assured him.

Holding her gaze for a silent exchange of words, he scooped the child into his arms and ran back down the path to his horse. He effortlessly climbed into the saddle, cradling Bailey close, and the horse took off down the trail. Mindy walked back to Maggie, tears streaming down her cheeks. Her heart broke for Bailey and her parents. How scared they all must have been.

Grabbing Maggie's reins, Mindy heard a whimper behind her. She turned to find the dog staring at her. He'd followed her expectantly. "Oh no. I'm sorry. I almost forgot about you." Mindy bent down and held out her hand. He slowly made his way to her, probably wanting more jerky, but she didn't have any to give him. Once he was close enough, she rewarded him with a scratch behind the ears. "You were a good dog. I can't leave you here." The poor boy had no meat on his bones and he needed a bath and brushing. She picked him up with little effort and climbed into the saddle.

Situating him between her legs in the saddle so he wouldn't fall, she reached for the reins and clicked her tongue. "Let's go, Maggie."

Dog looked up at her with big brown eyes as if to ask where they were going.

"You stayed with her, didn't you, boy?" Mindy patted the dog's head.

He continued to stare, while his body shook in fear.

"Listen, I know you have a story but I'm saving you too. Don't worry. You'll be safe too."

Maybe he understood her or maybe he sensed the concern in her voice, but his shaking stopped.

They road for a few hours, taking the trail slow and easy.

The temperature had risen but she still needed the coat—Creed's coat.

She looked up through the branches of the trees into the blue sky and prayed that the little girl would be okay.

Ahead on the path a squirrel ran. Birds chirped. The mountain brought so much peace.

"I need to tell Creed, don't I? I need to tell him about Jane," she said to no one.

The dog perked up his ears from where he slept snuggled against her.

"It's the right thing to do, no matter what happens."

Finally the clearing came into view and they rode to the spot where Creed had left his truck and horse trailer. Creed climbed from the driver's side of the truck, giving her a wave.

"How is Bailey? Did the paramedics come?" She didn't see the girl so that was a good thing.

"They came and hooked her up to an IV and gave her oxygen. Sheriff Conley said he'll call me with any news."

"Are you doing okay?" She saw the worry glint in his eyes.

He swiped off his hat and tore a hand through his thick hair, a sign of his agitation. "Maybe if I'd made it to her sooner." He shrugged. "Let me help you down. I'll take the dog."

She handed him over and slid out of the saddle. "Creed, don't do that to yourself."

His breath came out in an imperiled hiss. He put the dog down who loyally stayed by her side. "Let's get the horses loaded and get back to Hawke Landing." He took the reins from her and started for the truck and trailer.

Mindy called the dog to follow. He even obeyed when she told him to "stay". "For the time being I think I need to give you a name. How about Savior? Yes, I think that's a fitting name."

While Creed loaded up, she grabbed her empty coffee cup and a full water bottle and poured Savior some. He lapped it up thirstily and when the cup was empty, she poured more until he drank it all. His fur was matted, and he had a cut on his neck that was in early stages of healing. "You were out there for a while weren't you, fellow."

Hearing the trailer door slam shut, Mindy picked up Savior and climbed into the passenger seat, settling him in her lap.

Creed gave her a curious look. "I couldn't leave him behind," she explained.

"No, that wouldn't have been good. He's not wearing a collar so there's no clue who he belongs to."

"You did good, Creed," she said softly.

"Only if she survives." He turned on the engine.

As they drove away, they were both wrapped in their thoughts. The music played in the background as she stared through the window at the scenery that passed.

They reached Hawke Landing and he parked the truck near the stables. "I'm going to take care of the horses. Do you want to wait or go on in with Willow?"

"I'll wait."

When he finished, he didn't say a word. They walked into the building together for a second time that morning. Willow stood and greeted them. "Fresh pot of coffee is on."

"Thank you, Willow," Mindy said when Creed remained silent.

"I'm going to go change," he muttered.

She watched him stroll down the hall and a second later the door closed softly.

Willow rounded the desk, giving Mindy an understanding smile. "Welcome to the unfortunate times of being in Search and Rescue."

"Does he always get this solemn after a rescue?"

"Pretty much, especially when it's a kid."

"Do you have very many lost kids?"

"More than you'd think. Who do we have here?" Willow petted Savior. "He looks like he's lived through a storm."

"I think he has. We found him with Bailey."

"How about I take him, find him something to eat, and you go to Creed?"

"If you don't mind." Mindy did want to help him.

"Not at all." She took the shaking dog from Mindy.

"Go on, Savior. You need to eat," Mindy encouraged him.

Heading down the hallway, she knocked on the closed door, hoping he'd speak to her. She wasn't sure if he preferred being alone after a mission.

"Come in," came Creed's mumbled reply.

She opened the door and found him dragging his shirt off. Perfect timing. She closed the door and stood there, giving him space. "Are you okay, Creed?"

"You keep asking me that," he tossed his shirt onto the bed.

"Because you are giving me reason to ask."

His shoulders slumped some. "She was so small. So cold. When I save children, I think of Livvy. What if it was her?"

"I'd say all first responders feel the same anguish." She took the few steps between them and wrapped her arms around his waist, pressing her cheek against the warm skin of his back. He smelled so good. Felt so good. He laid his large hands over hers.

"I'm glad you came along," he said in a throaty mutter.

"I'm glad I was there too."

He turned and faced her, gently cupping her cheek with his callused palm. "Mindy."

"Creed."

"You drive me crazy," he said on an exhale of breath.

"The feeling is mutual." She smiled.

He lowered his mouth, but music interrupted the moment.

Chapter 13

HIS PHONE RANG from the bed where he'd tossed it earlier.

A part of him regretted that he'd turned the ringer back on. He wanted to stay here with Mindy a while longer before he had to welcome the world back in and all its flaws.

"You should get that, right?" she asked in a soft, alluring voice.

"Yeah, I guess I should." He grabbed the intrusion off the bed and glanced at the screen "It's Sheriff Conley." He clicked his phone. "Yeah?"

"Hi, Creed. Sheriff Conley. I wanted to let you know that Bailey woke up. Looks like she's going to be all right. Her parents are here with her now."

Relief spread through Creed. He wanted to pop open a champagne bottle, and he didn't even like the stuff. "Great to hear. Have you been able to ask her any questions yet?"

"Not too many except that she asked about the dog. Did she have a dog with her?"

"Yeah, she did. We have him with us. Is he hers?"

"No. Apparently she chased after him last night and lost her way back. The parents want to keep him. Can they pick him up?"

"Hang on." He covered the mouthpiece of the phone. "The parents want to come pick up the dog for Bailey. Is that okay?"

"That's wonderful," Mindy exclaimed.

He said to the Sheriff, "He'll be here at Hawke Landing."

Then he hung up and tossed the phone back on the bed. "Where were we before the interruption?"

"I'm gathering that was good news?"

"Very good news. Bailey is awake and her parents are with her. Now, where were we?"

She took a step closer, standing on tiptoe and kissed him.

His cell beeped. Mindy pulled back. "Shit!" he muttered, giving her an apologetic shrug. "Grand central station all of a sudden."

"It's okay," she ensured him.

He grabbed the phone and glanced at the screen. It was Boone. "I'll ignore it. It's just my brother."

Why the hell was Boone texting? They just talked earlier.

Another beep.

Where are you, bro? B.

Why aren't you answering? B.

Do I need to call? B

Respond, dick. B.

"He's a pest," Creed growled.

"He'll probably keep sending them until you answer." Mindy chuckled.

Beep. Beep.

Hey, are you ignoring me? B.

Finally, Creed tapped in, *I'm busy. Leave me alone.*

Any news on the girl? B.

She's fine but you won't be if you don't stop bothering me. C.

Fine, douche. B.

Good, asshole. C.

He stuck the phone inside his locker and closed the door.

Another beep sounded. This time it was Mindy's phone. She dragged it from the pocket of his jacket and looked at him. "It's Daddy. I better get it." She chewed on the edge of her nail. Her father never called her.

"Sure." He'd planned on kissing her, but it didn't look like fate wanted to let him experience some pleasure.

She answered, "Yeah I'm with Creed now. I'll put it on speaker phone."

"Hi, Rusty. I'm here."

"Bo called me. One of the goats is having a difficult time kidding. He can't get a hold of the vet and I'm an hour away. How close are you?"

"I'm at Hawke Landing." Guilt rushed through him. Creed knew exactly which doe. He had guessed this would happen. She was young and had been carelessly left in a pen with a seven-week old rutting buck. This had happened a handful of times in the past which resulted in dead does and kids. "I'll be there soon."

Hanging up, he swiped a hand through his messy hair. "Were you serious when you said you wanted to get your hands dirty on the ranch?"

"Yes."

"Well then. Now's as good a time as any to learn."

~~~~~

Mindy and Creed stood outside of the goat stall monitoring the behavior of female one-forty-seven. As soon as she laid down in the fresh straw, she started licking herself and wagging her tail. "You got this, Jazzie."

"Who named her?" Mindy asked.

"I did. I've been keeping an eye on her, so I thought it made sense just to name her instead of calling her "goat". Jazzie sounds much better."

Creed had a rare compassion for the livestock that she certainly appreciated and admired.

After thirty minutes of pushing, Jazzie's kidding wasn't advancing and the vet hadn't shown up. Bo had an appointment for his leg and couldn't stay.

Picking up the bag Creed brought with him, he opened it. "We're going to step inside, very quietly. She's friendly, but we don't want to upset her any more than she already is. Have you ever helped deliver a kid before?" he asked.

"No, I haven't. Please tell me you have."

"A few times. Goat deliveries usually go smooth." Inside the pen he bent and visually examined the doe. "The back hooves are visible so we need to get the kid out."

"So what do we do?" She bent next to him, anxious to help.

Jazzie lifted her head and looked at them in curiosity.

"Relax, girl. This won't be long," Creed comforted her.

"Poor thing." Mindy loved the goats. They were so sweet.

"I'm going to help ease the kid out. You reach inside my bag, grab one of the towels and a pair of gloves." He took the gloves and pulled them on. "You keep the towel and be ready."

Mindy watched him gently take the hooves of the kid and slowly pull. Mindy found it hard to believe that someone as large and gruff as Creed could be so gentle. The kid came out in one
~~~~~

messy, wet plop and was covered in a mucus like lining. Creed grabbed the teeny animal up into his arms and laid it in the center of towel that Mindy held.

"Firmly wipe off the placenta sac."

"Okay." She did as Creed advised.

"Be sure to clean around the eyes, nose and mouth to help the little fellow breathe. Look at him, he's coming around. Looks like he'll survive."

Mindy felt her chest expand. "He's so tiny."

"You should name him."

"I want to call him Hope. I think he's clean." She held up the baby wrapped in the stained towel.

Creed shook his head. "Now you rock Hope."

"Rock him?" Was he kidding? "What?"

"Swaddle him like you would a human baby, then rock back and forth. That helps get the remaining liquid out of the lungs."

Quickly swaddling the wet bundle up in the towel, she cuddled Hope while rocking. Tears came to her eyes. She wasn't sure how much time passed, but Creed touched her hand and she looked up at him. "Yes?"

"Let's try giving him to Jazzie so they can bond. She needs to feed him."

Relinquishing the kid, she smiled as Creed laid Hope next to Jazzie and she instantly took to her baby against her. The teeny boy snuggled closed and fed.

Mindy felt like she'd done something amazing.

And later when she and Creed were washing their hands under the water hose, she couldn't stop smiling. She hadn't felt so alive in a while.

"That was so incredible. I've never witnessed anything like it outside of my own child being born, but it's different. I could do this every day."

"No, you don't want to do this every day. This is a problem when we must intervene during delivery. We have to have controlled breeding, otherwise we're going to lose livestock."

"Has that been a problem?"

"Some carelessness on the part of some hands," he muttered, holding the stream of the water above his head and allowing it to pour over him. His shirt was stained from the birthing process.

She fought the urge to stare at his torso. "On Bo's part?"

He dropped the hose, wiped the water from his eyes and looked at her. "As foreman it's his responsibility. He's a great guy but he's dropped the ball a few times lately."

Mindy hesitated then said, "Are you pushing him to retire?" She knew what Bo had said but she was curious.

"No, I'm not pushing him, or anyone, to retire. He made that choice on his own decision."

"Bo's been here for a lot of years. He's more like family than a hand," she pointed out, swiping her palms down her thighs.

"I'm glad you're concerned for him, truly, I am. I realize how long he's worked this land. I'm all for keeping Bo on, and your father for that matter, but sometimes a man has to make a difficult choice, Mindy. This is hard work for even the younger hands."

"You mean once we reach our expiration date we should just give up?"

"Mindy, you know that's not what I meant. No one says they must give up. May wants to spend more time with Bo. Rusty wants to enjoy life a little. He's worked from sunrise to sunset for how many years? And let's face it, neither man is getting any younger."

"I've noticed that Daddy is tired." She heard the pounding of hammers and looked out into the distance where the new bigger barn was being built. "What happened to the old barn. It wasn't that old."

"Didn't Rusty tell you why we're building a new barn?" Creed's tan faded.

What? Something else he forgot to tell her?

"No."

"One night he went out to check on a foal down. I'm not sure of the details, but he somehow broke a lantern and the place went up like a bale of hay. We tore it down, or what was left of it."

"Were any of the horses hurt? Was my father hurt? Had he been drinking?" She felt her stomach turn.

"He managed to get the horses to safety, but the barn couldn't be salvaged. After that night he decided it was time he took a backseat." He blew out a long breath and stared out into the distance. "Mindy, I'm not one to stir up trouble, but Rusty's not been himself for some time. Hell, he's still as feisty as a wasp, but since the heart attack he's slowed down. I don't think he wants anyone to know just how much."

"Thank you for telling me. I suspected he's been hiding something for some time." Mindy never could tell her daddy a thing. "I need a shower".

"So do I."

"We can take one…I mean, at the same time…not in the same bathroom. You're free to use the shower up at the house." She felt her face flush.

"I understood what you meant." One corner of his mouth played with a smile. "Do you need some help scrubbing your back?"

"I can handle it." A trickle of warmth spread into her inner thighs.

"As much as I like the thought of us showering "together" I need to go home. Can we talk later?"

"Sure. Of course. Yes."

"Want me to drop you off up at the house?"

"No. I'll walk. I'd like to stick around awhile longer with Jazzie and Hope."

He smiled. "See you later."

Eventually she made her way up to the house and into the bathroom to take a shower. Turning on the water, she adjusted the temperature, stripped off her clothing and stepped under the spray. It had been a long day. She'd forgotten how busy things could be around Cooper's Hawk.

By the time she turned off the water, she was as pink and wrinkled as a newborn pig. Wrapping a towel around her, she stepped out of the bathroom followed by a puff of steam. She felt better and was still excited that she'd helped deliver a baby.

Her phone! It was ringing. Running, she hit 'talk' by the fifth ring.

"Hi, mom!"

Mindy smiled in gratitude. "Hi, honey. How's school?"

"It's going great. How are you?"

"I'm good. Guess what? I just helped deliver a baby goat. It was amazing. I'd forgotten how wonderful it feels to help on the ranch."

"Mom, you sound…different."

"Different? How?"

"Happy."

Mindy sat down on the end of the bed. "I am. I like being here. I feel like I'm living again."

"That makes it harder for me to tell you something," Jane said in a low voice.

"Honey, what's wrong? You can tell me anything?"

"I saw Dad today." There was uncertainty to her daughter's voice.

"You did? How'd that go?" Mindy laid back on the bed, pulling the towel from her wet hair.

"He and Sian got married last night," Jane said it with an obvious carefulness. "At the courthouse."

"Wow. I knew they were planning on getting married but not so soon." She sat back up and used the towel to soak up the water dripping from the ends of her hair.

"There's more. They got married so fast because she's pregnant."

"Oh…okay." Mindy felt a blow to her chest. Swallowing the unwanted emotion, she cleared her throat. "That's nice. Tell him I said congratulations."

"I wanted you to hear it from me, but she's seven months along."

Mindy tossed the damp towel aside. Although she didn't want Branch back, a part of Mindy felt hurt. He never wanted to have a child with Mindy.

Unfortunately, a woman's internal clock ticked a lot faster than a man's and, at her age, she guessed her window of baby opportunity was dwindling.

"Mom? You okay?"

"Yes. Of course, sweetheart. I'm truly happy for them." She forced her voice to stay level. She didn't want Jane worried. "I'm sure you're excited to have another sister or brother."

"Another?" Jane's chuckle vibrated the line. "Are you pregnant too?"

"No…never. I meant I'm sure you're glad to have a brother or sister soon." Mindy squeezed the phone.

"Sort of. I think it'll seem more real when its actually here."

Feeling her throat clog, Mindy said, "Thank you for telling me."

"I guess. I just want you to be okay."

"Honey, don't worry about me. Be happy for your father and Sian."

After a few more minutes of talking about Jane's classes, they hung up and Mindy dropped onto the bed, feeling the sting of tears. She'd wasted so many years.

Chapter 14

"*THIS ISN'T FAIR!* I'm tired of living like a prisoner here," Livvy said dramatically.

"So I'm keeping you prisoner now?" Creed sighed.

"Why can't I call Mom? Are you afraid that she'll let me come live with her?" She crossed her arms over her chest, acting like her world was crumbling around her cute, pink flip flops since he'd told her she had to earn her phone back by doing chores on the farm.

"I'm not keeping you from calling her," he pointed out. "You can call her any time.".

"Really?" Her face twisted. "How am I supposed to call her, or anyone, without a phone?"

Creed bit his lip to keep from reminding her that her mom hadn't called in months to check up on her, but he didn't want to hurt Livvy. "You can call her using my phone. Keep it on speaker phone."

"See what I mean! Prison."

He took out his phone from his front pocket and laid it on the table. "It's up to you."

She whipped the cell off the table like a gunfighter at the Okay corral. On the fifth ring Mel finally answered, "Hi, sweetie. How are you? Did you get the gift I sent you last week?"

"No. I didn't." Livvy paced the floor.

"Oh, I'll have to track it. You're going to love it. I'll give you a little hint. It's what all the hip young girls are wearing here in New York. Consider it an early birthday present."

"My birthday just passed."

"Yes, of course. I knew that."

"Why haven't you called, Mom?"

"Sorry, hun. You know I'm so busy right now with the new series. It's so much fun working here in the big city. I've met so many people."

Creed's chest twisted as he watched the beginning of disappointment spread over his daughter's face. Every time she spoke to her mother it ended with more hurt and anger for Livvy. Creed didn't understand why Mel didn't just tell the truth. Livvy was getting too old and wise not to see through the cracks and lies. She knew her mother had only started shooting the new TV series in the last three weeks.

"Dad's being mean. I had to call you from his phone because he won't let me use mine. I hate it here. He's going to make me do chores on the farm. I can see why you left." Livvy rolled her eyes and gave Creed a smirk. "I want to come there with you. Can I come live with you? Please." Sadly, that was the first sliver of vulnerability Livvy had shown in months.

Mel's heavy sigh rattled the line. "Livvy, you know-"

"Mom, please! I can't live here another second. I'm going to scream."

"I'm on set for twelve hours at a time, sweetheart. Who would keep you company?"

Livvy's eyes lit because she must have seen a window. "I can stay by myself. Then when you have a day off, we can go visit all those shops you talk about."

"Unfortunately, I don't have any time off. Remember, I explained how hard it is to be an actress?"

"It's okay, Mom! I'm fourteen now. I can stay alone." Her bottom lip trembled, but her stubborn pride kept the tears at bay.

"Liv, I'm sorry. It won't work. Cooper's Hawk is where you belong. I must concentrate on work and not be worried about your safety being here all alone. I promise that as soon as I can I'll send you a plane ticket and you can come and stay for a bit. How about before school starts? We can plan on shopping till we drop and there are so many fun and exciting things to do out here. You'll love it. Just be patient. Okay?"

Moisture filled Livvy's eyes, but she bravely sniffed them away. Silence filled the line.

Then Mel said bitterly, "Put your father on the line."

Without a word, Livvy handed over the phone, spun on her heels and took each step up the stairs like she was pounding a nail into the wood. Creed turned off the speaker. "I'm here."

"Why did you let her call? Is this a ploy to make me look bad? You know I can't take off work right now."

"I didn't *let* her do anything. She misses you and wanted to speak to you—or rather she hoped she could plead her case and you'd come get her." He took the phone into the kitchen.

"Can't you control her?" Mel bit off.

"Yes, thanks for asking," he growled. "That's what I'm doing. Giving her some accountability." Why did speaking to his ex feel like a drill being inserted inside his temple? He believed two people couldn't dislike each other more. He didn't hate her, but truthfully, he'd rather stay as far away from her as possible.

"Explain to her that I'm working hard. This wouldn't be a time or place for a teenager. That's where she should be, with you, at least for now. Remember, that's why you insisted we stay in Cooper's Hawk when we got married." She always threw that fact up in his face, as if that was why things crumbled between them.

"I'm not your cheering section, Mel. You need to explain those things to her yourself."

"I did but she doesn't seem to listen," she moaned. "Why bother."

"I need to ask you a question. I know it was a long time ago, but I'm curious. When Mindy Sage came back during the time you and I were first going to get married, did you speak to her?"

Her rude groan rattled the line. "How am I supposed to know?"

"Come on, Mel. Search your memory," he pressured.

"If you insist. Maybe I did. I don't know why it matters. After all, she did leave. Anyway, count your blessings. Why this question? Please don't tell me you're still brooding over the past with her. Didn't you do that enough when we were married," she crooned.

He wasn't about to get into the good, the bad and the ugly of their marriage. "Just curious, like I said. Did you take a letter that she left for me in my truck?" He didn't want to believe that Mel would have been so underhanded, but he believed Mindy.

"Is this an inquisition? Are you asking if I did something to some letter? Wow, this is ridiculous. I never call because of this reason."

"You didn't call. Livvy called you." He gripped the phone tighter. He knew this conversation would only go in circles. "Forget it. Take care of yourself." He clicked off.

He turned and looked up, seeing that Livvy was standing at the top of the stairs, giving him the stink eye. "Livvy, I—"

"This is all your fault! She hates you and that's why she hates me!" There was enough heat off her words that she shot invisible venom into his bloodstream.

"I can't deny that she hates me. That's obvious, but she doesn't hate you, Livvy. She wants to see you, but—"

"Why are you lying to me? I'm fourteen. Not four. You can't keep me a kid forever!"

He tore a hand through his hair. "I'm not..." But he was. "Okay, I guess I am. Cut me some slack, kiddo. I have no idea what a teenage girl needs and I'm doing my best."

"Am I supposed to thank you?" She turned and stomped away.

He dropped down on the chair and sunk his face in his palm. Lord help him. He couldn't win for losing when it came to his daughter.

The phone rang again and he stabbed the 'talk' button, "What?"

"Whoa there, bro." It was Boone.

"Sorry. I was just walking off the battlefield with Livvy."

"Did you win?"

"No. She has bigger guns. What's up?"

"Guess where I am?"

Creed wasn't in the mood for guessing games. "On the other end of the phone."

"Good one."

"How the hell should I know?" he said grumpily, feeling a little guilty that his brother was getting the shockwave over the arguments with Mel and Livvy.

"I'm at Pelican Hawke."

"Good for you. So?"

"And I think there's someone here who you might want to see."

Creed hadn't been at his brother's bar in months.

Hearing a woman's laughter, Creed's heart kicked up. That melodic sound was very familiar. "Who was that?"

"Mindy. Apparently, she's drinking away some feelings."

"Good for her."

"Did you do something?"

"Why do I always get the blame?" Creed rubbed the tension out of his forehead.

"Don't bite my head off. If you don't care then I guess you don't care."

Creed resisted the urge to run out the door. Time had passed and he couldn't run as if he still needed to protect her. He didn't have his house in order so how in God's name could he try to fix someone else's? After all, she was an adult and if she wanted to have a misery drink then so be it. He could use one too.

Then Creed heard a man say, "How about another dance, pretty lady?"

"And who is that?" Creed pressed through clenched teeth.

Boone chuckled. "Hey, you said you didn't care."

"No, brother. You said it. What the hell? You either answer my question or I'm going over to your place and put Nair in your shampoo."

"Like that scares me. I could use a cut."

"No, but if I use your toothbrush to clean out the toilet you'd be scared." They'd played enough dirty tricks on each other growing up that Boone knew better than to pretend he wasn't worried.

"Fine. That's the cowboy she's been dancing with for the last hour."

"And you're just now calling me?" Before Boone could answer, Creed muttered, "I'm on my way." He started for the door then stopped. *What the hell am I doing?* If Mindy decided to dance with someone, she had that right. She had a freewill. The last thing he should do was go running after her.

He went into the kitchen, poured a glass of water and downed it.

Then washed the glass.

Scrubbed the already spotless counter.

Swept the clean floor.

Bounced a rubber ball he found in the junk drawer.

Then cursed a blue streak.

Strolling into the living room, he grabbed his hat from the hook and practically ran to his truck.

Yeah, he was an idiot for doing this. Mindy no longer needed him, but why did he still need to be needed? No, he wanted to be wanted. Especially by her.

Those were his thoughts when fifteen minutes later he pulled up in between two trucks at Pelican Hawke and climbed out. Several strides took him through the front door and into the crowded honky tonk. Nothing new. The place always drew a crowd, as much for the food as for the alcohol. A live band was playing on stage which brought a crowd from surrounding counties.

Creed always respected that Hank had taken over the place and turned it into a reputable business.

Searching through the swarm of people, Creed finally found Boone sitting at the bar.

"Where is she?" Creed asked once he stepped up to the bar, waving at Hank who was working the bar. He didn't usually bartend these days, not since he'd hired help.

"Hello to you too," Boone chuckled. "Right there." He pointed a finger.

Following the path, Creed found her on the dance floor. He felt a crushing blow in his stomach. She was dancing—or rather arousing the attention of more than one man with the shake of her hips and shimmy of her bottom. Her hands were tangled in her hair as she moved smoothly to the beat of the country song.

My God, he'd never seen a more beautiful woman.

The long-sleeved white shirt was tied at her waist, and the black lace cami underneath gave a teasing glimpse of firm breasts. The waist of her cut off jean shorts rested low on her hips, cinched by a leather belt. The swaying and shaking of her hips reminded Creed of a dangerous pendulum.

Long, toned legs went on for miles and miles, down to ankle length cowgirl boots with an intricate western design carved into the leather. The longer she was back in Cooper's Hawk, the more he was seeing the girl again who didn't care what people thought. In his opinion, she'd been a little buttoned up when she first came back, not that it had deterred his attraction in any way.

He'd been staring so intently that it took him a good solid two minutes before he realized she wasn't dancing alone. Some cowboy was bumping and grinding the air close to her.

Creed laughed, but it quickly turned to a growl when the man got a little too close. Boone elbowed Creed. "Relax there, partner. She's been keeping him at a decent space."

The dancing hillbilly rested his hands on her hips and pulled her closer. Creed felt the buried protectiveness rear its head. "You call that reasonable space, do ya?" A football field would have been too close with the way the stranger had his blood thirsty eyes on her firm bottom.

Mindy created more distance between them.

"The tequila shots must be working."

Creed shot his gaze on his brother. "Tequila?" He knew exactly what Tequila did to her—for her. He lifted off his hat, threaded his fingers through his hair and fixed his hat back into place.

"A couple at least. What did you do to her?" Boone leaned his elbows back on the edge of the bar.

"What did *I* do to her? I didn't do a damn thing. I thought I made myself clear over the phone?" Creed turned his attention back to the dance floor, reminding himself to breathe.

"Hell, I just figured." Boone shrugged, lifted his beer bottle and took a long swig. "Want a drink?"

He could certainly use one. "No." He needed to keep his wits about him.

Hank came over and shook his head. "Oh I see. A pretty brown-eyed cowgirl can convince you to come inside your brother's bar, but when he asks you are too busy," he quipped. All three brothers looked similar. Dark hair. Whiskered, broad jaws. All over six foot and two hundred pounds of solid muscle. People said when the three of them got together they could be intimidating. Probably why they never got into fights with others growing up. You fought one Hawke you'd have to face them all.

"If I wanted to see your ugly face I'd come in more often," Creed joked. Although he and his brothers played a little harshly, they loved each other. He never had to question if they had his back.

"Yeah, yeah. It's like looking in the mirror, right bro? Just a better version."

"You both are ugly. I bet when I was born mama was celebrating that she finally popped one out that couldn't scare away the vermin," Boone tossed his two cents into the mix.

"Yeah she celebrated but much later when she praised God that you were born with good looks because you wouldn't get very far with half a brain." Hank and Creed fist bumped.

"That's why you always loved the Wizard of Oz. You wanted the brains like the tin man," Hank teased.

"It's the lion, dumbass." Boone snorted.

"You're both stupid. It's the scarecrow," Creed said with a sniff. When the sitter came over she turned on the Wizard of Oz and made them watch. The brothers had been happy when she moved and Abby decided her boys no longer needed a sitter.

"Oh shit!" Boone muttered, his eyes as wide as silver dollars.

Following his brother's glare, Creed found Mindy and the cowboy dancing to a slow song.

Creed gritted his teeth.

"Creed?" Hank tapped his shoulder.

"What?"

"Don't bust up anything in my place. You got it? The last time you got pissed over her you rammed your fist into a wall and broke a few fingers."

"I'm fine. I'm not jealous." Creed denied the charge of anger that coursed through him.

"Oh? Did I use that word?" Hank laughed.

"So you always look like you're constipated?" Boone dared.

"Don't worry. I won't break anything unless it happens to be a man's jaw. But that won't happen. She'd never forgive me if I acted like a jerk."

"Damn, bro. Why the hell are you still sitting here? If I felt this much jealousy over a woman, I wouldn't be sitting back watching her dance with another man. I'd make her mine. Isn't it about time you took the initiative?" Boone patted his shoulder. "That's not being a jerk. That's stepping out of your bubble."

Hell, maybe his brothers were right.

Pushing off the edge of the bar, Creed weaved his way through the crowd, hearing a few greetings from patrons and shaking a couple of hands until he finally made his way to the unsuspecting couple. The cowboy dancing with Mindy was the first one to see Creed.

"I didn't know she had a husband," the man blurted, dropping his hands to his sides.

Creed had his eyes on wide-eyed Mindy. Her bottom lip trembled. Her cheeks were rosy and flushed from dancing. He'd never seen her more beautiful. "I'm not her husband," he finally said to the man, but Creed kept his eyes glued on her. She seemed a bit uncomfortable.

"We're dancing, Creed." Her smile was forced.

"You don't mind if I cut in, do you, Cowboy?"

Without hesitation, the man booked it.

"What are you doing?" she said in a lowered voice so the other couples on the dance floor couldn't hear.

"Just wanted to dance." He grinned. "If we stand here much longer, we're going to have a lot of explaining to do when the rumors start blasting around town."

"And whose fault is that?" There was slight slur in her tone. He'd seen her drunker, but the glossiness in her eyes told him she'd had a few too many.

Because they were quickly becoming the center of attention, he wrapped his arm around her waist and dragged her against him. A little squeal fell off her lips. He bent his mouth close to her ear and whispered, "Pretend you like being in my arms. We don't want to give people too much to talk about, do we?"

"You should have thought about that before you stormed up here like a general at Invasion of Normandy." She placed both of her hands against his chest. Was this her way of keeping him at a safe distance?

"I told you. I wanted to dance."

"You? Dance? Since when?" she whispered.

"Since the last two minutes ago. You should feel special." He grinned. "You know I have two left feet."

"Oh, was this a ploy to make me feel special or make me feel like we're back in high school and you're scaring away all the competition?" She lifted her gaze and he felt her spine stiffen.

"Are you kidding?"

"So you're going to deny that you scared them away?"

"No. I'm denying that they were ever any competition," he said without humiliation.

"What if I wanted to dance with Hamil again? He's a great dancer." The corners of her mouth played with a smile.

"Hamil? That was his name?" He snorted.

"Yes. He owns a ranch outside of Cooper's Hawk. He rode on the rodeo circuit too. Won lots of rewards."

"Hamil looked as uptight as his name sounds."

"Did you come here to pester me?"

The growl gurgled up from deep in his chest and rumbled in his throat. He wrapped his arm tighter around her waist, not caring that others were still looking. "Behave yourself."

"Or?" Her eyes were challenging.

"Let's not play games, Minnow."

"Trust me, I'd be the last one who'd play games."

"Are you suggesting that I do?"

"If that's how you'd like to take it."

"I never did like it when you drank tequila," he rasped.

"So let me guess. Was it Boone or Hank who called to tell on me? Just like old times," she huffed. "Can't those fellows mind their own damn business? I thought we were having a good time talking about the past. Bonding over making fun of you."

"Neither told on you."

"Really? Then why are you here looking like a bear?"

"Damn, Mindy. You know why I'm here."

She pulled back an inch to look up at him. "No, I don't."

He sucked in a breath. "I can't let you make a mistake—"

"You *can't* let me make a mistake?" She laughed but it was as cold as an arctic blast. "Let me inform you of something, Creedy Hawke. You *don't* control me. It's not your place to *let* me do anything. I have the right to move on just as much as anyone else does."

He blinked. "What the hell is going on? Did I miss something?"

"You certainly have."

"When will you forgive me?"

"Maybe never."

He growled. "Just so you know, I spoke with Melody earlier. I asked her about the letter and she said she had no clue what I was talking about."

Her brows scrunched. "So what are you saying? That I lied about writing you?"

"Mindy, that's not what I'm suggesting."

"Then what are you saying? Maybe you're lying. Maybe you knew it was from me and tossed it and you just can't admit it."

Slumping his shoulders, he gave his head a jerky shake. "I'm tired of the arguing. Think whatever makes you happy."

The song ended, he dipped his hat, and left her on the dance floor.

He could have easily stormed back, swept her up into his arms and carried her with him. But he knew he couldn't force her into anything. If she wanted him, she needed to come to him.

Passing Hamil's table, Creed bent and said to the man, "She's all yours, buddy."

Dipping his hat, Creed strolled through the door and didn't look back.

Chapter 15

CREED SAT AT his desk at Hawke Landing, looking over quarterly reports for the chartered flights. He rubbed his tired eyes and leaned back in the chair. Stretching his legs and hooking his boots on the corner of the desk, he couldn't seem to concentrate. After leaving Pelican Hawke, he had jumped in his truck and came to work. He'd called his ma and let her know he wouldn't he home tonight and to watch Livvy.

He glanced at the clock above the door. It read twelve fifteen. Maybe it was time to call it a night. Turning off the light, he left the office and strolled down to the bunker. Removing his boots and his shirt, he laid down on the bottom bed and relaxed his aching muscles.

Tossing and turning, sleep eluded him although he was dog-tired.

The rain picked up and pelted the tin roof.

Any other night he could have slept a few hours, but tonight he had a lot on his mind.

Images of Mindy filled his cluttered brain.

A craving unlike any other flowed through his veins, making him feel like a madman. He should never have walked out onto the dance floor looking like a foolish dick. Jealousy never looked good on anyone, especially a man his age.

Rolling onto his stomach, he punched the pillow twice and laid his head into the center.

Suddenly the pillow was too soft.

The bed too lumpy.

And his body too hard.

His phone lit up and then dinged from the end of the bed.

He thought about ignoring it, but responsibility made him grab it and read the screen. His heart almost leapt out of his chest. Why was Mindy texting?

Where are you?

He tossed the phone and laid his head back down.

He needed sleep, not another round with the woman who loved to argue.

Two minutes slowly crept by.

Not responding.

Nope. Not happening.

But what if she needs me?

Reaching for the phone he tapped at the keyboard. *Where are you?*

You're not allowed to answer a question with a question. M

Just did. C

What's wrong with you? M

You. You're what's wrong with me C. No sense in lying.

I see your car. Open the door. M.

With a growl he pushed off the bed and strolled down the hall to the double glass doors, peering into the darkness. He could see the headlights of a car and a second later the silhouette of someone running toward the doors. Unlocking the door, he held it open for Mindy. By the time she made it inside she was soaked and the car outside had driven away.

"Your ride is leaving," he muttered.

"It was an Uber." She shivered.

He almost felt sorry for her until he realized she'd been using his jacket as an umbrella. "Here, you can have this back." She handed him the dripping coat then he saw the bottle tucked under her shoulder.

"Gee, thanks. Is that why you came out here? To give me my soaked coat back?" He hung it on a hook next to the door. "By the way, how'd you know I was here?"

"I had the driver take me out to the farm. When I didn't see your truck, I figured I could find you here. You're always here." Her hair clung to her wet, rosy cheeks and the shirt had become see-through.

"Why are you here?" he urged.

"I brought an old favorite. Apple whiskey." She held up the unopened bottle, giving it a little shake.

"You think you need more?" He lifted a brow.

She lowered her eyes to the floor for a brief second. "I guess I was feeling sorry for myself and that's why I went to Pelican Hawke. I shouldn't have been so ugly toward you."

"I know you don't trust me," he said. "I guess I deserve some ugliness, but I'm here now, Mindy. Let me be here for you." His heart was ripping apart.

~~~~~

Mindy wasn't sure why she'd come, but she was here now, and she couldn't turn away.

His words made her knees weak. Her inner thighs clenched.

She wanted him. That was honestly why she came.

When he'd walked out of Pelican Hawke, she felt like a part of her had left with him.

It was time they had a heart-to-heart.

"Do you have glasses around here?" First, she needed more liquid therapy.

He smiled, nodded, and motioned for her to follow him. He took her into the room with the bunk beds and she stepped inside. His shoes were sitting by the bed and his shirt was tossed over the end. The door closed with a soft click.

Mindy watched him stroll over to a cabinet and take down a stack of plastic cups. He took two and turned them over on the desk. She handed him the bottle and he poured a small amount into each cup.

"Here you go."

She took the cup and sipped the mellow whiskey. Rolling her tongue over her lips, she made a throaty moan. "Remember when we snuck a bottle of this stuff out of daddy's cabinet? First alcohol we tasted and I spat it everywhere. It certainly goes down better with age."

"A lot of things get better with age." His warm gaze spoke volumes.

He backed up, opened one of the lockers, and took out a T-shirt. "Here. Put this on."

She hesitated.

His laughter made her shiver. "It's a shirt not a snake. Get out of those wet clothes before you catch your death." He sat down on the edge of the desk, looking at her over the rim of his glass.
~~~~~

She was cold and wet, all the way down to her itty-bitty thong.

Taking the shirt, she placed her glass on a nearby shelf. She looked across the room at Creed.

"What?" he muttered.

"Turn around."

"I've seen everything before. A few times." His voice was as smooth as the whiskey.

"Probably so, but I'm not that young girl anymore. My body has changed."

He gave an easy shrug, pushed up from the bed and turned his back to her. "Why do women do that?"

She unbuttoned the wet shirt and dropped it to the side. Then the cami. "Do what?"

"Think that age is a disgrace to their body. I love your new curves. The new confidence I see in your eyes. It's sexy as hell." The divulging of his words made her tremble inside.

Unhooking her bra, she dragged the damp material away and her nipples budded, from the combination of his words and the cooler air. "I think it's wonderful that you feel that way, but Branch felt differently."

"Fuck your ex-husband. If he couldn't deal with a smart, sophisticated, beautiful, mature woman that speaks of his low character."

She smiled at Creed's back as she reached for the T-shirt and read the front, "Hawke Landing Search and Rescue." Pulling the soft cotton down over her shoulders and torso, she hugged it to her skin. "Don't get me wrong, I've long gotten over him. Hopefully Sian's body tightens back into place once she has the baby. He might not feel the same about her then."

"Is that the woman he left you for?"

"Yes. I just found out yesterday that he married her and they're expecting a child." Toeing off her boots and socks, she then unbuttoned her damp shorts and slid them down her legs. She started to leave her panties on but decided against it.

Thankfully, she'd shaven her legs. She smiled at the silly thought.

"So that's why you needed the emotional drunk?"

"I was celebrating my freedom." Scooping up her clothes, she said, "You can turn around."

She hung her damp things over the top bunk to dry. She lifted her chin to find Creed's simmering gaze on her. "What?" She curled her toes against the cool hardwood floor.

"You. In my shirt. I'll never look at it the same way again." He emptied his whiskey and poured another.

"Thank you. It does feel better than the wet things." She picked up her cup and sipped, feeling the warmth pool into her stomach. "How often do you stay here?"

"Not often. Tonight I worked late and decided to catch some ZZs."

"Did I wake you?"

"No. In fact, I couldn't get my mind off you. So why did you come?"

"I-I came to see you, Creed." She took a step forward, inhaling him into her greedy lungs. How could one man smell so good? Be so powerful. Every part of him was big and strong.

A deep, reverberating jolt rocketed through her. He watched her with such emotion, such appreciation and desire. She needed to believe she could be herself with him. She could be vulnerable and he'd never hurt her. Holding up her empty cup, she said, "Pour me another, Cowboy?"

"Good thing you didn't drive. I'd have to take your keys." He picked up the bottle and poured a little more into her cup.

"I'm a smart drunk. Not that I do it often. I just felt I needed a little liquid therapy." She saluted him with her cup then turned on her feet and examined the room. "By the way, your mom called and said Livvy wants to take lessons with me." She stopped in front of a row of framed pictures of Creed and his brothers.

"Really? I didn't know."

"Does it bother you that she wants to take lessons?" She turned to face him, wrapping her fingers around the cup.

"No. Should it?"

"No, but I thought I caught a hint of disappointment in your voice."

He shrugged and swiped a hand down his whiskered jaw. "I'm grateful that Ma has helped with Livvy, but there are times I feel like my daughter will never listen to me while she has Ma as a sympathy vote."

"I don't think it's a sympathy vote, Creed. You said yourself you work a lot. Livvy probably depends upon her grandmother.

Have you spoken to them about how you feel?" She took a step closer, sipping the whiskey.

"I do, but I don't think I get my point across."

"Nothing new," she teased. "Although, I do think you've learned a lesson or two in communication since I was last in Cooper's Hawk."

"Let's just say I've watched my brothers a time or two and learned what not to do with the ladies." He chuckled.

Swallowing the last bit of whiskey, this time she poured herself more. "Oh, so you think you know women, huh? Let me be the judge of your knowledge. Let's pretend I'm a stranger. What come on would you use to get my attention?"

"Mindy…"

"Creed. Are you shy?" She rolled her tongue over her lips.

"Fine." He set his whiskey aside. "Don't laugh." He rolled his shoulders and clenched his hands open and shut as if he prepared for a boxing match.

"I can't promise there won't be laughter involved."

"Here it goes." Clearing his throat, he smiled. "Hi, sweetheart. Do I know you? 'Cause you look a lot like my next girlfriend." He broke out into a full grin. "How was that?"

"Terrible."

"Terrible? Why?"

"Because it's cheesy. Try something else. This time something better."

He crossed the short space between them, holding her gaze intently. Her spine tingled and her toes curled. "Most people experience love, but then there are those who don't just love but they fall mindlessly. I don't just love you with all my heart. I love you with all my circle. Hearts can break. They can stop beating. But a circle, it's infinity. It flows on forever and ever and ever, just like the love I have for you."

Her breath stilled.

Her knees quivered.

"Well?"

Clearing the butterflies from her stomach, she finally managed to gain her voice, "That's better. Much better."

"Just better? Are you telling me that didn't do anything for you?"

Nervous, she gulped down the rest of the whiskey. The sudden rush of dizziness made her slightly wobble. He grabbed her gently and held her close. "Whoa there, sweetheart. I see you're still a lightweight."

She stared up at him, feeling herself wavering between logic and desire. "Honestly, if you use that line on any girl, I think she'd fall for you."

"How about you, Minnow? Could you fall?" His whiskey-laced breath brushed her cheek.

"Creed…"

"Do you trust me?" He cupped her cheek, sending warmth into her bloodstream.

"No." But she did. It was herself that she didn't trust. What if she got hurt again? "Yes," she finally admitted. "I've always trusted you. That's why it hurt so much when I came home and you were no longer *my* Creedy."

He smiled and it rained heaven into her soul. "You know I'd never hurt you on purpose, right?"

"These feelings feel an awfully lot like pain, Creed."

"That's because you keep fighting them."

"Do you still like me?"

"Like you? Just a little."

"I have to tell you that I came here tonight because I didn't want to be alone." She watched his expression.

"You have to be clearer than that, sweetheart. Do you want me, or do you just want to be held tonight? Call me crazy but I'm picking up some confusion. I won't be a salve, not for you. I can't risk losing myself again."

"Both." She moistened her lips.

He took her cup and placed it on the shelf, and with a tangled growl he picked her up into his arms and carried her to the bed. Flipping on the reading lamp clamped to the headboard the dim light cast a golden glow over them. She felt exposed lying on the bunk, feeling like all her weaknesses were laid out for him to see. Her body shivered and she brought her arms up around her body.

"Don't hide yourself from me."

"Okay." Placing her arms at her sides, she swallowed hard.

"I want to see all of you."

"You first," she whispered.

He chuckled and stood.

"You've always been a beautiful man, Creed." She lowered her eyes to the waist of his jeans that sat low on his slender hips.

With a flick of his wrist, he undid the buckle of his belt and pulled the leather from the straps, sending an echo bouncing off the walls. Then came an unsnapping of a button, the familiar scrape of unzipping, and a push of denim down long legs until finally he stood in front of her, wearing only thin boxers. The flap came open revealing dark, crisp hair. He sat back down beside her hip.

"You're like a fine wine, Mindy. You've gotten better with age. Don't let a man like your ex dictate how you feel about yourself. Any man with a brain and eyes would agree that you're beautiful."

"I look different," she admitted shyly.

"Better than ever." His husky voice vibrated her nerve endings.

"I'm older. I've had a child. I have some stretch marks and my breasts aren't as perky as they once were."

"So what?" Creed lowered himself and kissed her, teasing her lips. She moaned in delight at the phenomena he tweaked inside of her. He pulled slightly back, their gazes meeting, and she threaded her fingers in his thick hair.

"I used to be positive, saw the good in everyone and anything. I came back to Cooper's Hawk to find that girl again, or at least a sliver of her. I don't know what tomorrow brings, Creed, but I do know that I've learned a valuable lesson in never letting things slip through my fingers. I'm not sure I'm good for anyone right now though. Does that make any sense?"

He touched his finger to her chin. "You're saying you haven't found yourself again, right?"

"Right. When I say I'm not the same person, I'm not only speaking physically," she said. She needed to get the boulder off her chest. "I have baggage. Branch did a number on me, but I was in the wrong too."

"Do you still care about him?"

She shook her head. "No, I don't but shouldn't I feel a little jealous that he's married and having a child? I'm not. I'm only hurt because I didn't recognize the signs that he and I just weren't in it for the long haul." She blinked back unshed tears.

"Sweetheart, you have to let the past go so you can live in the future. You wouldn't be the first who overlooked the obvious."

"I care for you, Creed. I don't think I ever stopped, but you don't know everything about me—" She lowered her face.

He hooked a finger under her chin and lifted her face, catching her gaze in his. "Listen, Mindy. I like you just the way you are. Neither one of us is free of baggage, kid. If this is too much for you—"

"No." She sat up, palming his cheek, feeling the whiskers scrape her skin. "That's not the path I wanted this to head. I just, well, I just…I don't know. I'm sorry that things went as they did when we were eighteen. If I could go back and fix some things I would. I need you to understand that."

"Listen, I regret the past too, but maturity tells me that maybe things happened for a reason. I was a kid, immature, and needed to do some growing. If you'd ask Mel, I'm sure she'd tell you that I wasn't an award-winning husband. Was it because I was with her? Or because I was still too wrapped up in myself? Livvy taught me a lot about caring for someone other than myself. I'm not saying I didn't care for you, I told you that I loved you, but life rotated around me. What if we would have married and you started hating me because I was an idiot? Hell, maybe you were the only one who could have kicked me into shape. Problem is, we'll never know, will we? All we can do is head into the future with an open mind."

Why did the valiancy in his gaze make her want to cry? To cuddle up in his arms and confess all her sins? "It appears since I've been gone you've grown compassion."

He swept a piece of her hair off her cheek. "If it helps, I wasn't unscathed when you left. You were the one and only woman who ever got close enough to break my heart. I don't think all the cracks ever did fill in."

A powerful man like Creed admitting weakness touched her deeply. He could come across as a tough guy, but he'd always been caring.

She'd always had an emptiness within her—a void inside her heart. Slowly that vast emptiness was being crammed with love. Things weren't that easy though. They had children. And she had a secret. Would he ever understand why she moved on?

"Will you ever forgive me for being stupid? For not chasing after you?" The emotion in his voice sent tears rolling down her cheeks.

He used the callused pad of his thumb to swipe the moisture away. So gentle. So powerful. So Creed. He'd always wiped her tears away, her hurt, and been the shoulder she'd leaned on when she didn't even know how much she needed him. "I forgave you a long time ago. I just now acknowledged it."

"I still love you, Mindy. Not the girl you were, but the person you are now. I see how kind, loving, caring and beautiful, inside and out, that you are."

Lifting herself, she kissed him lightly on the lips, his cheeks, his eyelids, then pulled back slightly. His eyes reflected an emotion she'd never witnessed before. "I like you a little." She held up her fingers with an inch between them.

"Is that so?" He tickled her, causing her to erupt into giggles.

When the laughter faded, his lips were back on hers, soft, inviting, amazing. He dragged her in close, pressing their bodies together, igniting more internal flames. This wasn't your run of the mill kiss shared between two horny people, but a kiss filled with emotion, desire and appreciation. He flicked his tongue inside, then tugged and nipped with his teeth…so gentle and yet so needful. She didn't have the desire to fight the all-consuming feeling any longer. She sunk against his chest in an invitation to take her.

She crawled into his lap, her knees on either side of his hips, the apex of her moist thighs pressed against the proof of his desire, and yet he didn't move too fast.

He tangled his fingers in her hair, deepening the kiss, while a deep moan escaped his throat. She rocked against him, gyrating her hips against his, turning the simmer to boiling point. They spent the next few moments kissing and re-learning each other.

Creed lowered his hands, wrapping his arms tight around her, pressing his cheek against hers. "There's something wrong with this picture," the gruffness of his voice made her body tremble.

"Yeah?"

"You've had too much to drink."

"I'm not drunk." He narrowed his gaze accusingly. "Okay. Maybe I am, but the whiskey hasn't lessened or changed my desire for you."

"I want that. Damn do I want that, but I'm afraid to move too fast. Afraid to screw up things between us again. I want you to trust me. I certainly don't want to take you when you've had too much to drink and then you regret it."

She pulled back, looking down at him with a narrowed eye. "You don't want me?" Rejection filled her chest.

"No, sweetheart—I mean, yes, I want you more than my life." He kissed her chin. "Yet, wanting you isn't enough. I need to prove to you that I'm more than a hard dick. You deserve more."

"Uh…have you noticed that I'm not complaining?" She lifted a brow. "Or are you playing hard to get?"

He chuckled and she felt the rumble low in his chest. "No." He brushed the backs of his knuckles down her cheek. "When it happens it's going to be amazing. Monumental. There will be no doubts left in us."

"You have doubts?" Mindy swallowed hard.

"Sorry, sweetheart. Yes. Not in you. But doubts in the fact that sex complicates things."

Confusion flickered inside her. "Sex complicates things. Hmm. Really?" Was she hearing right?

"Do you ever stop arguing?"

"Sometimes."

"Here. Take this off." He reached down and grabbed the hem of the shirt, lifting it over her head. He smoothed his gaze over her breasts, his eyes reflecting a desire that she hadn't seen in a long time. He made her feel beautiful, although she knew she shouldn't need any man to do that for her.

"My God. You're like heaven on earth." He blew out a breath. "It's going to take every sliver of control that I have to be a gentleman, but I want to hold your naked body."

"Are you sure that's what you want?"

"No."

She laughed. "We had sex while I was drunk before," she said.

"Yeah, and you see where that got us?" He cocked a thick brow.

She could see his point. Although, she didn't feel like she was being illogical because of the alcohol but she respected that Creed was a pure gentleman.

He laid her back onto the bed and shifted beside her, wrapping a beefy arm around her and pulling her into the hard curve of his body. "If I can't find relief in one way, this is the next best thing. I like this. A lot." He nuzzled his face in her hair.

She smiled, falling into the cloud of warmth surrounding them. He was so warm she didn't need a blanket. "I hear what you're saying but something else didn't get the memo." She wriggled her hip against his bulging erection.

"Yeah, it's a bit stubborn, and painful."

"I could ease some of the tension," she teased.

"And there'd be no stopping. It'll come, Mindy. Trust me, it'll come."

"What an ironic choice of words."

He swatted her bottom playfully. "Quit teasing me. Go to sleep."

Chapter 16

CREED OPENED ONE eye and stared up at the top bunk. Hearing soft snoring next to him, he turned his cheek and saw the face of an angel. Mindy still slept and had her cheek pressed against her palm. Tendrils of her hair had fallen over her forehead. He gently lifted the silken strands away.

A soft purr came from her throat a second before her eyes fluttered open. Her big, smoky-brown eyes were surrounded with smeared mascara. She looked damn sexy. She blinked several times, staring back at him. Her plump lips curved into a sweet smile.

A smile meant they woke up with no regrets.

She stretched her arms over her head and he skirted his gaze down her naked curves, feeling himself grow by leaps and bounds. He hesitated at her perky breasts and his mouth salivated. He'd been a perfect gentleman last night but this morning the wolf in him was rearing its head.

"Mornin'," he said in a husky voice.

"What time is it?"

He lifted himself on his elbow. Just over her shoulder, he saw the half full bottle of apple whiskey. He reached for his phone and read the time. "Six."

"How long have you been awake? You should have woken me." She grabbed the T-shirt from the bottom of the bed and held it against her nakedness. Disappointed, he groaned.

"I just woke up." He rubbed the sleep from his eyes.

She swept her gaze down to where his excitement was visible. He reached over, ready to kiss her when she dodged his touch. "Sorry. I have to go."

"You what?"

Mindy climbed over him, more confident in her naked body which made him want her even more. He flashed her his best smile and squinted when he felt the overwhelming neglected pressure in his groin.

"I have to go," she repeated.

"Come on. Come back to bed."

"Your people will be getting here soon."

He watched her prance across the room, her firm bottom jiggling slightly. "Not for at least another hour. You know what we could do in that hour."

She picked up her shirt and shook it out, looking back at him. "You had your chance last night but remember…you're not wanting to make any mistakes."

Damn. He should have known those words would come back to haunt him. "I'm not drunk. You drunk?" He grinned.

"You go on and flash that sexy smile at me, but it'll do no good, Creed Hawke. I don't plan on getting caught here with you. And I have an early morning lesson and I won't miss it." She grabbed her clothes and sat down at the end of the bed, pulling on her bra and then wrinkled shirt with a frown.

He stretched across the bed and walked his fingers down her bare hip and paused at the dip where the crease of her leg met groomed apex. "Ten minutes more?"

"No."

"How about five minutes?"

"Not even five."

"You're killing me, you know that?" He pointed to his erection.

"No one has ever died from a hard on."

"Are you punishing me?" he scoffed

"Not at all."

He sat up and leaned against the headboard. "Fine. I don't want you to stay anyway."

"Good. We're on the same page. Behave yourself."

He reached out, snagged her arm and gently hauled her back into bed on top of him. "How can you expect me to behave myself when I have you here with me?"

"You'll just have to pull yourself together." She giggled. "By the way, you shouldn't want me here either when people start arriving."

"Who cares. I don't," he growled as he kissed her forehead, her cheeks, the tip of her nose.

His cell vibrated.

"Oh, and there's your phone."

"Again, don't care." He swept his hand upward on the back of her thigh and squeezed her tight bottom.

"What if it's important? What if it's Livvy or your mom?"

"Neither text me. They call."

Mindy pushed up on his chest. "It doesn't change the fact that I have a lesson in an hour. I need to shower," she whimpered and rolled out of bed again and reached for the scrap of red that had fallen on the floor. He watched her wriggle the sexy silk up her long legs and he grew three times the size that should be legal. He'd never wanted a woman as badly as he wanted Mindy Sage.

He pushed up, easing his lower body against the torment of an erection. If only he had another hour with her. Hell, he'd take fifteen minutes. Quick and sweet would work too. "I had other plans for today. I wanted to take you to breakfast."

"I don't eat breakfast."

"Then lunch."

"Don't worry. You don't have to do this. I still respect you." She winked playfully then grabbed her shorts.

It almost did him in to watch her climb into the cut offs and drag them up her lush thighs, buttoning the material that fit her slender curves like they were made specifically for her.

"I really am leaving." She came around the side of the bed, gave him a quick kiss on the lips and she stopped at the closed door. "Oh shit!"

"Forget something?"

"Oh, just that I don't have a ride." She pivoted and gave him a smile.

"Does that mean you can stay?"

She gave him a shame-on-you smirk. "No, that means you're going to be kind and sweet and give me a ride back to my car."

Slumping his shoulders, he realized all the bitchin' and moanin' wouldn't change the fact that this wasn't going to happen. "Fine." He climbed from bed, swiped his jeans off the floor and stuck his feet into the legs. As he dragged them up over his "problem" he squinted in pain. He looked over at Mindy who didn't have any sympathy for his predicament. From his locker he grabbed a clean shirt and pair of socks and sat down on the bed. "How about I see you later?"

"I'm sure you will. Cooper's Hawk is pretty small."

"Ouch. This rejection is hurting."

"I'll let you keep the whiskey. It should help."

He spotted her smile before she turned. Once he was dressed, he grabbed his keys and phone and he set the security system.

Chapter 17

CREED STOOD ALONG the pockmarked rail looking out onto the ice rink as Mindy showed Livvy a move that involved turning. He had no clue what the name of it was, but Mindy looked beautiful as she performed the step that sent her body twirling in one spot.

Livvy attempted the same move.

She didn't quite hit the target, but he liked seeing her smile at the failed attempt instead of stomping off angrily. She'd come a long way in the last three lessons. Seeing Mindy and his daughter on the ice together made Creed fully aware how much he cared for them both.

He patted his pocket where he'd shoved the velvet box that morning. He'd kept it with him for the last two days, waiting for the best possible moment when he could prove to Mindy that he wanted her and planned to never let her go—if she'd have him. The diamond ring would change their lives. For the better. Livvy liked her. He loved Mindy. And he hoped her daughter would approve too.

They came off the ice, laughing, and took a seat on the long bench to remove their skates. He joined them. Livvy looked up at him, smiling and his heart tugged.

"How's she doing?" he asked Mindy.

"Wonderful. She's a natural. At the rate she's going she'll be doing single loops in the next few months," Mindy said. Her hair was pulled up showing off her diamond earrings and long neck. She became more beautiful each day. "Remember, Liv, it takes confidence. Fear becomes concrete in our skates."

Creed stared. He couldn't wait to have Mindy alone so he could kiss her again.

"Dad? Did you hear me?" Livvy laughed.

"Sorry." He cleared his throat and dragged himself out of his musing.

"Can we pick up pizza?"

"Sure." He turned his attention to Mindy. "You want to come along?"

"Well, I don't know—"

"Come on, Mindy," Livvy pleaded.

"How could I possibly say no to that?" Mindy slipped on her jacket and then her boots. "I have my car. How about I grab my things, lock up the rink, and meet you both at the farm?"

"Sounds good." He was glad Mindy agreed. He would have hated to start pleading too. "You ready?" he asked Livvy.

She grabbed her bag, lifted it over her shoulder and nodded. "See you later, Mindy."

Creed and Livvy walked outside together. "You like her, don't you?" he asked.

"Yes. She's great."

"Yeah, I think so too," he admitted.

"That's obvious," Livvy said and opened the passenger door and climbed into the truck.

He went around to the driver's door and lifted himself in the driver's seat. "Obvious, huh?"

"Dad, I'm not a child. I can see the way you look at her."

"How would you feel, you know, if Mindy and I…well—"

"Dated?"

He was leaning more toward marriage. "Okay, dated."

She gave a quick shrug. "Dad, you're too old to be asking for permission." She unwrapped a piece of gum and pushed the strip into her mouth.

"I'm not asking for permission."

"You're not?"

"I guess I am at least to some extent. I want you to be happy."

"I think she likes you too." Livvy dug her phone out of her bag.

"Why do you say that?" The hair on his neck lifted. He hadn't been this excited in a long time.

"Because she talks about you a lot."

He liked hearing that. "Are you wearing a new perfume? It smells familiar."

She unzipped her bag and took out a small perfume bottle. "Mindy bought me this. She said she remembered what Mom wore."

"That's a thoughtful gift."

With a nod, she dropped the perfume back into the bag. "I told her that I missed Mom's scent."

His phone buzzed from his pocket. He pulled it out and read the message from Mindy. "Something has come up. I can't make it for pizza. I'll explain later."

Dropping his cell into the center console he sighed. For the last few days every time they made plans to get together something came up.

~~~~~

Hearing Jane's laughter coming from the kitchen, Mindy hurried in and found her daughter sitting at the table eating chocolate mint ice cream from the container. Every time she and her Pop Pop saw each other the first thing they did was buy ice cream.

Jane looked up and blinked. "Mom, you look like you ran all the way here."

"I came just as soon as I got your text. What are you doing here? Is everything okay?" She placed a palm over her chest where her heart was beating like a drum. She immediately started assuming something bad had happened.

"Sheesh, Mom. It's okay. Calm down. Pop Pop picked me up at the airport and we've just been hanging out. Grabbed ice cream too."

"It's so good to see you here. You haven't visited since, well, I can't even remember." Rusty wore a smile that Mindy hadn't seen in a while. Maybe his granddaughter was exactly what he needed.

"It's been a long time," Jane said.

Mindy pulled out the chair between them and plopped down, dragging her gym bag off her shoulder and dropping it on the floor. "You really didn't answer my question. Why are you here? And you flew in? That must have cost a fortune."

"Pop Pop bought the ticket for me."

Mindy slid an accusing glance his direction. He completely deflected it. "Great, Daddy. What else are you keeping secret?"

"Don't get mad." Jane sighed. "I felt bad after I told you about Dad and Sian. So, I thought I'd come for the weekend."
~~~~~

"Why didn't you call me? I would have come to the airport to get you."

"Since Pop Pop gave me the money, I wanted him to do the honor." Jane smiled widely. "Thanks, Pop Pop."

"I'm glad I could be of use."

Mindy exhaled. "I'm fine, Jane. You didn't have to worry."

"Fine." Jane dropped her spoon into the almost empty container. "There's another reason why I came. I have something to tell you."

Oh hell. Mindy felt an invisible whack against her head. She was this age and a few weeks into her freshmen year at college when she realized she was pregnant. If Jane walked the same path…

A smile burst over her face. "I've met someone, Mom."

"You've met someone?" Mindy dropped back into the chair, grasping the edge of the table. Was she pregnant? Would that be the next revelation?

"I'm totally in love. His name is Jonesy. He's twenty-one. And he's majoring in Chemistry." Her cheeks flushed. "He's a nerd just like me," she squealed.

"Honey, you've only been at school for three weeks. When did you meet him?"

"The first day of class. He's in my biology. We doubled up for a lab and hit it off immediately. He asked me to dinner and we ate at the Hot Dog Caddy Shack and spent the night talking."

Mindy couldn't speak.

Jane blinked. "Mom, aren't you happy for me?"

"Of course." But she couldn't seem to force a smile on her face. Mindy had never liked surprises.

"But you have that look."

"What look?"

Jane shaped her face into a duplicate expression. "Like that."

"Like I'm constipated?" Mindy shrugged, blowing out some tension. "I'm sorry, sweetie. I'm just surprised. Eventually I'd like to meet him."

Jane and her Pop Pop exchanged a look. Mindy's stomach turned.

"You will, Mom. Soon," Jane said.

"How soon?" Mindy heard the toilet flush from the bathroom down the hall.

"Soon. Very soon," Jane whispered.

"Jane?" Mindy heard shoes hitting the floor and turned in time to see a tall, lanky boy step into the room. His dark hair was cut into a mullet and he had a long row of piercings.

"Hi. You must be Mrs. Sage." The boy—man—wore a large smile. His shirt read, "Parents don't like me because I'm cool."

Jane jumped up and stepped next to his side, grabbing his hand proudly. "Mom, I'd like for you to meet Jonesy."

Mindy stood and gave her daddy a lifted brow as if to silently say, "You could have warned me." Planting a smile on her face, she looked at her daughter who wore the same look she had the day she dropped the bomb that she'd decided to let a friend live in the guest room. The friend happened to be a homeless man she saw on a bench outside the mall and invited him home with her. She was fifteen at the time. She'd wanted so badly for Mindy and Branch to be proud because she'd helped someone. "Hi, Jonesy." Mindy held out her hand.

The young man shifted from one untied boot to the other then stuck his clammy hand in Mindy's. He shook it enthusiastically. "Nice place you got here, Mrs. Sage."

"Where are you from, Jonesy?" Mindy pulled her hand away.

"Tampa."

"Is that where you grew up?"

"My mom and I moved there when my dad went to prison."

Jane cleared her throat. "Mom, how about we don't interrogate him before he's had a chance to settle in."

"I didn't realize I was interrogating him. Sorry if that's how it came across, Jonesy. Jane, can I talk to you alone for a moment?"

"Jonesy, I'll be back. Sit down. Get to know Pop Pop. I'll miss you."

"I'll miss you too, sweet tart." They rubbed noses.

Mindy stepped out of the kitchen and into the living room. When Jane came in, Mindy said, "Well, *sweet tart*, you've certainly managed to surprise me once again."

"He's wonderful, isn't he?" Her eyes twinkled and her lips pursed.

Mindy knew this was a trick question. No matter how she answered it wouldn't be right. "I don't know him. Could you have warned me that you were bringing someone with you?"

"I thought you'd be happy for me."

"Did I say I'm not? I'm only suggesting that this is a bit—"

"What?" Jane crossed her arms over her chest, tilting her chin stubbornly.

"Surprising. He seems…nice but give me a chance to catch my breath. Okay?"

Jane dropped her arms. "Do you really mean it? You'll give him a chance?"

"Of course. Why wouldn't I?"

"He's not like other boys my age. I know the rings and tats—"

"Don't bother me. I am concerned with you rushing things."

"Don't worry. Can we go back into the kitchen?"

When they stepped in, Jonesy and Rusty were talking about World War one. He had to have the same conversation with everyone he met. About the planes, bombs and POWs. Jonesy seemed genuinely interested.

Jane stepped up behind Jonesy's chair and hugged him tightly. "We've already stuck our things in the guest room, Mom."

Mindy cleared her throat. "Jane, you'll be sleeping in *my* room and Jonesy you'll be in the *guest* bedroom. I'm sure Jane can show you around tomorrow. Right, Jane?"

Receiving a disgruntled look, Mindy waited anxiously for Jane's argument. Mindy was more than willing to give the new boyfriend a chance, but she wasn't ready to welcome him into her daughter's bed. Not this soon.

"Fine. Come on, Jonesy. Let's get settled in."

Once she was alone with her daddy, Mindy turned to him, tapping the toe of her shoe lightly. "You could have said something to me."

"How was I supposed to do that?" He lifted his hands in a gesture of innocence.

"Call. Text. Send smoke signals. You certainly found a way of getting ahold of me when I was a teenager and I was late getting home." She opened the refrigerator and took out a bottle of water. Hearing his laughter, she turned to him. "I'm glad you think this is funny."

"Remember all those nights I stayed up worrying about you? It's about time I can sit back and watch as you learn what it's like." His grey eyes sparkled.

"Daddy, I was a good kid. You didn't have to worry. Just as Jane is a good girl and I don't have to worry, much. Although it does seem a little quick, don't you think?"

Rusty shrugged a shoulder. "You never listened to me. I tried to tell you about Branch and you thought he hung the moon and stars."

"No, I thought Creed hung the moon and stars," she corrected him.

"A parent always sees things differently. I always liked Creed, thought he was a good boy, but I saw that fire in your eyes when he was around. Reminded me a lot of the fire your mama and I had when we first met. That scares a parent." He stood, walked over to her and kissed her on top of the head. "Looks like Jane might just have that same fire. You'll get through this. Might get some new greys, but you'll get through it." He strolled from the kitchen, his laughter fading in his distance.

"You're wrong. I don't already have greys." She glanced at herself in the reflection of the stainless refrigerator.

Chapter 18

CREED HAD JUST tossed the empty pizza box into the trashcan when he heard a soft knock. His heart kicked up in speed. Could it be Mindy?

Strolling through the house he pulled open the door and his smile dropped faster than the rain in Montana.

"Are you going to just stand there and stare or are you going to invite me in?"

After finally catching his breath, he frowned. This was the last person he expected to see on his doorstep, or in Cooper's Hawk. "What are you doing here, Mel?"

She gave a careless laugh that got stuck in her throat. "Nice to see you too, Creed." Melody had always taken care of herself. He couldn't deny she hadn't aged any and still looked as beautiful as ever, but he was grateful he didn't feel anything but anger and disgust at seeing her now. Those penetrating pale blues used to work him with magical wonder, but now they only worked up the bile into his throat. "You're really not going to invite me in?" she huffed, pursing crimson red lips that had obviously been on the receiving end of a few needles.

He stepped out onto the porch and closed the door behind him. "What are you doing here?"

Her mouth twisted. "I'm here to see my daughter. Do I need any other reason?" One thin brow popped up.

"Haven't you heard of calling first?" Although he wanted to be happy that Melody was here to visit with Livvy, another part of him, the part that had been blindsided enough to know better, worried about Melody's intentions.

"Are you trying to say I have to schedule an appointment to visit?"

"Didn't you just tell me on the phone the other day that you were too busy to see Livvy?" He kept his voice lowered.

She gave a throaty sigh. "I got cut from the show. It appears the producer has no idea how to work with real talent." She tugged at the hem of her gauzy shirt. She looked completely out of place in the tight skirt and tall heels with the background of fields. "I flew all this way. Rented a car. Did I do that for nothing?"

As much as it panged him, he couldn't deny that Livvy would want to see her. Sending her away until he had a chance to speak to his daughter wouldn't be the best effort on his part. Opening the door, he stepped back to let Mel pass. He caught a lungful of her sweet scent. That was her signature fragrance, the same one that Mindy had gifted to Livvy.

She stepped in glanced around the space and smiled. "I see nothing has changed." He couldn't ignore the significant disgusted undertone.

"A lot has changed really." He closed the door, squeezing the doorknob a little too tight

"If you say so." She made a sweep of her gaze downward then brought it back up and smiled. "You're looking good, Creed."

If she was expecting a return compliment, he couldn't find one.

She stepped forward and gave him a sounding kiss on the cheek. "Oh no. I left lipstick." She wiped it off.

"Mom? Is that you? Is that really you?"

The excited voice from the staircase made Creed and Melody both look.

"There's my sweet daughter," Melody said with a smile.

Livvy raced down the stairs and practically jumped into her mother's arms like she did when she was a toddler. "Why? How? I didn't know you were coming," Livvy said once she unwrapped herself from Melody.

"It's a surprise. I guess I should have called first." She gave Creed a side glance. "But I had the urge to come and see you and so I came. Just like that."

"I'm glad you did. How long will you be staying?" Livvy's words were rushed.

"I'm not sure yet. I guess it depends on if I can find accommodations. This town has never been visitor friendly." She rolled her eyes.

Livvy looked at Creed with a pleading gaze. "Dad?"

"What?" He already knew what was going to happen before it did.

"She can stay here, right?" Livvy encouraged.

"I'm sure your mom would be more comfortable staying somewhere else." Creed rubbed the bridge of his nose, feeling Livvy's gaze grow warmer.

"I wouldn't want to impose," Melody said innocently. "I'm sure your dad doesn't want his privacy intruded upon."

And there it was. Melody's famous manipulation tactic. To make herself more the victim and him more the monster. That's how it had been throughout their marriage, and since. He'd give her one thing, her acting skills had gotten better.

"He doesn't have privacy. And he works all the time anyway," Livvy said. "You have to stay here. I want you close while you're here."

Melody pulled Livvy in for a tight hug and looked up at Creed. "I'm sorry. I'm probably inconveniencing you but if it wouldn't be too much do you mind if I stay? After all, this was once my home too."

"Problem is, we don't have much space. The couch is lumpy. If we had the room, maybe, but…"

"She can sleep in my room. See, it's settled. You're staying," Livvy congealed.

"Great! I'm looking forward to spending time with my girl. Creed, would you be a doll and grab my bags from the back of the service car? And don't forget to tip the driver."

If it wasn't for upsetting his daughter, he would have told Melody to go away, but he wanted to keep the peace. So, he went to gather her things.

Outside, he greeted the driver who seemed agitated that he had been waiting. Creed offered him an apology and a large tip that brightened his mood.

The man in the suit grabbed the bags out of the trunk.

Creed looked down at the pile of suitcases. How long was Melody planning on staying? She'd never been one to pack light.

Inhaling the fresh air and rubbing his forehead, his thoughts jetted to Mindy. *Shit!* What would she think of Melody being here?

He reached for his phone from his back pocket and texted her.

Mindy. Are you busy? I need to speak to you when you have a chance.

He hit 'send'.

Grabbing the luggage, he carried them to the porch, working up a sweat in the process. He burst through the front door, mumbling, "What the hell do you have in here, Mel? Rocks?" When he didn't get an answer, he looked and found his mother staring at him, her gaze narrowed and her nose slightly wrinkled.

"So, I just found out that we'll be having an overnight guest." The squeak in Abby's voice reminded him how much she disliked Melody.

He gave her an apologetic grin. "Yeah, I just found out myself. Where are they?"

"Oh I'm sure Melody is making herself at home." His mother rubbed her forehead in irritation. "What is she doing here?"

"She said she's visiting."

Disbelief covered Abby's face. "Visiting? Nothing is ever so simple."

He dropped the heavy bags. "What was I supposed to do? Livvy would have hated me if I sent her away."

"Yeah, true. But don't ask me to be nice to her." She turned and stomped out of the room.

~~~~~

Mindy could hear Jane and Jonsey's laughter coming from the back yard and she couldn't help but smile too. They were laying in the hammock discussing their favorite movies. Mindy hadn't seen her daughter this happy in a long time. Over dinner she'd learned a lot about Jonesy and his desire to become a chemist and his plans after graduation.

Reaching for her phone, Mindy checked her messages. Creed had left her a message earlier.

She started to type a return message. Erased it. Started another. Then erased it too.

What could she say?

His daughter was here in Cooper's Hawk.

There was no excuse now why Mindy didn't tell him the truth.

Over the last few days she'd done a lot of thinking and pondering. She cared for him—no, loved him. Had never stopped. If
~~~~~

there was ever a chance for a future together her only choice was to be completely honest with him about everything, and that meant telling him that he was Jane's father. It would come as a shock, but hopefully, eventually, he'd understand and forgive her.

She started to call him when she heard a soft knock on the door.

Placing her phone on the table, she went to the door and pulled back the thin curtain. Mindy's breath caught.

She swallowed the lump growing in her throat as she pulled open the door. "Melody? What are you doing here?"

"Hello, Mindy. Just the person I came to speak to," she said in a smooth tone then turned to wave at someone in the car. "I think it's so amazing that Cooper's Hawk has Uber service. Who would have thought it possible?"

"And the town also has running water and indoor toilets," Mindy groaned and crossed her arms over her chest to keep from slapping the smug smile off the woman's face. "I don't know what you think we'd have to say to one another, but you're wasting your time."

"Let's be adults about this. If you're sleeping with my ex-husband, the father of my child, we should at least have an open chat." Melody opened the screen door and stepped inside without waiting for an invitation. She was still beautiful with large blue eyes surrounded in thick lashes. The red top she wore showed off deep cleavage and a small waist. "So how about that talk?"

"Come right in why don't you." Mindy sighed. Closing the door, she geared up for an ensuing argument like the last time the two had spoken. "Creed didn't tell me you were coming to town."

"Then we're on the same page. He didn't tell me you were back either, although I guessed." She sashayed across the room, stopping in the center then giving a dramatic flip of her long hair.

"I'm sure Livvy is very happy to see you."

"She's very happy." Her smile showed off an even row of sparkling white teeth. "Why are you back here, Mindy? You were living in...Florida?"

"California."

"Same difference." She waved a slender hand. The diamond on her middle finger sparkled in the lighting. "I thought we both learned our lesson about Cooper's Hawk."

Seeing the other woman's arrogant expression made Mindy's chest tighten. "I've missed this place."

Melody's brow snapped up. "I've never had those warm, cozy feelings. But that's me. I'm not a country girl at heart." She slipped her gaze down Mindy's T-shirt, cut off shorts and flip flips.

"It's late, Melody—"

"Do you have anything to drink? I'm a little parched."

"Water?"

"I was thinking scotch."

"No."

"It's no big deal. I won't be staying long."

Mindy snapped her jaws tight "Why are you here?"

"Oh, I was just curious." She smoothed her hands down her waist. "So you and Creed are an item again."

"No, Creed and I aren't an item." Mindy wasn't sure what they were doing…

The woman's chuckle dripped of acid. "Come on, no reason to deny the truth to me. You two always were…well, hooked at the hips," she slurred. "Livvy told me that you and Creed were seeing each other again. You look shocked. Don't you think my daughter speaks to me? Tells me what's going on?"

"I won't deny that I care for Creed, and Livvy too." Mindy had no reason to deny her feelings.

"Hmm, so I'm right. You're back and ready to sink your claws into Creed. I mean, how could I blame you? He still has it after all these years." She spun and faked interest in a picture on the wall. "Isn't it interesting how things have worked out?"

"What *things* are you referring to?" Mindy could see where this was headed, but it was like watching a horror movie and she couldn't turn away.

"Don't be daft." She turned back around to face Mindy. "You know what I'm referring to. How I ended up with Creed instead of you?"

Mindy lifted her chin, dropping her arms to her sides. "That's in the past."

"Sure it is, but I have my daughter to think about. I want to make sure anyone who comes into her life is, well, a perfect fit." Her crimson mouth puckered.

"I can understand your concern, but with all due respect, I think Creed would never bring anyone into Livvy's life that isn't respectful or deserving."

With another wave of her hand as if she could wipe Mindy's words away, she sniffed loudly. "He's always been blind when it came to your friendship. I really never knew what he saw in you." She shrugged. "But I must say, you're not that skinny, freckled face, dirt under your nails girl any longer either."

"And you're still the beautiful woman you've always been."

Melody ran her fingers through her hair and grinned from ear to ear. "It takes some work."

"I'm sure it does. Can I ask a question?"

"Go ahead."

"What happened to the letter I'd written Creed?" It was time Mindy had the answers she deserved.

"Letter? What letter?" Melody played naivety like a role in a movie.

"To use your play of words, don't be daft. You know what letter I'm referring to."

"Just as I told Creed, I have no idea what letter you're describing. Whatever would I have to gain by taking a letter?" She snorted and her face tuned pale.

"You'd have a lot to gain. You'd have Creed."

"Really?" She grunted. "I already had Creed, honey. Lock, stock and barrel."

"If that were true you wouldn't have felt any risk with me being in town. You wouldn't have taken the letter and things would be much different now."

"Wow, you really are delusional. Fine, if it makes you feel better, I do remember something about a letter. I might have set it aside and forgotten to give it to him. Completely unintentional and definitely not out of fear that you'd come along and get him back."

And there came the truth.

Finally.

"Mom, do you know where the extra blankets are?" Jane stepped into the room and came to a sudden stop. "Oh, sorry. I didn't know you had company."

"Hello. I'm Melody, an old friend of your mothers. And who might you be?" Melody oozed fake interest.

"I'm Jane. Mindy's daughter."

"Oh…well…" Several expressions flickered across Melody's face before realization planted itself there. "Well, well, well. I didn't know you had a daughter, Mindy. How old are you, Jane?"

Mindy felt her heart drop into her stomach.

"I'm eighteen. I just started my freshman year at college."

"How exciting." She gave Mindy a I-caught-you grin.

"The blankets are in the chest in the guest bedroom," Mindy said, feeling choked.

"Thanks. Nice meeting you." Jane left.

Watching her daughter leave the room, she then turned her gaze upon Melody who looked like she was the cat who ate the canary. "Hmm. Looks like someone has a big secret."

So obviously Melody hadn't read the letter, at least not all of it. "I don't know what you're talking about."

Melody glided toward Mindy, leaning in and whispering, "I'm not a math wizard but I think I can calculate what nine months gets somebody. Now I know why you really came back to town. It wasn't for Creed. You were pregnant." She pulled back slightly, holding Mindy's gaze in a lock.

"Melody—"

"Don't Melody me." Her laughter was cold. "Are you worried that I'll tell Creed? Now why would I do that?" She sneered.

"I plan on telling him. It's between us."

"Really? I think you're wrong about that. I have a daughter involved in all this. Not to mention, Livvy and Jane look like sisters. Creed definitely has prominent genes, doesn't he?" She shrugged. "Do you think he'll ever forgive you?" Her gaze had turned frosty.

Mindy wrapped her arms around her stomach. She kept her mouth closed.

Melody stepped over to the door. "If I were you, I'd go back to where you came from." The closing of the door was a finality.

Chapter 19

CREED HEARD A noise and a second later he felt the bed sink. He'd been fast asleep so it took some time to force his eyes open. His breath came out in a hiss when he saw Melody. "What the hell are you doing, Mel?" he bit out.

"Livvy's bed is way too small," she cooed. "You have this big bed all to your lonesome, Creed. You don't mind sharing, do you, honey?" She reached out and tangled her fingers in his hair.

He blinked, sleep quickly leaving his body. He roved his gaze down the tight-fitting T-shirt that landed high on her shapely thighs. "Melody, it wouldn't matter if I was sleeping in a bed the size of this house it'd still be too small for the both of us."

She showed no signs of being hurt by his blunt words. "Come on, Creed. Don't you ever get a hankering for old times. Remember how good we were together? How wild and sexy we could be?" She scooted closer, roaming her fingers down his chest, his stomach, to the sheet that was tossed over his lap. No denying, they used to be hot together. She could suck a raisin through a straw and enjoyed showing off her skills. They could go all night until he could barely walk the next morning. Yet he didn't even feel a tingle south of his waist. Over the years he'd learned there was a heck of a lot more important than a roll in the sack. Hell, if he was still the cowboy who thought with his dick, he would have Mindy in his bed twenty-four seven, if she'd take him. But he wanted more. Needed more. And Melody didn't meet any of the criteria.

When she swept her hand lower, rubbing his flaccid body, he wrapped his fingers around her slender wrist and lifted her hand off his body. "Save your actions. It won't happen."

Her fuller bottom lip puckered. "It's okay. Livvy is fast asleep. She'll never know." She leaned in, but Creed sat up straight, taking the sheet with him to cover himself.

"This isn't about Livvy," he groaned.

She pushed herself up and the wide neckline of the shirt lowered, revealing the tops of her large naked breasts. "Please tell me this has nothing to do with Mindy Sage."

So, Melody knew Mindy was back in town. "Is that where you'd gone earlier? Doesn't matter. Even if Mindy wasn't here, I'd still feel the same. What we had is history."

"Fine. I'm good at keeping a secret, not as good as some, but I won't tell a soul. I'm offering you me."

"No."

Rolling her tongue along her satin smooth lips, she smiled. "I'm not looking for a relationship again, Creed. But I have to say, I miss you in a hundred ways." She dipped her gaze to the sheet. "I haven't been able to find a man yet who has your moves."

"Save yourself the embarrassment. The only thing getting off here tonight is me off the bed." He jumped up, wrapping the sheet around his hips.

An ugly expression covered her face. "My God, this really is about Mindy, isn't it?" She pushed off the bed and paraded up to him. The hem of the T-shirt stayed around her flat stomach. "What a pathetic story." She laughed.

"You're jealous of her, aren't you?"

"What? Me jealous of *her*? I think it was the other way around." She crossed her arms over her chest and wrinkled her nose.

"She had no reason to be jealous."

Several exasperated expressions flicked over her face before the frown shaped her full lips. "Just as I thought. You never did get over her. You want to blame me for the demise of our marriage, but you were the problem, Creed. I'm sick of everyone thinking Mindy is such an angel. You're mother. Your brothers. And now Livvy. I can tell you she's far from innocent."

"Save it, Mel. This won't change anything. You lied about the letter and many other things."

Stomping her foot, she stormed to the door, dragged it open, and looked back at him with a deep-rooted vengeance. "Did you know Mindy has a daughter?"

"Yes, I don't mind—"

Her snort sounded more like a choking sound. "Well, you should. Take a good look at her. I wonder if you'll be in Mindy's corner then," she ground out.

"What are you talking about?"

"Oh, I think you know. It doesn't take a genius, Creed. Goodbye!"

He stood there for a long time after Melody left, trying to wrap his head around what she'd said—or rather what she didn't say. What the hell was she talking about? What did Mindy's daughter have to do with any of this?

He dropped to the bed and stared at the door.

His heart raced.

His spine tingled.

Mindy had said she came back to Cooper's Hawk to speak to him nineteen years ago. Even writing him a letter explaining why.

Why hadn't she just come to see him?

Unless…

He jumped up from the bed, pacing the floor.

How old was Jane? Had Mindy told him? She was just starting college, so eighteen or nineteen?

Could it be possible?

Could Mindy have been carrying his child?

Melody had read the letter Mindy had written.

Creed dressed and left his bedroom, taking the stairs quietly and stepped outside. He couldn't sleep. It was still early and Mindy wouldn't be up. His mind whirled like a washing machine and every muscle ached.

Taking a seat in one of the rockers, he sat there as the fingers of light crawled across the sky and he heard a rooster crow. The time had come that he got some answers.

Driving to Sage Ranch, he greeted Bo and other hands with a wave as he drove by, heading toward the house.

He pulled up next to Mindy's car. Creed sat there staring at the front of the farmhouse, waiting for any sign of activity. Mindy would be coming out soon. He knew she'd been checking on the livestock and feeding the goats every morning.

If Jane was his daughter, why had she kept the truth from him?

Because he hadn't met her at the ice rink when she came back to town?

The Mindy he knew and loved wouldn't steal his daughter from him. Wouldn't take away all the firsts, his family, a part of him.

But she had been keeping a secret. She said so herself.

Burying his face in his palms, he rubbed the tension from his forehead. What did he want? If he prayed that Jane wasn't his daughter, then he felt like a jerk. If he wanted Jane to be his daughter, then he could never forgive Mindy and he'd lose her. Keeping his daughter a secret would be the biggest betrayal. How could anyone get over something like that?

Lifting his head, he stretched his gaze over the windows of the house. A light was now on in Mindy's bedroom. A few minutes later he saw her coming from the back of the house to take the worn path down to the barn. My God, seeing her made his heart skip a beat. He wanted to be with her, spend the rest of his life with her. He wanted to believe this had all been a misunderstanding. But how could a nineteen-year-old secret be a misunderstanding.

Slow down, man.

Melody could be stirring up trouble. Something she had become an expert at doing.

He needed to get the answers from Mindy.

Get out of the truck, Creed.

Sitting there for a few minutes longer, he decided being a coward didn't look good on him. He'd never ran away from trouble, never feared what was on the other side of a door. If he didn't speak to Mindy soon, he'd explode.

He slipped out of the driver's seat and shut the door quietly. He followed the worn path down to the field and into the open doorway of the new barn. He heard clanking and rattling and he found Mindy bent over scooping grain into a large metal bucket. The enticing curve of her firm bottom sticking up in the air didn't deter the powerful curiosity rolling through his body.

Watching her, he replayed in his head what he'd say to her. What he would do if Mindy admitted what Melody insinuated. The second she stood up, swiping tendrils of hair away from her flushed cheeks, he felt a familiar ache in his groin. He wanted to stroll over, wrap her up in his arms and hold her there forever. The future he'd planned had become murky.

She saw him and after the surprise faded, she smiled, strolled over to him and set the bucket down. "Creed, I didn't expect to see you so soon."

He stood there quietly. His voice was lost somewhere between joy and fear.

Mindy must have sensed his internal tornado because the corners of her beautiful mouth dipped into a frown. "Creed? Are you okay?"

Shoving his hands into the front pockets of his jeans, he swallowed a large lump in his throat. "I didn't expect to be here either."

Several expressions flitted across her face. Her eyes widened slightly. Her shoulders slumped as if the gig was up. "You look like crap."

"I didn't sleep."

She averted her gaze. "Must be from the company you're keeping." Picking up the bucket, she carried it outside. He followed.

"Mel came to see you, I know." Another new piece to the complex puzzle. "What did you two talk about?"

Mindy unlocked the gate to the goat fence and stepped in. The herd came running, hopping excitedly from front to back hooves as she headed toward the goat house.

He followed her across the wet grass and waited outside the door of the small shelter as she scooped grain into feeders. "Well?"

Mindy lifted her chin to glace at him. "Don't you already know the answer?"

"You don't have any reason to be angry with me," he huffed.

"Maybe I'm not angry with you. Maybe I am. Hell if I know. Why are you here, Creed?"

"We need to talk."

Turning her back to him, she poured the rest of feed mixture into the last feeder. "Go ahead and talk. I just need to finish my chores."

"Mindy—"

She finally turned, dread lacing her lovely features. "I feel like Melody has been the puppet master for our relationship, or the lack of, for nineteen years. I know what she said to you. I saw the wicked look in her expression when she left here last night."

An invisible vice grabbed him around the throat and squeezed. "I need *you* to tell me. Mindy, tell me the truth."

She dropped the bucket and there among a herd of goat chomping away on their breakfast, his world turned upside down again. He could only stare. His breath came in heavy pants.

"Creed…"

"Let's not mince words. I need to know," he said in a low voice.

"I didn't know I was pregnant when I left Cooper's Hawk. I found out and I had every intention of telling you. I came back, but I learned that you and Melody were getting married. I was blindsided, hurt and angry. I went back and forth, unsure what I should do, but I settled on giving you the option. I wrote you the letter, telling you that I was pregnant and I was keeping her. I asked that you meet me at the ice rink if you wanted me, wanted us, but begged that you didn't come unless you were committed. My heart had already been broken. I swore that if you didn't show up, I'd walk away and never bother you again."

"That's the letter you left in my truck?" He had to force the words through thin lips.

She nodded. "I did wait. For hours. You didn't come. But Melody did."

"I didn't know." The words came out with a raspy exhale.

"I didn't know that at the time." She picked up the bucket and brushed passed him. Halfway across the pen she stopped and turned, tears streaming down her face. "I thought you had made your decision. I was scared, heartbroken, and unsure of raising a child alone."

"Where does Branch come into this picture?" he asked angrily.

"I met him later."

"How wonderful for him," he growled.

"I called you. Three years later. Twice in fact. Left you messages and again you didn't respond."

"I was doing a tour in Kosovo. We didn't have access to phones, no outside communication for months."

"Did you not get my messages?" She lifted a brow.

He rubbed the bridge of his nose. "I did, but I ignored them."

"So you decided you didn't want to return my call?"

"I was angry. Hurt. I didn't want to be friends. If I'd known about Jane—"

"Would you have reached out? Came to California? What Creed?" The tears had dried and there was a new desperation to her voice.

"I would have been her father. I *am* her father. Does she know about me?" The breeze swept across them and it felt cold on his skin.

"We never kept it a secret that Branch wasn't her biological father. I spoke of you. She's never asked to see you—has no clue you live here in Cooper's Hawk. I've always allowed her to take the lead, Creed. If she wanted to see you I, and Branch, would have allowed that to happen."

A solid punch came in the center of his gut. He had a daughter. Another daughter. Two children. His heart sank. Time with his oldest daughter had been stolen from him. Anger, sadness, uncertainty boiled up inside him. "But maybe I wanted to see her," he said quietly. "Apparently you, or Branch, didn't think of that."

"I understand—"

"No you don't." He jerked off his hat and tore a hand though his hair. "What if the circumstances were switched, Mindy? What if I kept our child a secret? Wouldn't you have expected me to continue to try to tell you about her? To try all options?"

"Creed, I didn't deliberately keep her to myself. I did reach out. Looking back it's easy to say what's right or wrong, of what should have been done. I was eighteen years old and pregnant. I was scared. Coming home to Sage Ranch wasn't an option because I couldn't raise our child here with the chance of running into you and knowing you didn't want us."

"I did want you…and I would have wanted my child."

"Is that right? If you wanted me why didn't you pick up the phone? Come to see me? Instead, you jumped into the bed of the first woman who looked your way."

"You can't throw Mel up in my face. I thought we were through," he gritted out.

"And I thought we were through too."

"Not good enough. We're talking about a child."

"I do understand that you're upset—"

"Upset? I don't know what to feel. No, I know how to feel. Betrayed."

"Don't you think I've been saddled with guilt all these years? Do you think this was the choice I wanted to make?"

"You knew me, Mindy. Better than anyone. Do you honestly believe in your heart of hearts that I would walk away from my child?" He could barely see straight.

A good ten second hesitation passed until she finally said, "No, I don't think you would. After seeing you with Livvy and how good you are with her, I can say that now with one hundred percent faith, but nineteen years ago you were a different man—a good man, but different. You know you were too. You had dreams that didn't include a wife and child." She took the distance between them and reached out, but he pulled away. "I'm sorry, Creed."

"If you really are sorry why didn't you tell me when you first came back weeks ago? How could you let me get close to you again while keeping this secret?" The betrayal grew like a boulder in his chest.

"I did plan on telling you. I would have told you. I wanted to tell you. It just seemed there was never the right time."

"That's easy for you to say. You don't get to pick and choose when you tell a man he has a daughter." He rubbed the bridge of his nose. "I can't be near you right now. I can't be trusted what I'll say." He stormed passed her.

"Creed? What will you do now? Jane is here."

He stopped, feeling like he'd been blasted with ice cold water. "She's here?" He kept his back to Mindy, not wanting to lose it in front of her.

"Yes. I want you to meet her. I want her to know you and Livvy."

"I don't know," he said in a whispered voice. He didn't think she heard him, until she answered.

"I realize you need some time to wrap your head around this. What about us? Can you forgive me?" There was a pleading lilt to her voice.

"I don't think that'll ever be possible."

Practically taking the gate off the hinges, he barreled through and kept his gaze ahead on the stretch of grass. At his truck, he looked at the quiet house, feeling tears at the backs of his eyes. Knowing he had another daughter changed everything. Not just for him but for Livvy too. How would he tell his daughter she had a sister? Would Livvy blame him? Despise him more?

Jumping into the driver's side of his truck, he turned the key and the engine roared alive. He wasted no time in slamming the gear into reverse, pulling out and taking the narrow lane too fast but not caring. He sped out onto the main road and pounded his palm twice against the steering wheel. How was a man supposed to feel in a situation like this? He had an adult daughter—a stranger for a daughter.

Anger pierced his heart, but the hurt, betrayal, sadness, and torment lingering in his chest almost made him feel like he had reached the depths of hell.

He wasn't an award-winning father by far, but he loved and cared for Livvy. Took care of her. Protected her.

His daughter Jane had grown up without him. Another man had been all those things for her, and from what Mindy had told Creed, Branch had cared more for his career than his family. This choked Creed up. He wanted to hate Mindy, rip every memory of her out of his heart and mind, but he'd been such an arrogant ass. She had been right when she said he'd had big dreams that didn't include a family. Hell, he knew Melody had been callous and bitter and yet he'd married her. That showed where he'd been emotionally.

He rolled down the window, filling his lungs with fresh air.

He wanted to punch something.

By the time he reached the farm, his anger had been fueled with more emotion.

Then he saw Melody's luggage sitting on the porch.

The second he stepped into the house he heard raised voices coming from upstairs. He took the stairs two at a time and walked into World War Three happening in Livvy's bedroom.

Melody was dropping clothes into a suitcase while Livvy stood by her desk, arms crossed and her eyes red.

"What's going on?" he asked from the open doorway.

"She's angry," Melody said without looking at him.

Blowing out a long breath, he stepped inside. "Livvy? What's wrong?"

No answer, she just stared at the wall.

He looked at his ex for some answers. "Melody?"

"Don't look at me like that," she muttered. "You've raised her to be spoiled."

Creed took a second to gain his bearings before saying, "You've been here for less than twenty-four hours and you've already wreaked havoc."

She lifted her chin high, wearing a cold grin. "Oh, I'm gathering you spoke to Mindy then? While you were off taking care of *that* situation you needed to be here taking care of your daughter," she slurred.

He chose not to fall into that dirty web. "Why is Livvy upset?" He could only deal with one problem at a time and right now Livvy needed him. He had never seen her this quiet.

"I told her that I'm leaving," Melody confessed then slammed the lid to the suitcase.

He looked over at Livvy, understanding her anguish. People came and went, and sometimes it broke a person's heart. He'd had his broken a time or two. He'd known this would happen, just didn't expect it to be so soon. "Why are you leaving now?"

"I received a call from my agent this morning. He has managed to secure a role for me in an upcoming made-for-television movie." Her eyes twinkled in pride, and arrogance. "I booked a flight for early this afternoon."

Creed swiped both hands down his face then turned to his daughter. "Livvy? Let's talk."

"Go away!" she said softly.

"Sweetheart, please. You still have a few hours until your mom leaves. Maybe you two can go for breakfast."

"I gave her that option."

"You lied!" Livvy turned her heated gaze on Melody. "You said you'd stay for a while. You even told me last night that you'd talk to dad about you and me going on vacation together." Livvy's shaky voice told Creed she'd been crying hard.

"I wasn't referring to this moment." Melody intentionally didn't look at Creed. "Honey, you have to understand that I can't refuse work. It's my career, just as one day you'll have a career that you'll have to dedicate yourself to."

She was met with silence.

"She gets this from you, you know," Melody whispered, rolling her eyes.

He shifted from one dirty boot to another. "Is that what you think? Why did you make all those promises when you knew you wouldn't keep them?"

"Don't blame me. I didn't know my agent would score a role for me. What? Am I supposed to refuse work and stay here? In Cooper's Hawk?" She wrinkled her nose in disgust. "Livvy, if you don't stop this behavior at once I'm leaving now."

No response.

"Fine! I'm leaving." Melody turned, grabbed her small suitcase and sashayed her way down the hall.

"Please leave my room!" Livvy said to Creed.

He sighed and stepped into the hall and headed for the stairs when he heard the bedroom door slam shut behind him. Taking the stairs, he practically knocked the screen door off the hinges on his way through it. He knew this would happen. Melody was a human tornado who swept in, wreaked havoc, then left a mess for others to clean up. That had always been her deal.

On the porch, he leaned his elbows on the rail and looked out into the distance. Creed had never been a sentimental man but having a daughter had helped him connect with the compassionate and understanding parts within himself.

Lowering his gaze, he watched a bird grab a worm and take off in flight.

He had his own worms to carry.

He'd listened to Mindy's voice messages when he got home from Kosovo. Stubborn and prideful, he'd erased them. He'd been angry, but mostly he'd been hurt. And now, all those emotions were tenfold. Jane was in Cooper's Hawk. He wanted to see her, but what would he say? Would she want to see him? Would she be willing to have a conversation with him?

Emotion bubbled up inside of his throat and he couldn't push it down.

So many lives were affected by the secret.

He had to take accountability for his own actions though.

Hearing the screen door screech, he looked over his shoulder to see Melody stepping out, opening a water bottle. When she saw him, she blew a tendril of hair off her face. "That child is out of control."

"She's not out of control. She's a teen."

"Whatever. It's just like you to excuse her behavior."

"Do you blame her for acting out?"

"Don't start with me, Creed. Let's not rehash that same argument we had the first time I left."

He narrowed his gaze, pushed off the rail and faced her. "No worries. We were at an entirely different time then."

"Why are you still looking at me like that?" She puffed out her bottom lip.

"I think you understand why without me saying the words."

"Come on, you should be thanking me. Mindy would never have told you the truth."

"Maybe. Maybe not, but you always did enjoy stirring up trouble, didn't you?"

"This has as much to do with me as it does you. I don't want Livvy to be hurt."

"Really? You say that as you leave her sitting in her room licking her wounds," he growled.

"Oh there it is. The perfect Creed. Let me guess, you want a medal because you stuck around. We both know if you'd stayed on the rodeo circuit you would have just as easily left Livvy with me. Why is it when men leave for a career, they're respected and admired but when a woman follows her career we're made to look like monsters?"

"No one has ever made you out to be a monster, Mel. But you have a teen daughter who is going through something. She needs a mother. At least a part time mother. I've never asked you to give up your career."

"Well, it looks like Mindy will be filling that void soon enough." She set the water bottle down on the rail.

"Don't pretend innocence. You did what you came to do. How'd you find out Mindy was here?" he prodded.

She lowered her eyes a mere second then looked back up, her blank expression back into place. "Livvy told me you and Mindy were seeing each other."

"So you didn't come for Livvy, did you? When we were on the phone and I asked about the letter you guessed Mindy was back." He chuckled coldly. "That's just wonderful."

"Nonsense. I *came* for our daughter. I just needed to see it with my own eyes." Something flickered in her expression. Something close to human kindness. "I think Mindy would make a good mother."

Creed lifted a brow. "Huh? Sorry, I'm lost. Did you just compliment Mindy?"

"Don't push it. You heard what I said. I'll never be the mother that Livvy needs and she certainly needs someone to keep her occupied."

So her intentions weren't entirely altruistic. "Livvy isn't a dog, Mel. She's a teen who has feelings."

"Of course. Anyway, I called a car to take me to the airport and it should be here soon."

"You already knew you wouldn't be sticking around until this afternoon?"

"Oh please! Stop being so judgy."

"You'd think I would have learned my lesson about you," he growled. "You're right, Livvy needs much more than you can offer."

"Whatever. At least I can admit it." She shrugged and lost some of the sneer. Reaching into her purse she took out an envelope. "This is a little late, but I think it's time you read it."

He saw his name written across the front. Taking the envelope, he shook his head.

"You know what that is?"

"Why, Mel?"

She gave a small shrug. "You were mine, Creed Hawke, and I wanted to keep my cowboy."

"But how could you be so evil to keep my daughter from me?"

"I'm a lot of things, but I wouldn't have been that cruel. If it makes any difference, I didn't read the letter. I had been watching Mindy when she came back to town and I saw her put the letter in the truck. When she left, I took it. I wanted to read what she'd written, but I didn't. I followed her to the ice rink, and I was going to give the letter back to her, but I was angry."

He stared down at his name. The envelope was sealed. He heard tires on rock and looked up as the black Escalade pulled in front of the house.

"Mel? What about the text messages Mindy said I sent you, telling you I no longer wanted her?" It was time he knew all the truth.

"Who leaves their phone in their vehicle? You made it too easy." She sighed.

He couldn't find words to respond.

"Creed, I know I'm the last person you want to take advice from, but if it's worth anything, don't waste another nineteen years living in a memory. You've always loved her, and I'd bet my next role that she loves you too." She gave him a weak smile.

The driver stepped out of the Escalade. "Ma'am, can I help with your bags?"

"Yes. Come get them."

Melody didn't look back as she climbed into the back seat of the SUV.

Creed stood there for the longest time. So, this was the letter. He folded it and shoved it into his back pocket for later.

Going back inside, he took the stairs two at a time, and knocked on Livvy's door. He felt relieved when she called out, "It's unlocked."

Stepping in, he found her sitting on the edge of the bed. Her face was pale and her eyes were red rimmed. "You okay?" he asked.

"Did she leave?"

He nodded and took a seat next to her. "She's gone."

"I hate her."

"No, you don't."

"Yes I do."

"She's still your mother."

"Barely."

What could he say? "She wanted me to tell you that she loves you dearly." He lied. But some lies were needed to make someone feel better.

Livvy looked up at him with a hurt gaze. "You're just telling me that." She was a smart kid.

"Not everyone lives up to our expectations, Liv. At times the dream is a lot better than reality."

Livvy rubbed the back of her hand across her nose. "Dad, I need to tell you something."

"What?"

"I heard what Mom said to you last night. What did she mean?"

He swallowed hard. "You know it's not right to eavesdrop."

"I'm sorry. I know I shouldn't, but she woke me up getting out of bed."

"There are a lot of things you wouldn't understand—"

"Stop treating me like a baby. I have a right to know the truth."

He realized he couldn't ask for honestly from someone else if he wasn't willing to give it. "You know I've told you that Mindy and I were once very close. I loved her, dearly. I found out that Mindy's daughter, Jane, is my daughter too."

Livvy's gaze narrowed. Her mouth slipped open and she slammed it shut. Several seconds floated by. "That means I have a sister?"

He nodded. "Yes."

"Does she want to meet me?"

"Honey, I don't know. I'm not sure she even wants to meet me. This is all new to me too."

"But if you and Mindy get married, we can all be a family." Her eyes twinkled with a vulnerability that struck Creed with the velocity of a lightning bolt.

He didn't want to hurt her more than she already was, but he didn't want to keep things from her. "Livvy, I don't think that's going to happen."

She jumped up from the bed, shaking her head. "Why? You said you loved her. She loves you. Why not?" she demanded.

"It's complicated."

"It's always complicated. That's what parents say when they've fucked up!"

"Livvy, watch the language." He stood. "I know you're hurt but—"

"But what? We can be a family, but you'd rather be alone for the rest of your life keeping me a baby!"

"Livvy—" He reached out.

She stepped back. "I want to be alone." She turned her back to him.

"Let's talk,"

"No. Leave," she said softly.

Respecting that she needed time to absorb all that had gone down, he stepped out of the room and closed the door behind him.

Going back downstairs, he sat at the kitchen table then took out the letter. Opening it, he smoothed the folds from the sheet of paper and read…

"Dear Creed,

I hope I'm doing the right thing but leaving Cooper's Hawk without telling you the truth would only break my heart more than I can bear. I'm sorry I didn't tell you before I left that I love you. Not like a brother. Or a friend. But I love you deeply.

The night we slept together we created a child. It's a girl. I've already named her Jane Elizabeth.

I know you and Melody are getting married and I'm not asking you to not marry her, but I guess I was hoping you loved me too. I needed to take a chance.

If you don't want me—and our baby—please, don't come. Please stay away. I will take your absence as an answer. I will never burden you with any of this. But if you love me, want our family, come to the rink. I'll be waiting.

With much love,

Mindy."

Dropping the letter to the table, he lowered his head as tears blurred his vision. It was the first time he'd cried in years. He cried for Mindy. For Jane. For all the years they'd wasted on pride.

How many more years would he waste?

"You okay?"

He found his mother standing in the doorway. "No."

"The walls of this place are thin." She tightened the belt of her robe and stepped over to the coffee maker. "I'm sorry."

"I am too."

"So, you and Mindy have a child together. That's a lot to absorb."

He didn't respond. He was tired.

"Coffee, son?"

"No."

"Some advice?"

"Ma, I—"

"Stop. I need to say what I need to say." She sat down at the table, placing her palms on the wood. "People make mistakes. I've made mistakes too."

"You?" He'd never known her to do anything wrong.

Her skin paled. "Your father and I went through a very rocky time years ago. He spent so much time out on the land. I know that he was working hard but I felt like a neglected wife. I'm not excusing my actions, I'm only saying how I felt. I had an affair. It didn't last long, but it was still an affair."

What the hell?

"What? Did Dad know?"

She nodded. "I told him. I couldn't hide it from him. He was angry, wanted a divorce, and took off and stayed gone for a few weeks. Do you remember?"

"I think so. You said he was away at a rodeo event."

"Yes. I couldn't bear to tell you boys the truth because then I'd have to tell you everything, especially about my mistake. And about your father's mistake too."

Creed blew out a long breath. "And what mistake was that?"

"He had an affair too. He thought I didn't know, but a woman always knows when her husband isn't quite doing what's right."

Rubbing his cheek, he cursed. "Why are you telling me this?"

"I'm telling you this to show you that you can forgive. I forgave your father and he forgave me and the next remaining years that we had together were spent happy—happier than ever. It breaks my heart to think we could have given up on us, our family, and missed those wonderful last years. I loved him dearly."

"Ma, thanks but we're comparing apples and oranges here. I didn't screw around. I lost my daughter. Mindy kept her from me."

She patted his hand. "You're missing the point, son. Get out of that stubborn head of yours and listen. Are you willing to give up on Mindy and what could be because you're feeling betrayed? Or are you willing to forgive and spend the rest of your days, however many that may be, with those you love? Think about what you could be giving up." She stood and went back to pour herself some coffee.

"Who was the man?" Creed asked in a low voice.

"It doesn't matter." She kept her back to him.

"It does to me."

She didn't even turn to look at Creed. "Rusty."

"Shit!" he bit out.

Getting up, he started to say something to his Ma, but he decided against it.

Instead, he went upstairs to try and mend things with Livvy. He knocked three times. No answer each time.

Turning the doorknob, it was unlocked.

"Livvy, are you ready to talk?" he asked as he stepped inside.

Scanning the space, it was empty. The window was wide open.

He rushed down the hall and checked the bathroom. His mother's room. He ran from room to room and didn't find her.

His Ma met him in the living room. "What's wrong, son? You look like you saw a ghost."

"It's Livvy. She's gone."

"What do you mean gone?"

"Her window was open. I think she climbed out. I'm going to check outside and ask the hands if any of them have seen her."

"I'll go get dressed." She was already hurrying toward the stairs.

Chapter 20

"*MOM, OF COURSE* I forgive you. You've never lied to me. You've always been open about Branch not being my biological father."

Mindy met Jane's sincere gaze through unshed tears. Since her run in with Creed that morning she'd been a blubbering idiot. Jane was doing her best to console Mindy after she divulged everything. Shifting on the couch, she plucked another tissue from the box and blotted her eyes. "Creed will never forgive me."

"I think you're wrong. I don't know him but if he's as wonderful as you've always told me he was then he'll realize you both played a role in this."

Mindy patted her hand. "He's a wonderful man, honey. I want you to meet him. Meet Livvy."

"What will you do, Mom?"

"I'm going back to California to take care of the house and then I'm not sure."

"Will you come back here to live?"

"No. I don't know. Probably not. Cooper's Hawk isn't big enough for Creed and me. He has every right to be angry. I should have tried harder. I made a mess of things."

"Yes, you should have, but I'm the same age you were when you got pregnant with me. I don't know what I would do if I faced the same situation. No one knows what they'd do unless it happens to them."

"How'd you get to be so smart, sweetheart?" Mindy sniffed.

"From you, Mom. Everything I am is because of you. You deserve happiness and if Creed makes you happy then fight for it. Show him that you're willing to fight and do anything you need to."

If only she had the same hope that her daughter had. Mindy had seen Creed's face though when she'd admitted the truth. He looked at her with such hatred, unforgiveness.

An urgent knock came on the door.

"Are you expecting someone?" Jane asked.

"No."

"I'll get it."

Mindy wiped her eyes and pushed her soiled tissue inside her pocket. The familiar voice at the door made her heart lurch. It was Creed. What was he doing there?

She stood at the same time he came strolling into the living room wearing a tight jaw and cold eyes. He swiped his hat off his head. He had worried lines around his pale blue eyes. "What is it, Creed?" Mindy knew something was wrong.

"Should I leave you two alone?" Jane asked.

Creed shook his head. "I'm sorry. I'm looking for Livvy. Is she here?"

"No. Is she supposed to be?" Mindy stepped forward, clasping her hands together.

"I-I thought maybe she would be, you know, since..." He darted a glance at Jane.

"Jane knows everything," Mindy blurted. "If you need to say something you can speak in front of her."

"Livvy knows too. Her mom left and I think the combination of everything made her upset. I went to check on her and she had snuck out of the window." He turned to Jane, twisting his hat in his hands. "Maybe one day soon you'd be willing to sit down and talk to me. I'd like to stay, but I need to go search for Livvy."

"We can all help," Jane offered. "We'll find her faster that way."

"Yes, we can," Mindy said. "Jane, go get your Pop Pop and Jonesy. I'll go with you Creed. Where would you like for them to search?" She grabbed her jacket off the hook and pulled it on, wondering if Creed would deny her from accompanying him.

Creed looked anguished. "Can you go to Hawke Farm where my mother is waiting. She'll know where Livvy's friends live and you can start there. Maybe divide up the locations."

Mindy and Creed hurried to his truck that was still running.

"Where are we going, Creed?" She asked once they pulled onto the main road.

"If she's anything like me, she'll find the one person she feels has always been there for her."

"Alex, right?"

He nodded.

"What happened, Creed?"

He tightened his grip on the steering wheel. "She's angry with me. Angry at everyone. She has reason to be hurt. I think we've all let her down."

"Why did Melody leave?"

He shifted uncomfortably. "Her career is waiting."

"Livvy must be so upset."

"Before Mel left she gave me something." The low huskiness of his voice made the hair on Mindy's neck stand. "The letter."

She looked across the bench seat, seeing the moisture in his eyes. Tears blurred her vision too. A pain unlike any other filled her. "I understand you'll never forgive me, but it's not too late for you to build a relationship with Jane. She's willing."

"Does she truly want that?"

"More than anything. Please understand that I've never hid her from you."

His exhale sounded like a moan of a wounded animal. "It's best we don't go there now."

"We'll find Livvy. She loves you. She's hurt."

"If anything happens to her—"

She reached over and touched his arm. His thick muscle flexed under her fingers. "Don't even think that. She's safe."

Silence fell between them.

Ten minutes later, he parked the truck in front of a two-story yellow house. He barely had the gear in park before he jumped out and stormed up the stretch of cobblestone walkway.

Mindy watched from the truck. Five minutes later he returned and slid behind the steering wheel.

"Is she here?" Mindy asked.

"No. And neither is Alex. They're together."

Chapter 21

HANGING UP THE phone, Creed dropped the device into the center console. "That was Sheriff Conley. Livvy and Alex have been found."

Mindy's cell beeped and she glanced at the screen. "It's Isabella. She said the ice rink was broken into earlier. By two juveniles." She looked across the seat. "Creed? Was it Livvy and Alex?"

"Bingo," he growled then jerked the steering wheel, doing an illegal U-turn on the road. He slammed on the gas pedal as they headed back toward Cooper's Hawk.

"Why? I could have let them in to skate."

"Something tells me they didn't want to do things by the book. Livvy's angry and wants attention."

"What will you do? What will Sheriff Conley do?"

"I'm going to ground her until she's eighteen." He felt his muscles aching in his shoulders. "Sheriff is a fair man."

"Grounding her until she's eighteen might be a bit overdramatic."

He flashed Mindy a dangerous glance. "And how would you handle this?"

"Well, I'd first ask why. When Jane was fifteen, she and some friends were caught drinking on private property. I was so angry and disappointed but after learning the truth things weren't as bad as they first seemed. She didn't know there would be older kids at the party or that they would bring alcohol. Feeling pressure, she took a sip of beer. She hated it so she didn't drink it. I grounded her for a few weeks. Trust me, I wanted to throw the book at her. Sometimes we must remember what it was like when we were kids. Peer pressure, hormones, social media…it's all tough. I even took Jane to see a therapist."

"She saw a therapist?"

"For a few months."

"Why?"

"Don't get panicked. She was going through a pretty hard stage. She got involved with the wrong crowd, had insecurities and she needed to speak to someone besides me about her feelings. Some kids need to talk to an unbiased person, someone they feel no emotional connection to."

"Did she ever tell you what made her feel like that?"

"A kid at school continually called her fat. She wasn't, but for a young girl that word can be very harmful."

"Mindy…do you really believe that she and I can have a relationship? Will she be willing to give me a chance? Or will we never be close?"

She shifted so that she was looking at his profile. "Yes, she'll give you a chance. Why wouldn't she?"

"I'm not doing very good with Livvy."

"Hey," she laid her hand back on his arm. "Trust me, parents all feel the walk of shame at times. There were moments I thought I must have been the worst parent around because Jane was rebelling. It turns out she wasn't rebelling as much as she was trying to find herself. We all go through stages where we lose our footing and must get back up and everyone gets back up at their own pace." A long sigh came from her. "I'm sorry, Creed. It wouldn't be fair to ask you to forgive me, but I do hope that one day you'll understand."

He stretched his gaze across the short space. "I wish I could say that I see that as a possibility."

The rest of the drive was in silence.

Chapter 22

PULLING OUTSIDE OF the two-story brick building with a fountain in front, Creed turned off the truck.

Mindy said softly, "I'm going to have Jane pick me up. You go on in and help Livvy. She needs you right now." He opened the door and she added, "And remember that it wasn't that long ago that you and I were kids and we snuck into the rink more times than we can count."

Creed didn't look back. He had enough on his plate than to take a stroll down memory lane right now.

Sheriff Conley was waiting for him when Creed stepped into the sheriff's office. "Thanks for coming, Creed."

Shaking his hand, Creed looked down the stretch of hallway looking for his daughter in one of the wooden chairs. He didn't see her. "What are we looking at, Conley?"

"Well, they didn't do any damage to the property. The door was left unlocked. Isabella is getting forgetful these days and said she must have left it unbolted. She also doesn't want to file any charges. Apparently, they snuck in the building to skate."

"Thanks, pal. Can I see her?"

"Sure. She's free to go. Just so we're clear I gave her a good scare, just as I remember that Conley Senior used to give us when we were kids getting into mischief."

"Why does it feel a whole helluva lot worse when it's our kids getting into trouble?"

"Our parents always said karma was a bitch." He chuckled and motioned for Creed to follow him down the long hallway. He stopped at a closed door marked "private". "She's pretty shaken up. I think she learned her lesson. The boy too." Conley dipped his white Stetson and stepped across the hall into another room.

Creed sucked in a breath and opened the door. Livvy was asleep on the couch inside. She looked peaceful. When she was younger, he'd read her to sleep and say a prayer that she'd always know how much he loved her. Creed had tripped somewhere along the way. He'd made big mistakes—just like his Ma had said. Everyone made mistakes.

"Dad?"

"Livvy?"

She jumped up from the couch. "Daddy!" She raced into his arms, clinging to him like she'd done when she was little. He felt her shoulders shake as she sobbed into his shirt.

He squeezed her tight against him, comforting her. "It's okay, sweetheart. I'm here." He held her until her sobs turned to whimpers and faded. She lifted her head, looking at him with red-rimmed eyes and trembling bottom lip. Moisture streaked her puffy cheeks. His heart swelled three times its normal size.

"Daddy! I'm so sorry. It wasn't Alex's fault. I made him go into the ice rink," she said on a rushed breath. "Please don't make us stop being friends."

"Come here." He pointed to the couch. They sat down next to each other and he took her small hand into his. "Listen, what you did was wrong, but Sheriff Conley said there's no damage to the property. Why did you sneak into the rink?"

"I wanted Alex to see my routine. I was so proud. He said he couldn't wait to see me skate. Isabella always leaves the door unlocked and I knew that. I'm sorry. We shouldn't have gone inside, but I didn't think it'd hurt. We just skated. That's all."

He swiped away her tears. He remembered how his mom had handled the situations when he and his brothers got into trouble, and they'd done some pretty bad things. She didn't threaten to go out back and get a switch like his father would have, but she would sit down, listen, and then give them a just and fair punishment. His Ma had been the best role model. Maybe he should have listened to her better. Creed was surprised what she'd confessed to him earlier, but it was important to forgive. No one was perfect. "Honey, it's not the end of the world. Just don't do it again. Okay?"

"I promise. I won't. *We* won't." She swiped the back of her hand across her moist eyes.

"And I'm going to make a promise right now and stick to it. I'm going to stop working so much and be home more. I'll hire more hands if I need to. I'm going to make you my focus from now on until you become an adult. You're the most important person in my life and you need to always know that. I'm going to ground myself because I've grounded you at times when I shouldn't have, when you were just trying to get my attention. That's my fault. Not yours."

"Does that mean I'm not going to be grounded now?" she asked hopefully.

"That's pushing it. You'll be grounded, but I'm not taking Alex away from you. He's a good kid and a good friend to you. But you two will need to start being accountable for what you do and how you do it. Not following rules can lead to danger."

"I will. I promise. I'll never do anything wrong again." She crossed her fingers.

He chuckled. "Although that sounds pretty darn good, we all make mistakes, even adults can make the worst."

"I want to meet Jane, Dad. She's my sister. I'm excited."

"You will. We'll make that happen. I want to meet her too." He'd only met her in passing earlier when he'd stopped at Sage Ranch. "I saw her today. You look like her. You both look like the Hawke family."

"I look like her?" The vulnerability he saw in her reminded him just how young she still was.

"Yes, you do. How about we get out of here? I spent enough time in here as a kid." He stood, reaching out to help her up.

"Dad? You were in jail?"

"Not behind bars, but in this room. One day I'll tell you about my brushes with danger if you promise to learn from my mistakes and not repeat them. The last thing this town needs is another misbehaving Hawke."

Chapter 23

CREED BRUSHED HIS hands down Maggie's neck. "You're a good girl." He'd brought her there after she'd sprained her leg during a mission. She'd stay at Hawke Farm until she recovered fully.

She clawed the ground as if to say, "Thank you."

Four weeks had passed since Mindy left Cooper's Hawk. She'd called him and told him she was heading back to California to take care of business. She didn't say whether she would come back or not, and he didn't ask. He'd wanted to, but he couldn't forgive her.

Jane and her boyfriend Jonesy had visited one weekend and they spent it getting to know each other. Although things were a little awkward at first, by the end of Sunday they'd made a lot of headway in becoming friends. Creed even had a "dad-to-boyfriend" conversation with Jonesy. He made it clear to the young man that he'd better respect his daughter.

Rusty had stopped to speak to Creed one afternoon, and he could see the man was a little uncomfortable. Rusty had apologized for the past. Creed had forgiven him.

"Dad?"

He looked up to find Livvy standing alongside the fence to the arena. "Is everything okay?"

"I want to speak to you." She waved him over.

Crossing the grass, he climbed over the top rail of the fence and dropped his boots down on the other side. Just as he'd promised he was spending more time at home and getting Livvy more involved in the chores at the farm, and at Sage Ranch. Since Mindy had left, Isabella had taken over helping Livvy with figure skating, but because she needed more, she gave Creed a number to call to set up lessons a few counties over. Livvy had been upset that Mindy was no longer teaching her, but she wanted to continue to skate.

He pulled off his gloves and pushed them into his back pocket. "What's up?"

"I spoke to Jane this morning."

"Great. I'm glad you two are talking every day."

"We talked about Mindy."

He swallowed hard, feeling an ache at the back of his skull. "I'm sure you two will have some discussions about her." He scratched his temple with his thumb.

"Jane said they are coming back to visit with Rusty this weekend."

Looking out into the distance, Creed saw nothing through his hurt and obstinacy. He didn't like feeling this way, but the betrayal had taken up residence inside him and he didn't know how to let it go. "Okay."

"Don't you care?"

"I care." He leaned into the fence. "I'll always care for Mindy but it's hard for you to understand what's going on. Sometimes a person is meant to care for someone from afar."

Livvy lifted herself to sit on the top rail. Her new cowgirl boots were scuffed and dirty. That was a great thing. She'd been doing her chores every day, without him asking. "Why? You two are crazy for each other, Dad. It's about time you stopped being obstinate."

"That's a new word."

"I read it in a book."

"Glad you're reading. And helping out more around here."

"I like working on the land, with the horses and goats. I especially like Hope."

"They'll grow on you fast." He liked seeing her smile.

"So, why are you so stubborn?"

"Have you looked at yourself lately?" He laughed. "It's in the Hawke genes."

She shrugged. "We're tough and stubborn. That's not a bad thing, unless you let something go when you shouldn't."

"Honey, although I'm flattered that you care for my wellbeing and relationship status, I assure you I'm okay."

"You say that, but I know better. Everyone wants love. I miss Mindy. I know you do too!"

Lying wouldn't help the situation. "I do," he said quietly.

"Thought so. So Jane and I have an idea."

"You do?" He couldn't wait to hear what they'd brewed up.

"Marry Mindy."

He blinked. "Let's say for theories sake that I still wanted to marry her, that doesn't mean she'd say yes. Livvy, she left. She wants to stay in California."

"She's in California because she can't be near you. That's what Jane said."

"There's a lot more to the story."

"Because she didn't tell you about Jane? Dad, sometimes I think you can't see the way things really are. She did try to tell you. Mom took the letter and you married her. Anyway, you love Mindy. Are you going to be stupid and wait another nineteen years?"

"You're not supposed to call your dad stupid. My goodness, girl. I don't think you're going to let up on this, are you?"

"Nope. Not until you listen. You were going to ask her to marry you, weren't you?"

"Yes," the answer came on the tail end of a sigh.

"And the only thing that changed is that we have Jane now. Right?"

How she said "we have Jane" made his heart fill with emotion. She was right. This wasn't a negative experience. He had another daughter and his heart expanded. A man could never have too much love—and he loved Mindy. Even after everything they'd been through. "So tell me about this plan you and Jane have manufactured."

"Well, since you've asked..."

~~~~~

"Honey, why do we have to go down to the barn? I'd like to get back on the road before dark," Mindy complained. She and Jane had taken a flight, rented a car and drove the few hours to Sage Ranch. The second she crossed the town limits into Cooper's Hawk she felt a sad heaviness. She didn't want to see Creed. Although she missed him—she loved him—she would only be overwhelmed with pain. He'd made his choice. He couldn't forgive her for the secret. Mindy would do everything she could from afar to encourage Jane to continue building a relationship with both Creed and Livvy.

But as far as ever fulfilling a dream with Creed, that was dead and gone...
~~~~~

"I told you. Jonesy and I wanted to see the goats before we leave. Right, Jonesy?" Jane looked up at her boyfriend.

"Yeah. I wanted to see the goats," he added.

"Fine. Then we'll go see them," Mindy caved. They'd both been acting weird for hours. Rushing her here and there. Why didn't they want to rush now?

It was a beautiful day. The sun was shining. The sky was clear and blue. There was a scent of sweetness mixed in the air. Oh how she missed the ranch.

Jane slid open the door to the barn and Mindy started to step in when she came to a halt. She had to blink twice to be sure what she was seeing was real. Creed stood a few feet away, smiling and holding a large bouquet of her favorite flowers. He looked handsome wearing a crisp white button-down shirt that emphasized the breadth of his shoulders and chest. The dark denims fit his long legs like they were tailor made for him and his boots were new. The whiskers were gone from his jaw and he looked younger.

Consumed with him, it took her a long moment before she realized he wasn't alone. Standing next to him was Livvy who looked like she was dressed in her Sunday's best. Her beautiful hair hung in long waves and the sea green dress was so pretty.

"Hi, Livvy."

The teen came forward and hugged Mindy. She blinked back tears.

When Livvy moved back to join her dad, Mindy saw that behind them was a small gathering of family and friends. Rusty, Hank, Boone, Bo, Isabella, and a few more familiar faces from her childhood. They were all happy to see her.

"What's going on here?" Mindy looked from Creed to Jane and back to Creed for an answer.

He swiped off his hat and handed it and the bouquet to Livvy. Sweat beaded his forehead and he looked both excited and worried.

"Creed?"

"Give me a chance." He took Mindy's hand into his. "If you can forgive me for being an idiot for letting you leave Cooper's Hawk a second time in a lifetime, I want to ask you a question." He reached into his back pocket, pulled out something, and bent to his knee.

Mindy realized he held a small velvet box in his palm. "Creed, this feels like a ..."

"Marriage proposal?" He lifted the lid to the box. Inside was a twinkling diamond surrounded by a circle of rubies. "When we were little we were playing in mama's room and we found this ring in a chest. You said it was the prettiest ring you'd ever laid eyes upon and one day you wanted a ring just like it. Remember?" She nodded, watching him through blurred vision. "Ma gave this to me to give to you. Sweetheart, I should have given you this ring years ago, but you know us Hawke's. We're a bit foolish when it comes to the matters of the heart."

Laughter sounded from those behind him. Mindy looked up and saw Abby using a handkerchief to wipe tears from her eyes. "I've always admired that ring, Abby."

"My mom would be proud to see it on your finger," she said. Rusty put his arm around her to comfort her.

"Will you marry me, Mindy? Only say yes if you're willing to tolerate me loving you for the rest of our lives."

"Creed, I thought you'd never forgive me." Tears fell to her cheeks.

"A wise person once told me that I could choose to never forgive you or forgive and see how happy we can be." He stood. "I love you. I'll always love you."

"Yes, Creed. Yes a million times." They walked into each other's arms. He swung her around then put her back on her feet, giving her a quick kiss on the lips.

"What do you think?" He wagged his brows.

"I think it's amazing that all these people have come to watch you ask for my hand in marriage." She smiled at the small crowd of people.

"Sweetheart, these people have come to watch us get married, that is if you really mean yes. I'm not taking the risk of losing you again. We even have Pastor Michaels here."

The silver haired man waved from where he stood behind Rusty.

"What?" She looked back at Jane. "Did you know about this?"

Her daughter nodded. "It killed me not to tell you, but Mom, isn't this what you want? What you've always wanted? You have my blessing."

"And mine," Livvy said.

Mindy looked at her father. "Daddy?"

"You have my blessing as long as I get to walk you down the aisle."

Turning her gaze to the man she had always loved, she nodded. "Yes, Creed." She laughed in excitement. "I'll marry you today, but what about a dress? I don't have anything with me except for what I have on."

"Don't worry," Jane said. "Pop Pop found something you might be okay wearing."

"I'll be right back." Rusty stepped around a wall then came forward, holding the pretty lace dress that Mindy's mom wore when she married Rusty.

"Daddy? Are you sure?"

"Your mom would have wanted you to wear this." He had tears in his eyes.

"Then what are we waiting for? I'm ready to become Mrs. Creed Hawke," Mindy exclaimed.

Everyone clapped and cheered.

That day fate brought a man and woman together—a love that not even time could fade.

Epilogue

MINDY GENTLY ROCKED on the porch as she watched Jane, Livvy and Jonesy tossing the frisbee. They were laughing and having such an amazing time.

Hearing a cooing sound, she lowered her eyes to the bundle of joy in her arms. Nicholas Rusty Hawke looked just like his daddy, of course. Thick black hair, bright eyes and a charmer at even a month old. Mindy's heart swelled. Nic had been a surprise, but a very joyous one. She once believed she'd never hold a baby of her own again, but fate proved it had a plan of its own.

Just like her marriage to Creed. Their love had withstood time. Now they were living at Sage Creek with their small family. Things had come full circle.

"Happy one-year anniversary, babe." Creed came up behind her, bent over and kissed her cheek.

"Did you speak to the builders?"

"They're going to break ground with the new house next week. Soon, sweetheart, we'll have our own home on the west property. Right there where we've shared so much history."

"I can't wait, Creed. I'm so happy."

"How is my beautiful wife and son?"

"We're wonderful. Right, Nic? How are the steaks coming on the grill?"

"I've had to threaten to shoo your father away at least a dozen times. Is he always this controlling when it comes to grilling?" Creed laughed.

"No clue, although I do remember him always calling himself the "grill master". I thought all men thought they were grill masters."

"It's going to take me some time to get used to that." He pointed at the scene around the grill.

Rusty and Abby were laughing and holding hands. "You know, I'm not so surprised. I mean, I am shocked that they had an affair, but I like that they can be happy. They're both deserving and going to be so happy traveling to Paris next month."

"Ma has always wanted to go there."

"And now she gets to. We'll miss them, won't we, little man." His little fists waved through the air.

"How about I take Nic for a bit?"

"Sure." She handed over their son and watched them together with pride. Mindy stood and joined them as they strolled into the grass.

"I can't believe they'll be getting married soon," Creed whispered, referring to Jane and Jonesy.

"As long as he treats my girl right." Mindy looked over to where Jonesy was teasing Jane by tickling her.

"He better," Creed growled.

A car pulled in and the back door opened. Alex jumped out and ran to meet Livvy. Mindy waved at his mother as she pulled away. Livvy wore such a sweet smile.

Mindy thought the crush was cute but had a feeling they'd be seeing more and more of Alex over the years if Livvy stayed on track. She'd become such a blessing, helping around the house, taking a leading role on the farm. She'd even recently signed up for her first competition in figure skating with Mindy as her coach.

Melody called once a week, but Livvy gave up asking her mom to visit.

"What if we decided to have another?" Creed surprised her by saying.

"Another baby? Don't you think we should slow down? If Jane and Jonesy get married, we could have a grandchild in the next few years."

"I guess you're right. I just look at Nic and see our love in him and it makes me so proud."

"You make me proud, Creed."

He bent and kissed her.

"Come on you two. Save that stuff," Livvy teased.

Not the end but only the beginning.

From the author:
Thank you for reading. Please leave a review and let others
know your thoughts.
Hugs,
Rhonda Lee Carver

At an early age, Rhonda fell in love with romance novels, knowing one day she'd write her own love story. Life took a short detour, but when the story ideas were no longer contained, she decided to dive in and write. Her first plot was on a dirty napkin she found buried in her car. Eventually, she ran out of napkins. With baby on one hip and laptop on the other, she made a dream into reality—one word at a time.

Her specialty is men who love to get their hands dirty and women who are smart, strong and flawed. She loves writing about the everyday hero.

When Rhonda isn't crafting sizzling manuscripts, you will find her busy editing novels, blogging, juggling kids and animals (too many to name), dreaming of a beach house and keeping romance alive. Oh, and drinking lots of coffee to keep up with her hero and heroine.

For other titles by Rhonda Lee Carver, please visit: www.rhondaleecarver.com.

Find me on Facebook, too! www.facebook.com/rhondalee.carver

Other books by Rhonda Lee Carver

Rhonda Lee Carver Books by Series

Tarnation, Texas Series
Hitched (Book 1)
The Cowboy's Son (Book 2)
Pour Me a Drink (Book 3)
Cowboy State of Mind (Book 4)
Big Hearted Cowboy (Book 5)

Mountain Force Series
Justice by the Lawman (Book 1)
Secured by the Lawman (Book 2)
Tormented by the Lawman (Book 3)

Lawmen of Wyoming Series
Protected by the Lawman (Book 1)
Wanted by the Lawman (Book 2)
Seized by the Lawman (Book 3)
Claimed by the Lawman (Book 4)
Sheltered by the Lawman (Book 5)
Taken by the Lawman (Book 6)

Saddles & Second Chances Series
Roman's Choice (Book 1)
Penn's Fortune (Book 2)
Weston's Trouble (Book 3)

Urban's Rush (Book 4)
Hugh's Chase (Book 5)

Cowboys of Nirvana Series
Cowboy Paradise (Book 1)
Ropin' Trouble (Book 2)
Smoke. Fire. Cowboy (Book 3)
Kissed, Spurred & Valentined (Book 4)
Cowboy is Mine (Book 5)
The Discreet Cowboy (Book 6)
A Perfect Cowboy Daddy (Book 7)
Cowboys Forgive (Book 8)

Second Chance Cowboy Series
Second Chance Cowboy (Book 1)
Second Ride Cowboy (Book 2)
Second Round Cowboy (Book 3)
Second Dance Cowboy (Book 4)
Second Song Cowboy (Book 5)
Second Burn Cowboy (Book 6)
Second Hope Cowboy (Book 7)
Second Sunrise Cowboy (Book 8)

The KNIGHT Brothers Series
Pride and Pleasure (Book 1)
His Weekend Wife (Book 2)
The Darkest Knight (Book 3)

Letting Go Series
Letting Go (Book 1)
Legacy (Book 2)

Without You (Book 3)

Rhinestone Cowgirls Series
Under Pressure (Book 1)
Pressure Rising (Book 2)
Pressure Point (Book 3)
Secret Pressure (Book 4)
Resisting Pressure (Book 5)

Studs in Scrubs Series
Hot as Hell (Book 1)
Dirty as Hell (Book 2)
Smooth as Hell (Book 3)

Buttermilk Valley Series
Unexpected Hero (Book 1)
The Lawman's Promise Book 2)

Wicked Wolves Series
Wicked Pleasures (Book 1)
Wicked Lust (Book 2

Other books by Rhonda Lee Carver (Not part of a series)
A New Year's Cowboy
Leather for Two: Wings of Steel MC
Fighting Flames
Double Dare
With Honor
Sin with Cuffs

Friends with Benefits
Dreaming Ivy
Castle's Fortress
Delaney's Sunrise
Diamond in a Rose

Have you read Bighearted Cowboy (Book 5, Tarnation, Texas)? Here is a bonus read...

CHAPTER ONE

"Don't push!"

"What's going on? What's wrong with my daughter?" The frantic mother stood by the table in the emergency room where her seventeen-year-old daughter was curled up in pain.

Charlotte Sophia had worked as a nurse long enough to ably compartmentalize her emotions from professionalism. However, a part of her wanted to wrap her arms around the scared young patient and tell her, "everything will be all right" but the proficient nurse in her knew time was of the essence to save the lives of the mother and the unborn child. "Ms. Hampton, your daughter is pregnant, and she is in active labor."

"Pre-g-nant?".

"Yes. She's having a baby. I know it's a shock, but I need you to be strong for your daughter. Missy," Charlotte directed her attention to the crying teenager. "Did you know you were pregnant?"

Out came two moans before she finally answered, "No. I didn't know. Am I going to live?" Frenzied-filled dark eyes stared up at her. "I feel like I'm being attacked inside."

"You're going to be fine." Charlotte wiped her face gently with a cool, damp cloth. "When did you first notice any cramping or pain?" Her intention was to get information while trying to calm Missy as much as possible. They were still waiting on an available doctor who could help deliver the baby.

"I left school early because I was sick. I went home and was playing a video game and winning too. You know, the one where the cyborg attacks California and—"

"Missy!" her mother reprimanded. "Stay on track, for God's sake!"

"Fine! I thought I was starting my period, the worst one of my life, but this sucks. Can you get it out? Can you give me something for the pain?" More tears flowed to mix with the streaks of mascara on her cheeks. "I have practice tonight."

"Listen to me carefully," Charlotte said evenly. "I know this is painful and you're scared. It's important that you stay calm and whatever you do don't push. So you play sports?"

"Soccer. I-I play soccer." She was in between contractions, but they were close together, so she didn't have much of a break.

"Ah, a soccer player. You're determined and strong. Just like you do in the game when you're ready to make a goal, you can do this, and you *will* do this, sweetheart. Just keep breathing and concentrate." Charlotte looked up at the teen's mother. "Stay with her and keep her relaxed as much as you can."

"Yes. I will, but where's the doctor? Shouldn't there be a doctor here?" Ms. Hampton looked like she was a thread away from collapsing. Who could blame her? "How could you do this, Missy? Wait until I get my hands wrapped around that boy's neck."

Patting the mother's shoulder, Charlotte gave her an encouraging smile. "It'll be okay. We won't let anything happen to your daughter or your grandchild. I know this is all a blow, but you can take care of the details of how this happened later."

Ms. Hampton gave a shaky nod. "I love you." She laid her hand on her daughter's trembling fingers. "I'm here for you. Now listen to what the nurse tells you."

Charlotte dropped her used gloves in the trash on her way into the hall where she said, "We need a doctor now!"

"They're still with the victims of the five-car pileup. We're trying to pull a doctor from somewhere. I'll call labor and delivery again to see why they haven't come and got her," Bristol said from the nurse's station.

That was how things tended to happen in the ER. Emergencies came in numbers.

"Nurse! Nurse!" Ms. Hampton yelled, "Come fast!"

Grabbing a pair of gloves from the box on her way into the room, Charlotte dragged them on as she stepped up to the table. Missy's white-knuckled grasp on the pillow and her glazed over eyes told Charlotte the baby was coming, doctor or not.

"I'm going to give you a quick exam to see how dilated you are, Missy." Charlotte's adrenaline spiked once she felt the baby's head. "Bristol! I need you in here now!"

"What's happening?" Ms. Hampton wrung her hands.

"We're preparing you daughter for delivery. The baby is coming. Bristol, we'll have to do this. Listen, Missy, I need you to turn onto your back and place your feet into the stirrups. This is Nurse Bristol, and we're going to help you through this. Just listen to everything we tell you."

Feet in place and her bottom scooted to the edge of the bed, Missy was panting and whimpering. Charlotte paused a second to work through her mind what to do in an emergency delivery. She'd never performed one alone, but she'd assisted in several deliveries in nursing school.

"I'm here! What's the status?" Dr. Noah swept in, tugging on gloves and covering his face with a mask.

"Patient's name is Missy. She's been in labor for approximately four hours. Baby's head is in the canal. She's ready to push." Charlotte stepped aside so the doctor could take his place at the bottom of the exam table.

"Hi, I'm Dr. Noah. Missy, Nurse Charlotte is going to help you push."

After twenty minutes of pushing, Missy delivered a boy who entered the world crying. They rushed him and Missy to labor and delivery where they would make sure mom and baby were okay.

"That was amazing, wasn't it?" Charlotte said to Bristol hours later when they met at the vending machines.

"Amazing? Could you imagine finding out your teen is pregnant twenty minutes before she delivers? Whoa…I don't think I'm cut out for parenthood. Do you believe she didn't know that she was pregnant?" Bristol stabbed a button and a Coke bottle dropped.

Charlotte shrugged. "Who knows. Kids today get so caught up in sports, and life, they sometimes don't pay attention to the monthly call."

"I guess, but I think she had to suspect something wasn't right. Anyway, how are mom and baby?"

"I called upstairs earlier and they're doing great. Fortunately, baby is healthy." Charlotte dug the needed amount of change from her pocket and dumped them into the coin slot for a candy bar and coffee.

"Who doesn't know that they're kid is pregnant? I thought Missy's mom was going to flip out."

"I'm glad they're both okay. This could have been a worse situation if she hadn't done the right thing by telling her mom that she needed help."

"You certainly were amazing," Bristol said as they walked outside to the employee break area. They took a table close to the water fountain.

"I did my job. I felt so sorry for both moms. I don't know how I'd handle the same situation if I were in their shoes." She bit into the chocolate and chewed thoughtfully.

"Are you sure about this?"

Charlotte looked up at her friend. "About?"

"Moving? Leaving the hospital."

"Very sure." She swallowed her candy with a sip of the terrible coffee. That was something she wouldn't miss.

"I'm going to be lonely." Bristol puckered her bottom lip. They'd been roommates and best friends since they met in nursing school five years ago.

"I'll miss you. Promise me that you won't eat ice cream for breakfast every morning. Eat something with real substance at least once a day."

"Maybe once a day." Bristol crossed her legs on the chair. "Things won't be the same around here without you. I'm going to have to deal with Hatchet Agatha myself. That's so unfair." She referred to their supervisor who ran the emergency department like a naval ship.

"You're going to be fine. Personally and professionally. You have Frank who seems to be keeping you busy these days." Charlotte picked a piece of caramel from her candy bar. "You two are growing closer, unless my ears deceive me." She wiggled her brows.

"You heard, huh? I'm sorry. I've become one of those pesky roommates. I didn't realize the apartment walls were so thin."

"It's okay. I put in my Raycons and fell right to sleep. I just pray Betty Sue turns out to like sleep more than she enjoys midnight booty calls," Charlotte teased.

"On a serious note, how do you know you'll even like Betty Sue?"

Charlotte popped the last bit of candy into her mouth and downed the rest of the coffee. "She's my cousin and she asked me to come. We haven't seen each other in a long time, but as kids we were close. Anyway, I need a change of scenery. I want to have more bedside time with my patients."

"But do you think you'll like working in a doctor's office? It's definitely a change of pace from working here."

"It's actually a clinic and from what I hear they keep pretty busy because the closest hospital is almost an hour away."

"So Texas, huh? You don't even own a pair of cowboy boots. You won't fit in. Stay here." Bristol put her hands into a prayer position and puffed out her bottom lip.

"Please understand. I need to get away from Ohio. I want you to come and visit soon. It'll give you an excuse to buy a new pair of jeans and boots."

"Don't you mean you need to get away from Lucy? She'd finally driven you away."

"That too." She couldn't deny that going to Tarnation had a lot to do with her aunt.

"That I can understand. It's time you put a stop to her taking advantage of you."

"I think it's the only way she knows how to show affection, by being abrasive."

Bristol popped a nut into her mouth. "That woman has never been affectionate. It's not in her DNA. So what does she say about you leaving?" When Charlotte didn't answer, Bristol's eyes widened. "You didn't tell her?"

"Not yet. I plan on stopping on my way to the airport in the morning."

"Well, since I can't convince you to stay, I might as well give you this." She reached into her purse and brought out a small box.

"You got me a going away present?"

Bristol shoved the box toward Charlotte who took it and popped off the lid. Inside she found a heart necklace. "Bristol! You shouldn't have. You can't afford this."

"Anything for the greatest friend alive. If it wasn't for you, I wouldn't have made it through nursing school. You kicked my butt when I needed it." Her eyes filled with moisture.

"Don't cry." Charlotte pulled her friend in for a tight hug.

"I'm not crying. You're crying." Bristol sniffed and pulled back, subtly wiping away the wetness. "Go and find yourself in Texas. If you don't, come back because you always have a place here."

They gave each other another quick hug and Bristol stood. "I've got to get back to work. Don't leave without saying bye to me." She rushed off.

Charlotte stayed a few minutes longer, taking in the beauty of the courtyard. She was both scared and excited to be leaving. Getting up, she threw away her trash and for the last time took the bridgeway into the emergency department. She was greeted by several co-workers and as she turned down a corridor, she helped an elderly patient who had dropped her purse.

She stepped behind the nurse's station and reached for the chart, opening it. She felt someone over her shoulder and looked up to find Agatha standing there, hovering. "I'm sorry that I'm a few minutes late. I'm going to check on my patient now." She hurried to be on her way.

"I wanted to stop and wish you well on your new journey."

Blinking, Charlotte couldn't remember in the three years that she'd worked at the hospital having Agatha say one pleasant word. "Thank you!"

The older woman started to step away, but she stopped, giving Charlotte a smile. "You're a very skilled nurse. If you decide you'd like to come back, I'm sure we can find a place for you here in the ER."

Charlotte had to mentally shake herself.

Although she'd miss her work family, she hoped she'd meet new friends.

And she remembered this the next morning when she took the cab to the apartment building where she'd grown up.

A familiar feeling of butterflies erupted inside her stomach as she was time machined back to the child who'd been awakened by a caseworker in the middle of the night and asked to pack her belongings in a trash bag because she was being taken away from home. The next events of that night and why she had been whisked away were all a blur, but she recalled how they'd driven for what seemed like hours until they pulled up in front of the apartment building where she'd call home for the next eleven years.

The caseworker, a pretty brunette with glasses, had come around to the passenger seat and told Charlotte not to be scared. She would be staying with her aunt Lucy. Clinging to her stuffed toy, a brown bear with a missing eye and rip in the belly, Charlotte had walked up the sidewalk in her dirty, untied tennis shoes to meet a relative she'd never met before.

Twenty years had passed, but the memories remained.

Asking the driver to wait, she slipped him a twenty, then climbed out from the backseat and made her way up that same long sidewalk and in through the double glass doors that had spider cracks from corner to corner.

The lobby smelled like mildew and musk, a smell that Charlotte didn't think she'd ever escape. Every time she smelled it, she jetted back to her childhood when she feared her own shadow. She'd been wary of everyone, unsure of who to trust or who to care for. Her patients had taken the place for the things she lacked in her personal life.

Up the stairs, she stepped over old man Hagley who was passed out. She took the empty bottle from his hand, set it aside, then continued up to the fifth floor and to the door at the end of the hall. Two seventeen. The seven had been turned upside down since Charlotte came that first day.

Inside, she looked around the cluttered apartment with a sigh of despair. Her aunt had a hoarding issue, as well a few other flaws. Magazines stacked as high as Charlotte was tall and filled trash bags piled into a mound cluttered the small space. A permanent odor hung in the air that came from many sources. The smoke-saturated curtains hung haphazardly from bent rods. The coffee stained blue and white linoleum floor had more holes than swiss cheese. The faux leather chair had peeled down to the netting. Charlotte smiled at the memory of how she and Lucy had dragged the secondhand chair from the dumpster, up the five flights of stairs and stuck it in their apartment. When Charlotte had complained, Lucy had given her the go-to lecture, "Stop being so selfish. Until you have a job of your own and pay the bills then you'll come off that hoity-toity attitude and do what's best. Remember I was the one who took you in when your mom didn't want you." As if she needed reminding…

Charlotte would never forget the humiliation on that Christmas morning, the ridicule of the neighbors watching as she and Lucy hauled the chair away as if it was a prized possession. How the kids had laughed at and bullied Charlotte when she returned to school, calling her "Trashy Charlotte". Months had passed, but felt like years, before they found someone else to pick on.

Even dumpster diving wasn't as humiliating as being responsible for going down to the corner bar for two a.m. pickups. It never failed that Lucy would drink herself under the bar and the bartender would call for someone to come get her. Charlotte would get scared walking the dark streets in the middle of the night so at fifteen she switched things up and started driving the beat up silver two door that had spongy brakes the few blocks to get her drunk aunt.

If only Charlotte could count the number of men that had come and gone over the years—all the "uncles" she'd met. Those memories had been tattooed into every brain cell as a constant reminder that one day she'd be better. She'd be a better mother when she had kids of her own.

Charlotte could only wonder how horrible her mother was that family court thought living with Lucy would be a healthier environment.

In Lucy's defense, she'd never been abusive and kept a roof over their heads and meals on the table, at least most of the time.

Movement caught her eye.

She picked up a magazine off the top of a stack and rolled it, smashing the cockroach against the wall. She tossed it into the trash and started to put the magazine back when she gave it a toss too.

Glancing around the clutter, she gave her head a little shake. She wouldn't miss this place. The day she'd moved out, working two jobs to help pay for nursing school and a small one room apartment close to campus, had been a liberating moment. Several curve balls had been thrown her way in adulthood, delaying her graduation by a few years, but she'd finally managed to graduate with honors. Learning to work through the past, it got sloppy at times, but she did day by day.

Charlotte had given up on trying to convince Lucy to move from the apartment where there were more bugs than people, but she refused. Stubborn ways kept her there. Just like keeping the old chair that had smelled like butt when they lugged it into the apartment.

She stepped through the narrow doorway into the room off the kitchen, a laundry-room-turned-Charlotte's-bedroom. The room wasn't much bigger than a closet, but she'd never had many things outside of a twin bed, small three-drawer dresser, and a lamp. It surprised her that Lucy hadn't done something with the space since Charlotte moved, not even using it to fill with useless clutter. Maybe she was hoping that one day Charlotte would come back.

Leaving the room, she closed the door behind her and breathed in deeply. Although she couldn't say that her every dream was about to come true, she did know she'd be in control of her own decisions.

In the living room, she picked up the empty beer bottles and overflowing ashtray and dumped them. Her aunt would be hung over this morning and Charlotte would come to the rescue as she'd done many times.

Taking bread from the cabinet, she checked the expiration date then placed a slice into the toaster. Thankfully, she found eggs and bacon in the fridge, leftover from the groceries she bought last week. And a moldy TV dinner that she tossed.

Once breakfast was prepared, she placed it on a tray and grabbed the coffee on her way out of the kitchen. The closer she got to her aunt's bedroom the stronger the scent of stale cigarette smoke and cheap floral perfume became.

Standing on the outside of the closed door, she breathed in for bravery. She could do this. She was an adult. Inhaling the putrid odor, she sneezed. Making her way into the room, she set the tray down on the nightstand.

Her aunt's snoring echoed off the bare walls.

Charlotte pulled the curtain back on the window and opened it a few inches. The sounds of children playing in the courtyard wafted in. She'd always liked the sounds of joy.

Turning on the heels of her Converses, she stared through the heavy smog at the sleeping figure laying under the piles of blankets.

A part of her wanted to let Lucy stay asleep, but she couldn't leave without saying goodbye. As much as she feared telling her aunt about the move, she needed to do the right thing.

Giving Lucy a gentle shake, it took several more attempts until she finally moaned, cursed, and farted. "What the hell?" she mumbled in a ragged voice.

"I made you breakfast."

Charlotte went to the dresser and stared at her reflection in the spotted mirror. Her long, dark curls were pulled into a messy bun, her usual look these days. She wore no makeup and couldn't remember the last time she'd applied foundation or mascara, and this morning she could have used a bit of concealer to hide the inky circles under her eyes. She'd tossed and turned most of the night and finally at the crack of dawn she gave up on sleep.

Today was a big day. She had to tell her aunt that she was leaving, and Charlotte wasn't sure what response she'd get. One could never know how Lucy would react when something bothered her. Making breakfast on a paper plate and the coffee in Styrofoam was one way to make sure so there was no china within reach to throw.

Her aunt finally crawled out from the wrinkled blankets, grabbed her dry vape from the nightstand and took a long drag before she glanced across the short distance with a blood shot glare. The redness of her eyes matched her rosy complexion. She'd stopped dying her hair black six months ago and her silver roots had grown out to ear length. "Why are you waking me up so early?"

"It's ten o'clock. Not so early and I needed to speak to you." Charlotte took the plate of food and set it on Lucy's lap which eased the crinkles around her eyes—some.

"You look…different," she said around a mouthful of egg.

"I'm wearing a new shirt." Plucking at the gauzy material, Charlotte sat on the end of the bed. Buying new clothes happened rarely for her, but she'd decided that a few new things couldn't hurt, like the pretty shirt and new jeans. And cowgirl boots. A woman heading to Texas needed to fit in. "Bristol said hello," she tossed in casually.

"Hmmph. I don't like her."

"She'd been there for me when I needed someone the most." Four years ago during a breast self-exam she'd discovered a lump in her breast. After going through a battery of tests the specialist diagnosed her with a rare condition, atypical hyperplasia, and they put her on hormonal therapy. She'd recovered, but she worried that sometime in the future that could change. The condition changed the entire dynamic of relationships and had destroyed her last with her fiancé.

In the process of getting healthier, she'd learned a lot about herself—and how she and Ryan, her fiancé of two years, had nothing in common. Agreeing to go their separate ways had been a very difficult choice, but a necessary one. She'd buried herself in work, helping others, and the rare times she missed him happened only when she felt sorry for herself, but ice cream was a miracle cure. And extra shifts.

"She dresses like a slut."

"That's not very nice of you, Aunt Lucy," Charlotte scolded.

"Yeah, yeah." She shrugged a bony shoulder. "Can't say a damn thing these days without offending someone."

"How are the eggs?"

"Good."

"I'm moving," she blurted.

The fork hit the plate, knocking food out onto Lucy's lap. "Moving? Where?"

"Tarnation, Texas."

She smacked her lips as if the words wouldn't come. "Whatever for? Do you know the difference between a cow and a dog?"

Charlotte stood and went to the window to look out where the children kicked a ball around the unkempt courtyard.

Why did she feel a sense of guilt for leaving? She could decide for herself where she lived, what she did in life. Over the years she'd felt an overwhelming obligation to her aunt. After all, she had taken Charlotte in when otherwise she would have ended up in foster care. Lucy had never been nurturing or affectionate, but she had been the only parent Charlotte had ever really known. "I'm moving there to be closer to Betty Sue."

Lucy's cold laughter filled the air. "Let me guess. She's one of your mom's relatives."

"Yes. My cousin." Charlotte anticipated the negativity that would come. It always did.

The mention of her mother always did bring out the worst in Lucy. "Your mother was a bitch and your father was a bastard. The little money he had he spent on gambling and the little he won he spent on alcohol. Never kept a job longer than two weeks and screwed anything with two legs. Forget about going to Tarnation." Her groan rattled the window. "You're going to stay here."

Charlotte planted a smile on her lips, not allowing her aunt to trigger more guilt. "I've already made arrangements. I even have a job waiting for me. I'm flying out today."

"What?" Lucy's lips thinned and the wrinkles around her mouth deepened into quivering trenches. "And you're just now telling me this? Why's the old lady always the last to know?"

"I want you to be happy for me."

"What about Ryan?" She grabbed her vape, inhaled, which sent her into a coughing fit. She gulped the coffee.

"What about him?"

"You can't tell me there's not a chance you two won't hook up again. I saw him the other day. He asked about you."

"No. Ryan and I won't be getting back together. Ever." Lucy didn't like many people, but she'd liked Ryan. She especially liked that he was a junior associate at a law firm.

"Why are you always making the wrong decisions?" Lucy moaned.

"I guess it's just in my genes."

The sarcasm went unpounced on.

"What about me? You know I don't get around much these days. My feet are killing me."

Lifting her chin and folding her arms over her waist, Charlotte said stiffly, "It's time I did something for myself. The doctor said you needed to walk more to keep the circulation going in your feet and stop drinking. I noticed by the empty bottles in the living room that you didn't take Dr. Kenworth's suggestion to heart."

As every other time when the drinking came up, Lucy changed the subject. "After all that I've done for you. You're going to treat me like yesterday's trash?"

"That's not what I'm doing, and you know it. I'm branching out."

"You can do it here. Stop talking foolish."

Charlotte cleared her throat. "It's already settled. I bought the ticket and there's no turning back."

"Fine," Lucy grumbled. "Then why are you here?"

"I've asked our neighbor to check on you. She has agreed. You like Jamie. Maybe you two can go to Bingo and stop at that diner you really love."

"I tolerate Jamie. That's all. I don't want her coming over here and checking on me and fussing."

Going back to the bed, Charlotte sat down. "I spoke to Marvin at the market. He said he's willing to give you your job back. He needs someone in the deli and a cashier. He promised he'll give you another chance as long as you stop in the next few days."

"What? I wouldn't give that uptight twerp the time of day. After the way he treated me? Pfft. Accusing me of stealing?" She inhaled loudly, pushed the plate off her lap and stood, a little wobbly at first but quickly gained her bearings. Pieces of egg rolled off her gown and dropped to the floor. "And how dare you go behind my back and speak to *that* man. I don't need you to arrange jobs for me." Her gray eyes turned a shade darker.

"I thought you'd want to go back. You worked there for twenty years and he was a flexible boss. And for the record, he didn't accuse you of stealing. Marvin only said that you'd made a mistake in cashing out."

"Sorry that I had lost a couple of dollars. I was tired." Lucy pulled on her short pink robe, brought out a full pack of cigarettes and started to light one when she met Charlotte's accusing gaze. "Damn." She dropped the unlit cigarette and pack back into her pocket with a disappointed groan.

"Martin said you'd been having a few rough nights there at the end."

"And you believe him?"

"I'm not taking sides. You need the job, Lucy. I don't mind continuing to help you out, that's fine. I'll send you money, but I can't stay here. I won't stay here."

Her aunt's shoulders slumped some. "Then go." She waved her spindly hand through the air like a fairy godmother with a magic wand. "I don't need you or your help. I'll find my own job too, thank you very much."

"I'm sure you'll find one."

"Selfish."

"Excuse me?"

"You're selfish. When your mom couldn't take care of you who swept in and did the right thing? I did. I didn't have to, but I did out of the grace of my heart and this is how I'm paid back. You get some shiny certificate and then everything here is useless. That doesn't surprise me. Your mother was the same way. Selfish to the bone."

Charlotte gritted her teeth, holding back the hurt that bubbled up into her chest. She'd heard this same argument so many times over the years and each one seemed to burrow deeper. Although her memories had nearly faded of the woman who people said she looked identical to, she'd held out hope that one day her mother would show up, wanting to fix the broken relationship—or maybe apologize for sucking at parenting. That never happened and after this long Charlotte guessed it never would. She had no idea where her mother had gone, if she was even still alive, but she wanted to believe that she'd turned her life around from drugs and crime. As a nurse, Charlotte had seen countless lives destroyed from bad choices.

New scenery was exactly what she needed.

Stiffening her back, Charlotte reached into her back pocket and took out the check she'd written that morning and placed it on the nightstand. She stepped toward the door and turned back only to say, "I'm sorry you feel that way, Aunt Lucy. Take care of yourself." She walked away.

In the hallway, she started for the stairs when she heard her name.

Jamie met her in the corridor. The friendly woman wore an encouraging smile and she took Charlotte's hand as she had so many times over the years. "Remember what I said, sweet thing. You go on and find yourself and leave your aunt to me. She'll be fine. She won't scare me away. I've learned long ago her bark is bigger than her bite."

"How will I ever repay you?"

"For what?"

"You've fed me, comforted me, inspired me over the years. You were the one who came to my school functions. Attended my college graduation."

"Honey, bite your tongue. You kept this old lady young. You make sure you stay in touch and when you're in town you stop by."

"I will." Giving the woman a quick hug, Charlotte hurried down the stairs before her tears overflowed. Once she was on the sidewalk, she sniffed back the emotion and gathered her feelings. She had nothing to feel guilty about. Lucy should be proud that Charlotte wanted to expand her horizon. Maybe one day her aunt would come around.

Cowboy Creed

CHAPTER TWO

Two weeks later.

Plucking a lollipop from the pocket of her scrubs, she handed it to the sweet little girl with big blue eyes and her blonde hair pulled back into two ponytails. "You were very brave, Isabelle." The eight-year-old didn't shed one tear during her immunizations.

"You were wonderful with her. You have such a great bedside manner." Isabelle's mom, a young brunette with bright eyes, shook Charlotte's hand. "I hope you'll stay here at the clinic. We need more caring nurses like you in this small town."

"I love being here. I haven't had much time to explore Tarnation, but the people I've met are amazing. Just like this little girl here." She patted Isabelle on the shoulder. "I'm glad her asthma is under control but if you see any problems let us know. Dr. Healey is finished so you're free to go."

She waved goodbye as they left then turned to Meka who was sitting at the nurse's station popping a raisin into her mouth.

"Patient's like her make my job much better." Charlotte loved that things were a slower pace here than back home in the ER. She enjoyed hearing their life stories.

"The next one won't hurt either." Meka smiled and handed Charlotte a chart.

Reading the name, she shrugged. "Brennan Colt? Has he been here in the clinic before?"

"He's a walk in. He was in a ranch accident and hurt his head and leg. He's ready and waiting." The pretty redhead went back to typing at her computer.

Charlotte stepped over to exam room three, lightly knocked then stepped inside. "Good morning." When she didn't get an answer, she looked up from the notes and to the exam table where her patient was stretched out awkwardly. He was about a foot too tall for the bed and he looked like he was about to bust out of the flowered paper gown. His hat was pulled down covering his face and his arms were extended above his head, his large hands clasped. She could hear his soft snores. Not many people fell asleep here in the office.

Jetting her gaze from his whiskered jaw, over his broad chest covered in blue and pink flowered gown to his bare legs down to the dusty cowboy boots, she smiled. She guessed a cowboy never took off his boots.

People had a way of doing things around these parts. She'd heard Betty Sue explain it with "beating to their own drum". Time didn't seem to matter in Tarnation. People were late, and if Charlotte was a couple minutes late, it didn't seem to matter. Back home she would have been ripped.

Clearing her throat, he didn't move.

Stepping over to the bed, she patted his shoulder. "Mr. Colt?"

He mumbled something inaudible then grabbed his hat, swiping it off his face. He blinked several times as his eyes adjusted to the light before his gaze came to her in curiosity. He had a few blood splatters on his cheek. "Hi," he said in a sleep raspy voice.

"Hi." She bit back another smile. "I'm Charlotte. I'm a nurse here. I hear you've suffered an injury. I'm sorry I woke you."

"Sorry, ma'am. I've been up since daybreak." He pushed himself onto his elbows and rubbed the sleep from his clear blue eyes. When he smiled, he showed off deep dimples and nice teeth.

"So you were hurt?"

"Just a minor injury. I was thrown by a horse."

"Oh, just that, huh?" In a millisecond of time she evaluated his long legs and the fresh bruising on his thigh and knee under crisp, dark hairs.

"I think we need a proper hello. Hi, I'm Brennan Colt." He thrust out his hand.

She hesitated before finally laying her palm against his, caught by the sudden warmth and tingles that shot up her arm. The calluses on the underside of his knuckles scraped her skin, not in a repulsive way, but more of a tweaking of her nerve endings. As she'd told Isabelle's mom, Charlotte hadn't had the chance to get out and tour the town, but she'd met a handful of cowboys—real cowboys who worked the land from dawn to dusk and liked their boots dirty and their hands dirtier. A sweet energy rushed over her. Pulling her hand away, she cleared her throat. "Nice to meet you, Brennan. Can you tell me where you're injured?"

The corners of his mouth lifted wider and his eyes dazzled with charm. "My left ankle and I have a little scratch on my head."

"How's the pain in the ankle?"

"I've had worse."

"That really didn't answer my question. Check out the chart. On a scale from one to ten, where would you place your pain?" She ran her hands down the thighs of her scrubs. The awareness remained in her arm.

"Four."

"Can I take a look?"

"Be my guest."

She had a feeling the cowboy had an overload of charm, but she was immune to mile-wide smiles and intriguing blue eyes. She focused on examining his leg, using the tips of her fingers to gently slide along the thick, muscular chord covered in soft hair. She paused at his knee. Nothing was broken so far. "I'll have to take your boot off."

"Go for it."

As carefully and slowly as she could, she dragged the boot off. Then the white sock downward and when she got to his ankle he jerked and cursed.

She looked up at him. "Still a four?"

"I'm a bit ticklish." There was that smile again. Too bad her nipples didn't get the message to stay professional.

Rolling the sock off completely, she laid it next to him. "And inflamed too. I don't think anything's broken but I'm guessing Dr. Healey will want an X-ray."

He gave a half shrug. "Whatever you see fit as long as I can get back to my chores this afternoon."

"I respect your work ethic, but you'll have to rest, at least today. I'm going to look at your head now." He had silky, thick hair and she parted the waves as she examined the cut. "You'll need a couple of stitches, but at least it has stopped bleeding."

"Could have been worse, I guess."

"I need to get your vitals." She reached for the blood pressure cuff and he held out his arm. She wrapped the cuff around his large bicep, realizing he was still staring up at her. Concentrating on pressing the bulb and not the deep dimples bracketing his plush lips she got the reading and jotted the number in his chart.

"Am I still alive?"

"Perfect blood pressure, but let's take a listen at your heart to make sure." Using the stethoscope, she leaned in and pressed the chest piece over his heart. She caught a scent of leather and spice soap. She liked it. His gaze was on her, making it hard to focus. "Heart's beating fine too." She dragged the earpieces off and hung the stethoscope around her neck. "One more thing. Your temp." She slid the thermometer under his tongue. "Now keep this here until it beeps."

While the thermometer worked, she made a few notes in his chart, but none of them mentioned that she needed her own blood pressure taken.

"I feel fine. It's just a bruise."

She looked up at him, seeing him holding the thermometer. "You need to keep that in your mouth," she gently chastised.

He sighed and stuck it back under his tongue.

Once it finished, she took it and dropped off the protector cover into the trash. "It's a bit more than a bruise, but I think you already know that."

"Trust me. This ain't nothing."

"How about we wait for the X-ray to decide on how bad it is." She smiled. "Dr. Healey will probably want some bloodwork too."

Did his color pale some? Were there beads of sweat across his forehead?

"Is it necessary?"

"Very necessary."

"For whom?"

"Mr. Colt—"

"Brennan."

"Okay, Brennan. Lab work is routine. I assure. If you're afraid of needles—"

He grimaced. "I'm not afraid."

"Okay then. I'll be right back. I want to speak with Dr. Healey." She stepped out and closed the door behind her. She met Meka's gaze who was smiling from one hoop earring to the other.

"Do you need some water? You look a little flushed."

Charlotte did need a cold shower, but she didn't say that to the other nurse. "He certainly is full of charm, isn't he?" She continued into Dr. Healey's office, asked if he wanted to see the patient or get lab work first, then she went back into the exam room.

"Dr. Healey would like to get the work up."

"If you say so. What if I resist?"

She searched his face, seeing the teasing lines around his mouth. "Do you give every nurse a hard time like this?"

"Only the cute ones."

Her throat constricted. She felt her bottom lip tremble and she ignored his flirting. This wouldn't be the first time, but it certainly was the first time she felt a sexual tension between her legs. Maybe it was loneliness, or maybe she simply found the cowboy attractive. After all, she was a woman who enjoyed a man's attention just as much as the next lady. Her career didn't give her steel walls of resistance.

She took out the items she needed from the medical chest.

When she turned back around, she found him sitting up, his legs hung over the edge of the table. One sock on and the other off. His hat was pushed back on his forehead. The hem of the gown had lifted high on his firm thighs. One thing was for sure, the cowboy didn't mind showing a little leg…or magnetism.

Placing the tools on the tray next to the exam table, she pulled on gloves and snapped them into place. "Do you have a preference of which arm I use?"

"Is neither an option?"

She didn't bother looking at him. "How about we try the left. I think I remember seeing some healthy veins. That'll make my job easier." Once he held out his arm, she wrapped the band around his bicep and pushed around on the veins that were like tunnels. "Yup, we have one." Tearing open a packet, she took out the alcohol wipe and cleaned his skin. "You'll feel a stick." Charlotte worked quickly, got the amount she needed then loosened the band. "That wasn't too bad, was it?"

He didn't answer.

In fact, he looked a bit pale.

"You should lie back and take it easy."

"I'm fine," he mumbled about the same time a blank expression flooded over his face.

She had no time to react before the cowboy came tumbling down.

*

Squinting against the overhead light in the exam room, he realized he'd fallen asleep. A second later he realized he wasn't alone.

Looking up into amber eyes, flushed cheeks on a heart shaped face, he swallowed hard. Was he dreaming? He'd been wishing before he dozed off that he'd find a perfect woman to make all his troubles disappear.

After he woke up fully, exchanged some words and she examined his leg, he felt a bit off his kilter by the beauty. Lord knew, he wasn't trying to come off as a desperate man, but when he got nervous, he tended to make a blatant fool of himself. He couldn't seem to wipe the smile off his face, until she pulled out the needle and then his world turned upside down, but not in a good way—at least not in the way he hoped.

Since he was a kid, he hated getting shots, or having his blood taken. He always got weak, but how could he tell the beautiful nurse? He realized he was a bit old to still carry the fear, but even now, he felt his head spin.

The last thing he wanted to do was be yellow bellied in front of her. He wasn't too good with the opposite sex, at least not like Baxter or his other brothers. Prime example…Dr. CC Peladora, the beautiful vet at Grinning Spurs. There for a hot minute he thought he was in love with her, but it just wasn't meant to be.

As the pretty nurse wrapped the tight band around his bicep, Brennan took the time to explore her features and some of the tension disappeared for a different kind of strain. Her dark hair was pulled up on top of her head, but a few unruly curls had escaped and hung around her high cheekbones. Her eyes were surrounded by thick lashes and a sprinkling of freckles scattered her cheeks. She smelled amazing…until she brought out the alcohol. The odor stung his nostrils.

His plan was to not look at the needle, but he'd never been one to learn his lesson.

He felt weak. A little wobbly. She said something, but he couldn't quite wrap his brain around the words.

Oh shit! He couldn't go down.

No!

But he couldn't control the blackness as it took over his body…